SATAN'S SOLUTION

America is drowning in debt, its leadership of the Free World compromised, its allies isolated and weakened, its position as the globe's most powerful nation under attack from a relentless China.

A China that sees the 21st Century as its century. A China determined to become the world's only superpower. A China whose manifest destiny is to stand astride a humbled America.

But, what so many accept as inevitable, a group of ultra-nationalist Americans refuse to accept. If the United States government cannot or will not stop China's relentless advance, it must.

The group has the money. It has the means. And it has the will. Even if the price of crushing China's ambitions for all time is the deaths of hundreds of millions.

BOOKS BY GRAHAM SHARP PAUL

HELFORT'S WAR*

Book I: The Battle at the Moons of Hell

Book II: The Battle of the Hammer Worlds

Book III: The Battle of Devastation Reef

Book IV: The Battle for Commitment Planet

Book V: The Final Battle

THE GUILD WAR

Book I: *Vendetta*

Book II: *Counterattack*

THE REDEMPTION OF KAL KARIUKI

Books 1 to 4 of the Helfort's War series are published in the United States by Del Rey Books, an imprint of the Random House Publishing Group, a division of Random House Inc., New York.

ACKNOWLEDGEMENTS

My thanks for their help concluding what must be one of the longest book projects in history go to two people.

My wife, Vicki, for her patience. I know the hours I spent at my desk, muttering and grumbling, drove her nuts from time to time, and understandably so.

And my brother, Alastair, for his editorial assistance and for pointing out when my plot devices crossed into 'readers will never buy it' land. In spe vivimus.

NOTICES

Cover design copyright © Graham Sharp Paul 2020
Cover photograph © Alamy 2020

Print edition ISBN: 978-0-6487685-2-4
e-Book edition ISBN: 978-0-6487685-3-1

DEDICATION

This book is dedicated to the men of the United States Navy's submarine service of World War 2.

Many sailed. Too few returned.

The journey to evil is made in small steps.

Michael Shermer, *The Moral Arc,*
2015

It is only to consult the history of nations to perceive, that every country, at all times, is cursed by the existence of men, who, actuated by an irregular ambition, scruple nothing which they imagine will contribute to their own advancement and importance. In monarchies, supple courtiers; in republics, fawning or turbulent demagogues, worshipping still the idol power wherever placed, whether in the hands of a prince, or of the people, and trafficking in the weaknessess, vices, frailties, or prejudices of the one or the other.

Alexander Hamilton, *Defence of Mr. Jay's Treaty: No. 1, The Argus,*
July 22, 1795

1944

The wind howled bitter across the plains of northern Manchuria. It snatched at the coats of two Imperial Japanese Army officers as they hurried into a windowless building, a raw-concrete box behind a floodlit barbed-wire fence. A sign on the wall said:

関東軍防疫給水部本部

731部隊 — 建物2A

認可されたアクセスのみ

危険

致命的なウイルス検査

塩素ガス

EPIDEMIC PREVENTION AND WATER PURIFICATION DEPARTMENT
KWANTUNG ARMY
UNIT 731—BUILDING 2A

AUTHORIZED ACCESS ONLY

DANGER
LETHAL VIRUS TESTING
CHLORINE GAS

Inside, the air was warm and acrid with the bite of chlorine. The Kempeitai detail behind the security post were on their feet, at attention, rigid.

One of the officers snapped his fingers. "The last hourly report. Now!"

A hand shot out with a sheet of paper. "The prisoners were checked ten minutes ago, sir," the sergeant said.

"Any deaths since you took over?"

"Eight, sir. Six in Cell 12 and two in 31. As ordered, I telephoned Doctor Sato to inform him ... but excuse me, Colonel Hishikawa, sir. I regret to report I could not understand his instructions."

"Because he's drunk, you fool. Call Lieutenant Miyashita. Tell him I want Sato sobered up and in my office in fifteen minutes."

The sergeant was already reaching for the telephone. "Yes, sir."

"Come, major," Hishikawa said as he stamped off down the corridor.

He stopped at the window into Cell 16. "Here we are. Come on, major, come on! Look inside."

Major Mori peered into the cell. Harsh lights bleached the color from the twisted bodies sprawled on a concrete bench. Emaciated and befouled, the ten men lay on filthy blankets, wrists chained to ringbolts high in the wall. "I don't understand, colonel. Who are these men? What is happening here?"

"The future." Hishikawa took a clipboard off its hook and ran his finger down the list of names. "Let's see ... The man nearest us is Lieutenant Kortenauer, US Army Air Force. He will be dead by morning. Doctor Sato won't be happy; he wanted him for vivisection."

The colonel leaned forward and banged hard on the glass. Kortenauer's blood-shot eyes flickered open. He lifted an arm, skin stretched across bones, a mosaic of black blotches and sores oozing blood and pus.

"General Kitano will be very pleased," Hishikawa continued. "He expected Americans would be much harder to kill ... If you do your job, major, there will be millions more like him."

Mori stared at the men behind the glass. The work Unit 731 was doing here was shameful. It dishonored the Japanese people. When the world learned of Unit 731's atrocities, the nation would stand condemned for all time.

"Excuse me, colonel," he said, "but I don't understand. What has this to do with my unit?" he asked.

"Everything, major, everything. Unit 731 has developed a new virus, Hemorrhagic Smallpox Strain 5524. It is lethal, as you can see. Under your command, the 209th will be the first unit of the Imperial Japanese Army to use the virus, in combat against MacArthur's army. 5524 will kill hundreds of thousands of his men."

Mori pasted a smile on his face. "It is an honor, sir."

"The future of the Empire rests on your shoulders, major." Hishikawa put a hand on Mori's shoulder. "Now, Doctor Sato is waiting to brief you. When he has finished, we will drink to your success. General Kitano has sent me a very fine bottle of saké."

•••

The Nissan sedan slithered away down the icy road. Major Mori sat in back, silent, hands deep in his pockets against the draft pushing through ill-fitting doors.

Ever since Guadalcanal, Mori had known Japan could never win this war. And nothing the monsters of Unit 731 did would change that. The Americans would annihilate the 209th before it ever got close enough to fire the grenades Hishikawa had developed, grenades loaded with Doctor Sato's smallpox virus.

His and Unit 731's gift to the world.

Not that it mattered, Mori reminded himself.

An officer of the Imperial Japanese Army followed orders, no matter how stupid, pointless, or barbaric.

•••

The last of the Chinese laborers trudged off the wharf as tugs, gray smudges in a sullen night, eased the *Maroku Maru*'s 10,000-ton mass away from the wharf.

Major Mori was happy to see the lights of Dalian recede into the darkness. Manchukuo was a miserable place: bitterly cold in winter, hot and sweaty in summer, its peasants sullen and resentful after years of brutal oppression. He had hated it from the day he joined the 73rd Infantry in early '38.

Happy to get out of the biting cold, he went inside, dropping down the decks to check on the two brass canisters which held the smallpox virus. They would be where he had left them, of course—in a storeroom deep inside the ship and guarded by his men—but he would not be taking any chances.

Not when Colonel Hishikawa had left him in no doubt what would happen should there be the slightest mishap.

—2—

Alan Mayer read the message one last time before he headed back to *Orca*'s control room.

```
NBF DE NKZQ
F NR 444
Z 011802ZMAY44
FM COMSUBSOWESPAC
TO USS ORCA
WD GRNC
TOP SECRET
BT
ULTRA X NO DIST X CONVOY DESIG CHARLIE FOX ONE ETD MANILA
072230ZMAY DESTINATION PULAU BIAK VIA SOTAYA CHANNEL AND
LENDARI GULF X ETA NORTHERN APPROACHES SOTAYA CHANNEL
110600Z MAY X CHARLIE FOX ONE COMPRISES 1 AK NAME MAROKU
MARU 1 DD 2 DE X MAROKU MARU IS VERY HIGH VALUE TARGET X
YOUR MISSION TO INTECEPT MAROKU MARU AND SINK AT ALL COSTS
REPEAT SINK AT ALL COSTS X UNTIL MAROKU MARU SUNK ALL
OTHER TARGETS ARE TO BE IGNORED REPEAT IGNORED NO MATTER
HOW ATTRACTIVE X SAFETY YOUR BOAT AND CREW NOT MATERIAL
X ACKNOWLEDGE WITH YOUR ETA SOTAYA CHANNEL AND
INTENTIONS X PERSONAL FROM ADM CHRISTIE X GOOD LUCK ALAN
X
BT
AR
TOD 011835Z MAY 44
```

Mayer's executive officer was waiting for him. "What's COMSUBSOWESPAC want now, skipper?" Matt Bronsen asked.

"This," Mayer said, giving him the message.

"Admiral Christie and the seat-polishers in Fremantle sure have it in for us," Bronsen said with a lop-sided grin, handing the message back.

"Seems so, Matt ... Wardroom in five with the charts, intel summaries, and everything we have on this ship the admiral is so keen on stopping. And get us running southeast at best speed while we figure out how to do this."

"Aye, aye, sir."

•••

Bronsen frowned. "I don't understand it. sir. The Japs have trouble finding enough ships to cover their convoys, but they have tasked three warships to escort one freighter. Why is the *Maroku Maru* so important?"

Mayer shrugged. "COMSUBSOWESPAC didn't say, not that it matters."

"I guess not, sir ... Provided we get close enough, sinking the *Maroku Maru* shouldn't be too hard. Yes, it's moving fast, but there's plenty of ship to hit. Our problem is escaping afterwards. The Gulf of Lendari is no place for submarines: shallow, only one channel out to the Pacific, and plenty of air-cover from the Jap bases on Pulau Biak and the Vogelkop. This is suic—"

"Stop!" Mayer snapped. "Don't say it. Don't even think it. Our orders; are they clear?"

"Yes, sir," said Bronsen. "They're clear ... Sorry."

"The Japs aren't invincible. They're over-stretched, short of assets, and the ships they have left are worn out. We might find a way to make it out alive."

"Yes, sir."

But Mayer knew his executive officer was right: *Orca* would only make it back to Fremantle if the *Maroku Maru* was a no-show.

•••

As *Orca* rolled southeast under a moonless sky littered with stars in their millions, Mayer dropped down to the control room and headed for his stateroom.

What, he wondered, had the codebreakers found to make the *Maroku Maru* so important Admiral Christie was prepared to sacrifice a boat and its crew of eighty to sink one Jap freighter?

He could not think of a single reason.

Mayer gave up trying to work it. Exhausted, burned-out, he collapsed on his rack and slipped into sleep.

—3—

Mayer was on the bridge the moment *Orca* surfaced at sunset, as he had been every night since they sneaked through the Sotaya Channel behind a small patrol boat to stay away from any Japanese minefields.

The rain streamed down his face. Furious in their intensity, a succession of monsoonal storms had reduced visibility to less than a hundred yards. Then, as fast as they had come, the storms would go, leaving clear skies and a view across white-flecked seas all the way to the horizon. Until the next squall arrived.

It was a tactical nightmare, unpredictable and dangerous.

The bridge loudspeaker boomed. "Radar. Pip bearing zero-five-zero at 15,000 yards. Contact intermittent."

"Clear the bridge," Mayer ordered, slapping the diving alarm. "Take her down. Make your depth four-five feet. Man tracking stations!"

He ripped his binoculars out of the target-bearing transmitter and stood back as the bridge crew poured down the hatch.

Streaming water, he dropped into the conning tower as the quartermaster dogged the hatch shut behind him.

Bronsen was already at his position as assistant approach officer. "It must be something big for the radar to see it through all this rain, skipper."

"I'm hoping," Mayer said. He wasn't; he was praying the new arrival was any ship but the *Maroku Maru*.

Orca steadied,

"Up 'scope," Mayer ordered. He checked all around; all he saw was blackness streaked with the dirty gray of waves and rain. He took one last look down the radar bearing. "Down 'scope. Nothing to see; this squall's a bad one. Steer two-eight zero, make turns for one knot."

The surface situation was sharp in Mayer's mind: *Orca* sat at the center with the radar contact seven miles away to the northeast, the mouth of the Sotaya Channel five miles beyond. He did not believe in coincidences; it had to be the *Maroku Maru*, on its way to Pulau Biak.

Another quick scan through the periscope. Nothing, and Mayer settled down to wait.

"Radar. Contact now at 12,000 yards, bearing zero-four-zero. Confirmed large vessel. He's heading southwest, captain."

Right place, right time, and heading in the right direction, thought Mayer. It had to be the *Maroku Maru*.

"Radar, I have three additional contacts, painting intermittent. One big, two small. They're the escorts, captain."

Mayer allowed himself a moment of satisfaction. His decision to attack submerged was the right one. COMSUBSOWESPAC had said he would be facing at least one Jap fleet destroyer; its speed, radar and advanced fire control systems would send *Orca* to the bottom long before he could maneuver into a position to make an attack.

"Target course and speed confirmed: two-two-five, nineteen," Bronsen said. "It's heading direct for Pulau Biak, skipper."

"The convoy commander has decided he's safe now he's made the Gulf of Lendari," Mayer said. "If he'd been zig-zagging we'd have missed him."

"You can't blame him; with the visibility so bad, he'd probably end up hitting one of the escorts. And our boats haven't sunk anything in the Gulf this whole war."

Mayer nodded. The US Navy had refused to send submarines into the Gulf of Lendari; it was too dangerous ... until a target which had to be sunk had presented itself.

Which would not be easy, not with the *Maroku Maru* moving at nineteen knots. Which was good and bad.

Good because thrashing propellers, water rushing along hulls, and wave noise would degrade the Japanese escorts' sonars. Mayer thought they would be all but useless. The weather was on his side too. The Jap lookouts would struggle to spot his radar mast and periscope amidst the wind-driven seas. And, with moonrise still two hours away, the night was dark.

Bad because it would be past and gone if *Orca*'s first—and only—torpedo salvo missed, leaving the escorts to hunt down *Orca*.

On balance, the *Maroku Maru*'s speed worked for him, Mayer decided. And *Orca* was where it needed to be.

Mayer swept the enemy ships' bearings with the periscope. Nothing. The seconds ticked by, information flowed in from radar and sonar, and still Mayer could not see the *Maroku Maru* or its escorts. The weather was deteriorating as the rain intensified, lashing the sea into a maelstrom. And the last light of day was fading fast.

Mayer's confidence sagged; he needed positive confirmation, and soon.

Again and again he ran the periscope up for a quick sweep all-round, then a longer look down the target bearing. But he could only see rain and waves lit by the last loom of twilight.

Once more, Mayer ordered the 'scope up. His heart kicked.

A dull, dark-gray blur filled the eyepiece. It cleared a fraction, enough to see the massive Sampson posts forward of the superstructure. "Target is confirmed. It's the *Maroku Maru* ... Target! Bearing ... Mark!"

"Zero-two-seven," a crewman said, reading the numbers off the periscope's azimuth ring.

"Down 'scope. Radar range?"

"9,000 yards."

"JP, contact," the low-frequency sonar operator said, "bearing zero-two-four. Multiple ships."

"Blade count on any?"

"Negative, skipper. Too many ships moving too fast."

The minutes crawled.

"Up scope," Mayer said.

The squall had passed. He could see three new patches of gray, fast sharpening into recognizable ships.

"Down 'scope. I have two Mikuras left and right of the target and an Akizuki-class fleet destroyer bringing up the rear."

Bronsen's eyes widened. Mayer knew how he felt.

The Mikuras were sub killers. If their depth-charges didn't sink *Orca* first, they would drive it to the surface where the Akizuki's eight 3.9-inch guns would send it to the bottom in minutes.

"I'm glad we like a challenge, skipper," Bronsen said.

"We sure do … Battle stations torpedo, rig for depth charge. Flood all tubes."

The general alarm filled the conning tower.

"Up 'scope!"

Maroku Maru was closer now, its bows punching waves away in sheets of white water. "Bearing … mark!"

"Bearing zero-two-seven."

Bronsen's voice was taut, his words clipped. "Target course steady two-two-five, speed eighteen. He's still on base track, skipper."

"Happy days," Mayer said. "Right, we're on. Standby everybody. Set turns for one knot."

"Turns for one knot, aye."

A quick check to confirm the *Maroku Maru*'s masthead height. "Height check," Mayer said. "Use seven-three feet. Range ... Mark!"

"Range five-two-oh-oh."

"QB, bearing zero-two-five, single-ping range," Mayer ordered.

"Target bearing zero-two-five, single-ping," the sonar operator said. "Standby ... QB range five-one-oh-oh."

The distance to *Maroku Maru* he had measured using the periscope matched the distance calculated by the QB sonar. Mayer's attack was coming together.

"Target angle on the bow now port three-five. Target drawing left. Down 'scope ... Range to base track?" he said to the junior lieutenant on the TDC. The poor bastard had married an Aussie girl just before joining *Orca* in Fremantle. He was having one hell of a first patrol; the way things were going, it would be his last.

And Mayer was sure the man knew it.

"Range to base track now one-two-oh-oh, sir."

1,200 yards. Perfect. "Control, rig for silent running."

"Rig for silent running, aye."

Mayer turned to Bronsen. "Open all outer doors fore and aft. We'll go with four torpedoes forward on an eighty track, longitudinal spread, forward to aft."

"Seventy track, four fish, longitudinal spread, forward to aft, aye ... Only four, skipper?"

Mayer knew why Bronsen was asking. "Firing six leaves me out of options, Matt. If I keep Five and Six back, I'll have one more chance to hit the target if we miss first time around."

The risks were huge. They both knew it.

"Assuming we hit the target," Mayer went on, "Five and Six can take the nearest Mikura. Then, before they've worked out what's going on, we'll come hard right to take the second Mikura with the stern tubes. We'll worry about the Akizuki later."

The yeoman said, "Ship is at battle stations torpedo, captain, doors open, ready to shoot."

"Next observation will be a shooting observation," Mayer called out. "Standby forward."

His mind's eye tracked the *Maroku Maru* as it crawled across the plot. He flashed the periscope up and down as the range shortened. The Japanese ships were close, but the weather was deteriorating as the next squall swept in.

Time was running out.

Now!

"Standby One through Four. Up 'scope ... Angle on the bow port eight-five, drawing left. Final bearing ... mark!"

"Three-two-two."

"Set," Bronsen called when the data was in the TDC.

"Range ... mark!"

"One-two-four-oh."

"Set."

"Shoot!" Mayer said as he slapped the periscope handles up and stepped back.

"Fire!" ordered Bronsen as he started his stopwatch.

"One's away," the yeoman said as he smacked the firing key, with two, three, and four close behind, the deck jolting as *Orca* spit torpedo from its tube.

"Run time is five-two seconds," Bronsen said.

His firing solution had been solid; Mayer knew his torpedoes would find their target.

—4—

Mori hated the *Maroku Maru*.

A day out of Manila, the weather had turned foul and the seas rough, throwing the ship around, a ship packed with men, equipment, and stores until it could take no more. The ventilation was capricious, fresh water was short, there was no salt-water soap, and everywhere the air was fetid with the smell of body odor, vomit, and the after-effects of too much alcohol.

The Imperial Japanese Army never ran short of rough, raw rice wine.

At least he was feeling better.

He had been lucky to survive the smallpox vaccination Unit 731 had given him. Unlike thirty-seven of his men; they had died in agony.

But not much better, thanks to the shipboard rumor mill, now in full flow. On the unshakeable authority of the last person spoken to, every man onboard knew there were American submarines out there hunting for the *Maroku Maru*.

Lots of them, apparently.

One of the ship's officers had assured him he need not worry. With the navy's escorts to protect them and zigzagging at twenty knots, *Maroku Maru* presented a difficult target. The Americans would need to be in the right position long before the ship arrived to have any chance of a successful attack.

And, in the vastness of the ocean, what were the odds of that?

The stench from his brother officers caught in Mori's throat. He would go on deck, he decided.

He headed for the upper deck and fresh air.

•••

The *Maroku Maru*'s bows slammed into the endless succession of white-flecked waves, sending a sheet of seawater whipping over the bows and back across the deck, its warmth a momentary improvement over the ice-cold rain sleeting down.

Mori had had enough.

Even the reek of unwashed, saké-sodden, sea-sick officers was better than this. As he reached for the door handle, the ship staggered into a trough. He stumbled back, lost his footing, and fell to the deck.

Wham ...crunch!

The *Maroku Maru*'s deck punched upwards.

Wham... crunch. Wham ... crunch.

An instant's calm. Then came the awful grinding, rending screech of steel ripped from steel as the crippled ship staggered to a stop, wallowing in the heavy seas.

Mori started to his feet, only to be knocked back to the deck by one of the crew. He grabbed the man's leg. "What's happening?" he shouted.

The sailor kicked Mori's hand away. "We've been torpedoed, you idiot." And then he vanished into the growing crowd,

Mori stood. The urge to run almost overcame him, but where to? The canisters with the virus! He had to get them into a lifeboat and off the ship.

He forced a path through the fast-growing flood of men pouring out on deck, panicked, confused, terrified, fighting and clawing and tearing at each other in their desperate struggle to reach wherever they imagined safety to be. For a moment, Mori made ground, but the torrent of foul-smelling, rice-wine-soaked humanity from below was too strong.

A shouting, screaming, swearing mob hunting for a way out of the nightmare engulfing the *Maroku Maru* swept him away.

The ship lurched, hung for an instant, then started into its death roll, heeling until the mass of men crowding the upper deck could no longer stand. Bodies surged into bodies, a stumbling, sliding, sprawling crush that drove Mori across the deck and into a winch, his chest racked across angular metal edges splintering his ribs, his screams lost in the mayhem of failing ship and dying men.

Blackness claimed him.

Two of *Orca's* torpedoes had torn holes in the *Maroku Maru* below Number 5 and 6 holds. The sea had poured in and rampaged forward. Ripping bulkheads aside, it erupted into an engine room already flooding fast from *Orca's* first torpedo.

The *Maroku Maru* gave up the fight. It rolled over on its side, hesitated, rolled back, then slipped by the stern into the depths of the Gulf of Lendari.

Few of those who made it off the ship survived for long. The seething vortex of a 10,000-ton ship plunging to the bottom pulled them under, leaving a handful on the surface to drift on wind-flogged seas into the night.

Ignoring the doomed ship and any survivors, the three escorts had turned to attack.

— 5 —

Wham ... wham ... wham...

The explosions shook *Orca*'s hull.

"Left full rudder. Steady on two seven-five. Up 'scope," Mayer said. A quick glance confirmed his hopes: Three torpedoes from his first salvo had hit *Maroku Maru*. It listed over to port until its upper deck touched the water, the rail thick with bodies. It was doomed.

Mayer put the 'scope onto the closest Mikura, now turning hard to port.

It was coming for *Orca*. It was also all but broadside on. Targets did not come much better.

•••

Against terrible odds, *Orca* had done well, its torpedoes sending the *Maroku Maru* and two Mikuras to the bottom.

But not before repeated depth-charge attacks had forced it to the surface, its hull too damaged to allow it stay submerged, pumps working furiously to keep the submarine afloat, the sea around it thrashed white by the Akizuki's salvoes

Mayer knew the torpedoes he had just fired at the Jap destroyer had little chance of hitting the Akizuki. It would not be long before its guns sank *Orca*.

He wished he—

The Akizuki had fired the perfect salvo. Shells punched through the pressure hull below the waterline and tearing great gashes.

Water flooded in.

Its slender reserve of buoyancy gone, the wounded boat hesitated, reluctant to leave the surface. But *Orca's* time had come. Amidst the shriek of escaping air, it half-rolled over and slipped beneath the waves.

•••

Eight hundred yards away and moving fast, the Akizuki was heeling hard when one of *Orca's* torpedoes from its final salvo blew an enormous hole below the bridge, a hole that swallowed hundreds of tons water in seconds, the sheer mass and speed of the inrushing sea blasting a path through one watertight bulkhead after another all the way to the stern of the ship.

The destroyer crashed to a stop, rolling in the heavy swell as its stern sank below the surface and its bows lifted skywards. Slowly at first, it slipped away, and then it was gone.

A fizzing column of bubbles and shattered debris marked the doomed ship's disappearance. Soon bodies appeared, released from the vortex to drift up into the night air, open-mouthed and slack-jawed in death.

•••

Dawn broke over the battlefield, empty now save for flotsam from the sunken ships. A few survivors drifted amidst hundreds of dead.

Soon the oceanic white-tip sharks arrived. At first, there were few. Within an hour, there were hundreds. They slashed through the dead and the living until the water ran red. Soon, the screams died away.

Sated, the sharks vanished.

•••

In June 1944, the Commander Submarines, South West Pacific, reported *Orca* overdue, presumed sunk in its patrol area south of the Philippines, final position unknown.

2023

The young man behind the reception counter glanced up.

Black shapes moved behind the frosted glass of the door into the office. Odd shapes. Four of them. No, five now.

Bulky. Large heads. Helmets?

He half-stood to get a better look. He still couldn't make them out.
He sat down and picked up the telephone to call his CEO's personal assistant. *Hi Jilan. Can you tell the boss that there's something weird going on outside ... No, I don't .... They look—*

With a sharp *krakk*, the door blew inwards.

On instinct, the young man had dropped his head an instant before a blizzard of shattered glass engulfed him.

He huddled over in shock, bleeding from cuts to his arms and head, ears ringing.

Hands dragged him to his feet.

A black-suited man shouted, "Your boss! Where is he?"

Dazed, the young man wiped blood from his eyes. Like everyone in Beijing, he knew better than to argue with State Security. *I'll show you. This way, please.*

As one of the agents followed the young man, he kicked aside the brass plaque blasted off the door.

> ### 中国达斯勒企业。建立一个更美好的世界。
>
> Sino-Dassler Enterprises. For a better world.

—2—

The water carafe, lead-crystal and heavy, flew across the boardroom table and shattered against the wall.

Luke Dassler did not react. When his twin brother was in one of his rages, staying quiet was the only safe option. Years of savage beatings had pounded the lesson home.

Incandescent with anger, chest heaving, face mottled red with rage, heavy lids slits over small, gray-blue eyes, Mark Dassler was as tall as Luke was not, his once-muscled upper body long since gone to fat. "Goddammed scum!" he shouted. "How dare they steal from me."

Luke allowed himself to breathe again. Mark had stopped throwing things and was talking again, usually a sign he wasn't on his way to the emergency room. "Uh ... What's happened?"

Mark's face fractured into a sneer of contempt. "You are a waste of time, Luke. I still don't understand why Dad split the company between the two of us."

Luke knew why: to stop his brother destroying himself and the Dassler Corporation. He had done his best, but it had never been easy. If Mark wasn't a psychopath, he was close to being one.

"Come on, Mark," he said. "Tell me what China's done now."

Mark pushed a thick document across the table. "A Ministry of State Security front company has acquired Sino-Dassler for one US dollar. That's the sale and purchase agreement, hand-delivered by the MSS's Beijing Bureau after they blew the office door in. They told Jakob Lubiç to sign it or it'd be ten years before he and his family saw daylight again."

"Jakob signed the agreement under duress. It's void. We must sue; Sino-Dassler is worth well over a hundred billion."

"You are a half-wit," Mark Dassler spit. "No Chinese court will ever rule in our favor. Sino-Dassler's not ours anymore."

"This is unacceptable."

"Oh, really? Why don't you complain to the Great Navigator? Oh, wait! There's no point. He'll just tell you to go fuck yourself."

Luke Dassler put his hands up. "You're right. So, what do we do?"

"I tell you what we won't do: ask the US government for help. It's lost its balls ever since the Chinese told us to go fuck ourselves after the COVID-19 fiasco. And we're no better. All we do is talk while the Chinese steal our assets. If we don't stop them, they'll end up running the goddammed world."

Mark leaned forward. "I am not waiting for the government anymore," he went on. "We are going to make the Great Navigator and his commie friends pay, only this time there'll be no rules, no limits. We will do whatever it takes, and that is a promise."

Mark Dassler bared his teeth in feral anticipation. "And we don't have to do this alone. China's screwed over thousands of American businesses; it won't be hard to find people who want to help us make it pay. Right, I have a meeting. I'll catch up with you later … and clean up this mess."

Luke sat, silent, as his brother left. He knew what Mark meant by 'whatever it takes': something very, very ugly.

It always did.

And Mark Dassler always kept his promises.

2028

Two inches short of six feet, Joe Lessart was a broad-shouldered man with his Bahamian mother's milk-coffee skin and his father's blue eyes fringed by a mop of wayward curly black hair.

Cheeks red-tinged with anger, he glared at the man sat across Hydra Research's boardroom table.

Joe respected Adam Kuprovic, one of America's richest investors and a legend in the pharmaceutical industry, thanks to his ability to pick winning start-ups.

But Joe did not like him. Not many people did.

He had done his best to build a relationship with Adam which went beyond their shared interest in Hydra Research. Joe had even tried talk about Adam's time in the marines. The man had ended up a staff sergeant before going to college on his way to becoming an investment banker. Since Joe hadn't even graduated the marines' officer candidates school—thanks to a broken leg—it had been a short conversation.

Joe turned to the man sitting beside him. "For chrissakes, André! The day-to-day management of BT-677's Phase 3 trials is not a board matter. Tell him."

André Tanadi put a huge hand on Joe's shoulder. A large man, he was as calm as Joe was agitated. "Settle down. Adam's only asking to be briefed more often."

"No way! I am Hydra's chief executive. I'll decide what to tell him and when."

Adam stood and headed for the door. "Enough of this bullshit, André. See if you can kick some sense into him. We've almost closed the sale of Hydra to Courelle. We cannot afford any surprises."

Joe slumped back in his chair. "You told him you agreed, didn't you?" he said as the door slammed behind Adam Kuprovic.

André shifted in his chair, his tongue flickering across his lips. "I, um, ah... Well, not in so many words ... Okay, okay., I did."

Joe could not decide whether to laugh or scream. André was a terrible liar. Friends since college, he loved him for it.

"I give up. We'll do it Adam's way."

"Pity you didn't say so up front," André muttered as he headed for the door. "I'll go tell him."

Joe wasn't happy, but this was no time for a fight, not with Hydra Research so close to releasing BT-677, a vaccine which would defeat influenza for all time. A vaccine he hoped would make him and André very rich.

But only if Adam closed the sale of Hydra to Courelle Biologique. The negotiations seemed endless.

He sat back, rubbing eyes gritty with stress and fatigue. Work was a grind. André was frustrating. Adam was a pain. His girlfriend, Klara, was moving to DC. And something was up with his grandmother. Nothing life-threatening, he hoped; he hated the thought of losing her. With his parents long dead, she was all the family he had left.

Klara... wasn't he supposed to...

"I am so screwed!" he muttered when he remembered. As he reached for his cell, it rang.

Klara started to unload before Joe could say a word.

"You are such an asshole, Joe Lessart," she snarled. "Bellini's, eight o'clock, remember? I had to beg Marcello for a table. I felt so stupid sitting there on my own, waiting for you to turn up."

"I'm so sorry. Things are busy at work."

"Always the same excuse." Klara's voice was sour. "Our relationship has become a lie, Joe. You pretend we are equals. We are not. If we were, you would have been here. I have forgotten how many times you turn up late or not at all. You only want me on your terms, never on mine, which is why you don't want me to go to Washington."

"But I do," Joe protested. "You have to go."

"Whatever … This relationship is broken, and my move to DC won't fix it. Nothing can. We are over. Go find somebody else to manipulate."

Then she was gone.

Joe knew she would never be back.

—2—

Joe dropped his cellphone into a pocket. "That was Adam. Courelle Biologique have signed. Hydra Research is now all theirs. Which means, my friend, each of us is a millionaire two-hundred times over."

André folded Joe in a rib-crushing bear hug. "About time."

"For chrissakes," Joe squeaked, "put me down. You're killing me!"

André let Joe go. "Sorry. I was starting to worry."

"It's what you do best … Remember what we said at the end of our last Java Sea trip?"

A broad grin split André's face. "We wanted to spend the rest of our lives wreck diving?"

"We sure did, my friend. The expedition boat we saw for sale on the East Coast. I think we should buy it."

"We can now. And we should. It's perfect."

"I'll call the broker. Are we still calling it the *Sophie Scholl*?"

"She's one of my all-time heroes too," André said, "so the *Sophie Scholl* it is. Listen, I'm beat. I will see you tomorrow. Oh, by the way," he added, "Celia Vandergraaf is our new president. Not that she'll be able to make a difference."

"Which is why I've ignored the whole business," Joe said.

Once André had gone, he flopped into a chair, too wired to sleep. Flicking on the television, he stepped though the channels to CNN.

A reporter was talking to camera against a backdrop of thousands of Celia Vandergraaf's supporters, a raucous sea of red, white, and blue peppered with excited faces waving placards and flags.

Joe switched the television off. America was in mired in a debt-fueled crisis of its own making, a crisis China was busy exploiting. Vandergraaf had to be unhinged to want the presidency at a time like this. Nobody in their right mind would take the job.

Not that he cared. The world, Hydra, Courelle, Klara, could all go to hell. He and André would buy a boat and go diving.

—3—

The USAAF's 308th Bombardment Wing's records were unequivocal: Late in July 1944, a patrol of B-25 Mitchells out of Pulau Owi had sunk the Japanese destroyer, *Kumotori*, in the Gulf of Lendari off the north coast of West Papua.

And the *Kumotori* was going to be the *Sophie Scholl*'s first prize: a virgin World War 2 wreck, never dived.

So where was it?

For days, they had plowed up and down, the side-scan sonar seeing sand, rocky outcrops, an occasional fishing boat, but no destroyers.

By the time midnight came and went, the sonar screen was a blur. Joe's patience was exhausted. He left the control room and went forward onto the bridge.

Budi, the first officer, had the watch. "All quiet?" Joe asked.

"We have boats from Manokwari and Sorong, but fishermen stay home. No fish. All gone, I think."

"Why am I not surprised? I'm done. Night, Budi."

"Sleep well, Joe. I call if sonar find anything."

André was still up, sprawled out in the saloon. "I was wondering how long you'd keep going. Still nothing?"

Joe shook his head. He took a beer from the fridge and found himself a seat. "I was so sure we'd find the *Kumotori*. I think the B-25s sank another ship ... if they sunk anything at all."

"The 308th was sure they had."

"Hah!" Joe snorted. "I'm surprised the boys even flew. The weather was terrible. Those B-25s would have had trouble hitting a city block."

André leaned over and patted Joe on the shoulder. "Japanese Navy records confirmed the sinking. The *Kumotori* is out here somewhere. Don't worry, we'll find it. Fear the patient man and all that."

"I guess."

"And be happy the Chinese haven't found it first. You know, we were so lucky; we dived the South China Sea, the Gulf of Thailand, and the Java Sea before they salvaged all the wrecks."

Joe's face darkened. "Bastards. Those wrecks were war graves."

"The Chinese salvage companies don't give a shit. As far as they are concerned, China won the war all on its own and they can do what they like … Come on, Joe. Cheer up! Why own the world's best dive boat if we can't waste our time looking for wrecks?"

Joe shook his head. "Best dive boat? World's most expensive, you mean. All I seem to do is send money to Rikki Tengarran back in Semarang. And I worry about the man. I have never seen someone bet the way he does."

"Relax. All Indonesians like to gamble. Besides, Rikki has plenty of his own money. And he's family, as well as a very competent ship manager."

Joe laughed. "You've introduced me to a lot of Indonesians over the years, and most seem to be relatives of yours. How many are there?"

"Never stopped to count. Hundreds, I suppose if you count all the cousins. Us Hokkien Chinese are big on family."

The phone rang. Joe waved a hand at André to pick up.

"Yes, Budi … Oh, wow … Yes, I'll tell him."

André hung up the phone and turned to Joe. "Budi says the sonar's seen something interesting. Come on."

They climbed into the cool darkness of the bridge.

"What've you got, Budi?"

"Two contacts. One large, one small."

"Worth another run?"

"Oh, for sure."

"Then let's set up a new track."

Joe and André went into the control room, a small compartment behind the bridge packed with screens busy with data flowing from the ship's suite of sensors. The returns from the side-scan sonar cascaded across the largest display, a mass of orange displaying every feature across a 400-yard-wide swathe of the seabed as it passed under the side-scan sonar towed behind *Sophie Scholl*. Joe rolled the sonar trace back the way they had come.

"There!" André said.

Joe stared at the screen. There was no doubt what he was looking at: the shadow of a large merchant ship black against the mass of yellow and orange echoes reflected from the seabed, the wreck's hull, masts, its superstructure etched in exquisite detail.

"Oh, you beautiful, beautiful thing," Joe whispered.

"Four Sampson posts forward. Gun mounts bow and stern, superstructure amidships, docking bridge down aft. We're not looking at the *Kumotori*."

Joe ran a finger over the image. "No ... It looks familiar, but I can't place it."

"Check the other contact," André said.

Joe rolled a cursor across the screen. "Four hundred feet long. Raked bow, two turrets forward, two aft, a tower bridge. The stack's gone, though. A Japanese fleet destroyer, for sure."

André frowned. "We've got a merchantman and a Jap destroyer. Why aren't they in any of the combat reports?"

"Maybe whatever sunk them didn't survive long enough to get one away."

"We should finish the side-scan runs to see what else is out there. And, once we've had the ROV video the wrecks, we'll go diving."

Joe grinned. The remotely operated vehicle was André's favorite toy.

•••

The ROV inched towards the last of the five wrecks the *Sophie Scholl*'s sonar had discovered. An orgy of broken steel, André had called it, barely able to contain his excitement.

The screen filled with video from the ROV's high-definition camera. A shape materialized out of the blue-back gloom. It lay on the sand three-hundred-ten feet below the surface, half-canted to port, bows-on to the ROV, which Joe started moving down its length.

André leaned forward. "It's a submarine, as we thought. That explains the other wrecks, and why none of this appears in the patrol reports. The sub didn't live long enough to send one."

The forward deck gun swam past, and now the distinctive arrangement of a US fleet submarine's bridge appeared, shears holding periscopes and radar masts.

Joe and André said, "American!"

"Why was he taking on four Japanese ships inside the Gulf?" Joe said once the shock had worn off. "Was the skipper insane?"

"Insanely brave, more like it. One channel in and out, shallow water, attacking a target protected by three escorts."

"I'm hoping the wrecks will tell us something. Happy to start with the merchant ship?"

"Try stopping me," André said.

•••

Joe followed the line down to the wreck. The cobalt water, vodka-clear, darkened until only a faint blue circle remained overhead.

A black shape appeared from the gloom.

His torch picked out a ship's bow, the fo'c's'le cluttered with anchor gear and windlasses. He drifted to stop above the deck. He swung around to look at the shape rearing over him.

This ship was Japanese. Joe had seen the same gun mounting on other wrecks.

André joined him. "All good?"

His helium-distorted voice was metallic through the speech processor.

Joe checked the handset tracking his rebreather's status. "All good. Let's see if we can identify this gorgeous piece of steel."

He swam over the bows and into the void. Ten feet out, he turned, as he did with every wreck he dived. He loved looking back at a ship, imagining how it must have appeared in its prime. For a minute, he hung there, stunned. The wreck was magnificent. Massive bows flared from the stem; the gun dominated the fo'c's'le; beyond, huge Sampson posts reached up into the blue. Behind them was the gray-on-black of the superstructure, five or more decks high. Below him, the hull dropped away to sit on a seabed of featureless gray sand.

"Come on, Joe. No time for sightseeing. We need a name."

André was right; they weren't that deep—250 feet—but it was deep enough. They had a lot of wreck to see and the levels of nitrogen and helium in their bodies were building fast.

They swam aft, torches sweeping across the hull.

An inconsistency in the steel caught Joe's eye. It resolved itself into a single letter welded to the hull: an 'M'. His fingers traced out the letters.

"It's the *Maroku Maru*."

André swam up to join him. "If this isn't one of the *Aikoku Maru*'s sister ships, I'm a cabbage."

Joe had to agree. They had dived the *Aikoku Maru* many times. Of the many wrecks in Truk Lagoon, it was his favorite.

Aikoku Maru, 22 August 1942 at Seletar, Singapore, sister-ship to the Maroku Maru.

Source: Imperial Japanese Navy

—4—

Joe walked into the saloon and collapsed onto a bench. The niggling ache in one shoulder was an unwelcome harbinger of decompression sickness. Intoxicated by the wrecks they had discovered, he and André had dived too often, too deep, and for too long.

In the end, an endless run of squalls had swept away the calm, sunny weather they had enjoyed early on, whipping up short, steep seas which made life too difficult for the two chase boats trying to keep station over the wrecks.

Conditions underwater had also gone to shit. Visibility had fallen to a few feet. Worse, the current had picked up; they had learned the hard way not to take it for granted. Two dives back, a vicious eddy had come from nowhere and ripped them off one of the Japanese escorts. They had aborted the dive and come up on their marker buoys. They found themselves alone and drifting fast with empty ocean their only company, the sea battered by rainstorms which whited-out surface visibility to zero.

The experience had been sobering. Even with their safety beacons bleating calls for help, the chase boats had taken an hour to find them.

With an effort, Joe looked up. "Hey, André! Enough?"

André rolled over and peered at Joe from bleary eyes. "Enough. Now let me sleep."

Joe ignored his body's protests and levered himself upright. "You are an idle bastard. I'll go tell the captain to recover our buoys and head for Semarang, shall I?"

Face down on the bench, André gave Joe the finger.

•••

Joe and André sat, feet up on the stern guardrail, content to let the ocean slip away behind the *Sophie Scholl*, its tumbling wake broken by a pod of dolphins, a turtle up for air, flying fish skimming silver inches above the sea. Time passed in companionable quiet as the sun dropped in the west.

"This could be huge," André said.

"Bigger than huge," Joe replied. "Against impossible odds, a US submarine sinks four enemy ships, only to be sunk itself. Jeez, talk about brave. This has to be one of the great untold stories of World War 2 … a story we have to tell."

"Only when we've done our research. Then we can talk with someone like National Geographic about a proper scientific expedition."

Joe frowned. "We'll have a problem keeping the lid on this. Everyone onboard knows the wrecks are down there."

"I'm ahead of you. I have told the captain we'll give the crew a cash bonus once we sign up National Geographic or whoever. Omar says they understand keeping quiet is in their best interests. And they're family."

"Ah," said Joe, "loyalty underscored with greed. A powerful brew … Where are you up to with the world's best private detective?"

"Don't let Skylar Rafiki hear you … I spoke with her. She's happy with the brief."

"Really? Tracking down old wrecks isn't what she does."

"She says it's just about digging up information. She also said finding out what happened to the *Maroku Maru* is a huge improvement on hunting down criminal scum trying to steal Hydra's secrets. And a lot safer."

"We won't be getting any death threats, for sure," Joe said.

André grimaced. "I hated them."

Joe reached across and patted André's hand. "Relax. They're all Courelle's problem now."

The *Sophie Scholl*'s captain called from the bridge. "Satphone call, Joe. Line 2."

"Okay, Omar," Joe said, levering himself out of his chair with a grunt. "Joe Lessart ... Oh, hi, Doctor Muller."

Joe said nothing for a long time before speaking again. "I understand. No, no questions. I'll do my best... Goodbye."

"Something up?" André asked.

"That was my grandmother's doctor. He says she has advanced pancreatic cancer and doesn't have long. He wants me back. Why didn't she say something was wrong?"

"You tell me. But we need to get you home." André paused for a moment. "Semarang won't work," he went on. "Manado's your best bet. There are direct flights to Singapore from there. I'll go brief Omar."

Joe slumped back in his seat, numb. Just when his grandmother needed him most, he wasn't there.

—5—

"I'm so sorry, Joe. Your grandmother was a fine woman. I always said she was the best thing the Bahamas ever produced. We'll miss her."

"Thank you," Joe said to the latest in a lengthy line of somber-faced mourners he did not recognize and whose names he would never remember. "I will too."

"Joe?"

A familiar voice.

He spun around. Klara! Tall, slim, elegant, in a simple black dress with a necklace of twisted gold against deep, honey-brown skin. She was beyond stunning. Her perfume brought back all the memories Joe had tried so hard to forget. "Thanks for coming. Grandma Lessart was fond of you."

"I liked her."

"I'm so happy to see you," said Joe. "I've missed you. Perhaps we could—"

"Stop right there, Joe! I am here to say goodbye to your grandmother, not because I wanted a chat with you. What happened between us is history. Best you forget it. And I'm seeing someone else now, a guy called Cal Grujic."

"Oh ... Cal Grujic? Is he the guy who broke the story of Defense Department staffers selling classified information on the dark web? Works for the Washington Post?"

"It is, and the story's earned him a Pulitzer nomination. He is a decent man, Joe, and we are happy. He suits me, and I think I suit him."

The cynic in Joe wondered if it was so simple. Klara was an up-and-coming star inside Homeland Security. Grujic was the Post's leading investigative journalist, famous for his exposés of criminality and dysfunction within the Federal Government's sprawling security apparatus.

Talk about a coincidence. Either way, lucky Cal Grujic.

He forced the thought away as unworthy. Klara was way too smart to let anyone exploit her. Grujic was the one who needed to be careful.

"Let's catch up next time I'm in Washington," Joe said.

Klara shook her head. "No, let's not. And don't try to call me. I'll just hang up."

"We can't talk? Come on, Klara! You owe me."

"I do not owe you anything, Joe Lessart."

"But after everything—"

"But nothing."

"Jeez! Why can't—"

"Fuck off, Joe," Klara hissed.

—6—

Joe cut the call. The *Sophie Scholl* was alongside in Semarang, and André was on his way home, though not before visiting with every member of his extended family.

Joe wanted his grandmother's place cleared and handed over to a realtor before André got back. Then they could start work on what they now called 'The Big Project'.

He went upstairs to start on the attic.

•••

Joe had saved the Royal Crown Cola box for last. Unlike the others—all stuffed with the detritus of a long life lived well—it was full of old notebooks.

He picked one out. As he turned its pages, he realized it wasn't the diaries he'd expected. It was a workbook, full of jottings on a range of topics in his grandfather's spidery hand.

The result was a chaotic mix of information, with headings ranging from thoughts on growing succulents to notes from a long discussion with a man called Artie Shaw on the non-existence of God.

Joe put the workbook back. He was tempted to throw the entire box out, unread. He knew his grandfather only from old black-and-white photographs; weren't these just the ramblings of man sixty years dead?

But the box did connect him to the man, a box Grandma Lessart had thought worth keeping. He owed it to her to find out why.

Joe put the box aside. He would go through it later.

•••

Joe had cleared the attic and the first of the bedrooms; the rest of the house could wait. He started to sort through the notebooks. Anything of interest went into one pile, the rest into a second.

By the time he had finished, the investigate pile consisted of two leather-bound volumes. Inside the front cover of one were the spidery, handwritten words 'Japan 1', inside the other 'Japan 2'.

Joe picked up the first of them and settled down to read.

•••

Dawn was close when Joe closed the second volume.

There was so much about Michael Lessart he had not known. A detective with the Los Angeles Police Department, he had joined the US Army after Pearl Harbor, rising to the rank of captain in the military police. After the war, he was seconded to the War Crimes Tribunal in Tokyo, one of the prosecution team drawing up the cases against former government ministers Okinori Kaya, Mamoru Shigemitsu and—until his death in June 1946—Yōsuke Matsuoka, along with thirty-six less famous war criminals, each case recorded as Michael Lessart had seen them unfold.

Joe sat back and rubbed his eyes. Interesting stuff, but he was exhausted.

About to toss the notebooks back into the box, something stopped him. He flicked back through Volume 2 until he found the page which had snagged his attention.

Joe frowned.

His grandfather's words nagged at him, faint but insistent. His subconscious had found some connection, but it refused to let it out into the light.

He would send the page to Skylar Rafiki.

She and her team of analysts with their search bots could squeeze information out of a block of granite.

If anyone could find the connection his mind refused to reveal, it was her.

December 9, 1945

Had a beer with Amos and Hector this evening. Both very angry with way things are being handled. Sanders and Camp Detrick are pushing MacArthur hard to finalize a deal to get Japs to supply all Nip germ warfare research results in exchange for indemnities, even though they killed thousands in their tests, including US POWs from Mukden camp. If those weren't war crimes, what are?

Two nights ago, Sanders' interpreter Naito (very drunk as usual) told Hector that Unit 731 had been part of a big operation to kill Mac's boys in SOWESPAC, though the Japs never made it that far. A US sub sank 731's ship after it left Manila on its way south. Naito denied it all later, like he always does. Slimy SOB. Something not right about him.

Hector will try to put pressure on Naito for more information. (though he's sure Sanders will try to stop him). If he can prove the Japs were planning a germ warfare operation, maybe Mac will agree to prosecutions. God knows, he should.

I said it didn't matter. Mac is not a man who likes to change his mind. My guess is he thinks it makes him seem weak. Glad I'm not involved in 731 investigations. The whole thing stinks.

Back to Yokohama next week to prepare for trial of Asao Fukuhara. He was commander of Fukuoka-17 POW camp and a real bad one. I hope we nail the bastard. I think we will.

—7—

André tossed the report onto the table, the words 'BT-677 Market Update and Forecast' on its cover. "Tell you something, Joe. We sold to Courelle too soon and too cheap Our wonder vaccine is going gangbusters. Give it five years, and influenza's history, gone the way of smallpox."

"Huh," grunted Joe. "Like I care. I'm just glad we won't be having any more meetings with Adam Kuprovic. I do not want to see him ever again. All the asshole cares about is money, money, money."

"He sure does."

Joe's cellphone rang. "Hi Skylar, I'm with André. I'll put you on speaker ... Go ahead."

"I'll be in town for a meeting this evening. Can we talk before then? Lobby bar, Manchester Grand Hyatt at four?"

"We'll be there."

•••

Skylar Rafiki was a solid, no-nonsense woman in her late forties. Joe liked and respected her. Her ruthless pursuit of the criminals trying to hack Hydra's secrets had put the FBI to shame.

"Let's get started," she said. "We have identified your submarine. The serial number of the four-inch gun you gave me matches the one fitted to the *USS Orca*. It was running out of Fremantle in Australia at the time. COMSUBSOWEPAC—navy shorthand for the Commander Submarines, Southwest Pacific, Admiral Christie at the time—reported it lost in June 1944, last position unknown."

"Well done, Skylar. But you didn't tell the US Navy, did you? I don't want them hassling us. They don't trust technical divers to leave their wrecks alone."

"No. You made that clear."

"Outstanding. Anything else?"

"Yes. We have identified the Japanese ships you found," Rafiki went on. "The two Mikura-class ocean-defense ships are the *Kanazuchi* and *Kansei*. And the Akizuki is the fleet destroyer *Tatsumaki.* They were the only ships in the area whose sinkings haven't been accounted for. All the Japanese Navy's records say is they were lost off the Netherlands East Indies in June 1944, last positions unknown."

"How about the *Maroku Maru*?"

"It left Dalian on April 24, 1944 for Manila, arriving there May 4. And then it vanishes."

Joe stared at Rafiki in disbelief. "The *Maroku Maru* was important enough to warrant a heavy escort. Surely there must be something in the archives?"

"No, there isn't, which is odd. Transports like the *Maroku Maru* always reported their positions at noon every day, along with course, speed, destination, and so on. Those reports were enciphered using the Japanese Army's Water Transport Code, which the Allies cracked in '43. As a result, the archives contain hundreds of pages of information archives about ship movements. They tell us where the *Maroku Maru* was the entire war, right until it left Manila. Then, nothing. The ship vanished."

After a moment's silence, Joe said, "The *Maroku Maru* must have sent daily reports. How else could Christie have known where to send *Orca* to sink it?"

"You're right. COMSUBSOWEPAC's records tell us *Orca* was patrolling five hundred miles north of the Gulf of Lendari targeting Japanese convoys transporting reinforcements to Davao. Only an intercepted signal could have made Christie divert it south. What's odd is there is nothing in Seventh Fleet or COMSUBSOWEPAC archives about *Orca* or the *Maroku Maru*, and there should have been. Which means one thing: The signals retasking *Orca* were destroyed, along with all the *Maroku Maru*'s records."

There was another silence, broken by André. "What about the original decrypted intercepts?"

"They were read and then destroyed," Rafiki said. "The US Navy was obsessed about hiding the fact its codebreakers were reading Japanese naval signals. We will never find the decrypt which prompted Admiral Christie to send *Orca* to the Gulf of Lendari."

"This is bad," André said. "Unless we can find out why the *Maroku Maru* was so important, all we'll have is yet another unsolved mystery."

"Which I hate, and Nat Geo does too." Joe turned to Rafiki. "How do we find out why *Orca* was sent south?"

"We are checking Chinese sources. Ditto in the Philippines and Japan. *Maroku Maru* was a distinctive ship, large for its day. Somebody may have seen something as it went south."

"Maybe they will give us something. We can't take this to Nat Geo until we have answers."

Rafiki got to her feet. "I'll get back to you when I have something new."

—8—

Every source Joe had dredged up said the same thing.

By 1944, the Japanese—desperate to stop the Allies' relentless advance on their homeland—were draining men from China and Manchukuo to buttress a defensive line which arced northeast from West Papua and the Netherlands East Indies through the Philippines and on to the islands of the western Pacific.

Many of those men had left on ships from the port of Dalian, but none of those ships had ever received the extraordinary protection given to the *Maroku Maru*.

Joe sat back and rubbed his eyes. There had to be a reason. Why couldn't he find it?

His cellphone cut his thinking short. Skylar Rafiki had texted him.

"Sorry so late," she had written. "Urgent. First place we ever met. Now. Turn off your cell and watch before leaving home."

●●●

Joe admired the view across San Francisco's Union Square as he walked into Skylar Rafiki's suite. "Very flash, Skylar. Tell me I'm not paying for this"

Rafiki waved him to the meeting table. "Relax. Another client is picking up the tab."

"Why the secrecy? I was worried for a second."

"You should be. You guys have ripped the scab off something nasty."

"From over half a century ago?" Joe said, shaking his head. "Come on, Skylar. I don't see it."

"Have you heard of Unit 731?"

"I have. The Japanese Army's biological warfare center, right?"

"Correct. And a nasty bunch they were too. Now, do you remember the December 9, 1945 entry in your grandfather's notebook? The one where a man called Naito said Unit 731 was part of an operation against MacArthur's forces in the southwest Pacific, an operation which never happened because the US Navy sank their ship after it left Manila?"

"Yes, I do. The whole entry still bugs me, but I can't work out why."

"Well, Joe, I have. You found the *Maroku Maru*, sunk by a US submarine. Your grandfather's file note from December 9, 1945, said Unit 731's ship was also sunk by a US submarine. All your brain was doing was asking if 731's ship was the *Maroku Maru*. Which I think it was."

Joe threw his hands up. "Oh, for fuck's sake! Of course! I can't believe I missed it ... But US submarines sank a lot of Japanese ships. Are you sure about this?"

"Your grandfather talks about a man called Hector, family name Tejerina. US father, mother from Hokkaido, born in Osaka, spoke fluent Japanese. Like your grandfather, he was an investigator for the War Crimes Tribunal in Tokyo. He worked on Unit 731 cases. He is long dead, but his widow, Marcia, still lives in Buffalo. She is ninety-eight next week, but her mind is still sharp. When I said we were trying to find out more about Unit 731, she said they were horrible, horrible people and would anything she could to help."

"Hector must have told her what he was up against," Joe said.

"You should read some of his letters; they're the stuff of nightmares. Lucky for you, Marcia refused to let the family throw out any of his stuff, keeping it all in a self-storage unit. She said we could go through it, so we did..."

Rafiki slid a folder across the table.

"...and we found this."

Joe opened it to find four pages of typewritten text, the paper yellowed with age. He started to read.

HJT/10-10-45/6344-D/SATO - 1

INTERROGATION OF SATO, NORIMITSU

Date & Time: October 10, 1945; 14:00

Place: Sugamo Prison, Tokyo, Japan

Present: SATO, Norimitsu, Captain IJN, Prisoner

H. J. TEJERINA, Captain US Army, Interrogator

Miss H. INUKAI, Interpreter

Miss A. L. DUNDAS, Stenographer

PREFACE

During interrogation of SATO on 5 October 1945 (Ref: HJT/10-5-45/6344-D/SATO), he stated that a shipment of the Strain 5524 virus from UNIT 731 was sent to Pulau Biak, Netherlands East Indies (NEI). Given the extreme risk such a consignment poses, MAJOR MORRISETT has directed a further interrogation be conducted to confirm the answers SATO has given previously are correct.

TRANSCRIPT OF INTERROGATION

(HJT) Captain SATO, were you the officer-in-charge of Special Research Office 21, Division 2, UNIT 731, Epidemic Prevention and Water Purification Department, Kwantung Army, based in Pingfang, in the area formerly called Manchukuo?

(NS) You keep asking me this. Why? I have answered this question many times.

(HJT) Answer the question.

(NS) Yes, from February 1942. I was sent back to Japan in 1945.

(HJT) Which section of UNIT 731 developed smallpox viruses for military purposes?

(NS) Special Research Office 21, which was part of Division 2.

(HJT) Who was in charge of Special Research Office 21?

(NS) I have told you this also. Always the same questions. Why?

(HJT) Just answer the question.

(NS) I was.

HJT/10-10-45/6344-D/SATO - 2

(HJT) What was Strain 5524?

A strain of the hemorrhagic smallpox virus. I perfected it in early 1943, though the vaccine took until 1944. It was difficult to develop one with an acceptable mortality rate. General KITANO said it was best work anyone in UNIT 731 had ever done. I felt honored. I still do. Our trials proved infection rates would be close to 100%, with a 98% fatality rate. Everybody must breathe. Until they can't.

(NS laughs)

(HJT) Was General KITANO the officer commanding UNIT 731?

(NS) Yes. He took over in mid-1942 from General ISHII, who became Chief of the Japanese First Army's Medical Section.

(HJT) The trials you did. Those were on humans?

(NS) Of course. How else could I prove the virus worked? Ah, wait. No, that's not right . . . I want to assure you I had nothing to do with other trials. I was a scientist not a murderer.

(HJT) We will come back to that at another time. Who decided to deploy Strain 5524 in combat?'

(NS) There was a meeting, in Tokyo, with General **SUGIYAMA**, Chief of the Imperial General Staff, in March or April of 1943. General **KITANO**, General **ISHII**, and the commander of Division 2, Colonel **HISHIKAWA**, were there. When **HISHIKAWA** returned, he ordered me to prepare 5524 for deployment. I worked with Division 3; they developed a grenade for using the virus in combat.

(HJT) When was the virus dispatched from UNIT 731?

(NS) In March 1944, I think. (PAUSE) Yes, it was.

(HJT) Which unit transported the virus?

(NS) The 209th Special Detachment. It had about a thousand men, I think, all with experience in battle. I had to brief their commander on the virus. He was a major. Mori, I think. I did not like him. He did not approve of 5524. No, he did not. I had briefed him on the virus and how to use it.

HJT/10-10-45/6344-D/SATO - 3

(HJT) How large was the consignment?

(NS) We packed vials of 5524 in padded holders inside two large canisters made of brass. The end caps were brazed on to make sure none of the virus could escape. They were very strong. Each canister held enough virus to kill many tens of thousands of men, hundreds of thousands if conditions were right. We also shipped enough vaccine in metal boxes to protect our troops.

(HJT) How was the virus to be deployed in combat?

(NS) We mixed the virus with fern spores to carry it through the air. It was dispersed from ceramic grenades fired from Type-89 launchers. They exploded above the enemy. They worked very well. The virus from one grenade can cover 2000 square meters.

(HJT) Where did the 209th Special Detachment take the consignment of 5524 after it left Unit 731?

(NS) To the port of Dalian to be loaded on a ship. Maroku Maru, I think. Colonel **HISHIKAWA** told me the navy had said it was very fast and the American submarines would not be able to catch it. Lucky for your soldiers the navy was wrong.

(HJT) Once the consignment was aboard, where did the ship go?

(NS) Manila, then Pulau Biak, in the Netherlands East Indies.

(HJT) Are you sure the consignment was not landed in Manila?

(NS) Colonel **HISHIKAWA** showed me the 209th's movement order. The virus was going to Pulau Biak, definitely.

(HJT) And what was the 209th Special Detachment going to do once it had arrived on Pulau Biak?

(NS) Their orders were to use Strain 5524 to destroy the army of General MacArthur.

(HJT to ALD) Please read back the answer to my question: Where did the consignment of 5524 go after it left Unit 731? Just the last sentence, please.

(ALD) Lucky for your soldiers the navy was wrong.

HJT/10-10-45/6344-D/SATO - 4

(HJT) Tell me, Doctor SATO, how were our soldiers lucky?

(NS) Because the ship with the virus was sunk.

(HJT) How are you so certain the ship was sunk?

(NS) Like I told you the last time, because it disappeared somewhere between Manila and Pulau Biak. Of course, it sank. What? You think it flew off to the moon?

(HJT) Please think carefully before you answer my next question. We need to be sure you are telling us the truth. Understood?

(NS) I understand.

(HJT) How can you be certain the consignment did not reach Pulau Biak?

(NS) Colonel **HISHIKAWA** called me to his office. It was the end of May 1944, I think. It was late. He was so drunk he had trouble standing up. He was angry and waving his pistol around. I thought he was going to shoot me. I have never been so afraid.

(HJT) Why was Colonel **HISHIKAWA** so angry?

(NS) General **KITANO** told him the Americans had sunk the ship carrying my virus canisters. The colonel said the navy was a crowd of incompetent fools, that they lied when they promised to protect the ship. Then he got sad. He sat down and cried. He said Japan could not win the war because of the navy's incompetence. I had to have the Kempeitai take him away. I never saw him again. I heard later you Americans killed him in the battle for Manila.

(HJT) So you have no doubt the consignment was lost?

(NS) No, none. It is at the bottom of the sea, lost for all time.

(HJT) Bearing in mind your life depends on the answers you have given me, is there anything further you would like to tell me?

(NS) No, I have told the truth. We should forget the virus and look to the future.

(End of interrogation)

Joe sat back. "Jeezus! That wreck contains two canisters of live hemorrhagic smallpox virus."

"It did all those years ago," Rafiki said, "but the virus can't still be alive … Can it?"

"Smallpox is very persistent under the right conditions. In the 1950s, some Dutch researchers stored infected scabs…"

Rafiki pulled a face.

"…in a laboratory cupboard. The virus was still alive a decade later. If you keep smallpox dry, cool, and stable, it can last a hundred years."

"And are the conditions right?" Rafiki asked. "On the wreck, I mean."

"As long as the canisters are still intact, then yes. Which means we have a nasty problem on our hands. Apart from samples kept in Russia and the US, smallpox is extinct in the wild… except now it isn't. And, if what Sato said when he was being interrogated is true, then we have no vaccines against 5524."

"I thought we had antivirals instead?"

"We do. Tpoxx and Tecovirimat are two of them. There are others, but nobody is sure how effective any of them are. None have been tested on infected humans, which is a huge problem. Plenty of antivirals work well on animals but not on humans exposed to a live virus. And 5524 sounds like a radically different strain of smallpox. Given Sato's research showed the standard vaccines didn't work, there's high probability chance the current antivirals won't either."

"Which means?" Rafiki said.

"5524 will kill hundreds of millions of people if it escapes … This is getting out of hand, Skylar. I think I need to talk with Homeland Security I'll call Klara tomorrow to set up a meeting."

"Hold on, Joe. Not the smart thing to do."

"Of course it is!"

"Twenty years ago, I'd have agreed with you. But since then we've had one president assassinated; the same bomb killed twenty-five members of Congress and hundreds of others. And then there were the Philadelphia, Chicago, and Seattle bombings; how many did they kill?"

"Thousands."

"Not thousands, Joe, tens of thousands. And those tragedies have changed Homeland Security, and not for the better. Now it can lock you up for six months, without any evidence, without a warrant, without judicial oversight. And why? Because some political appointee thinks you might be a threat to the United States. Not will be a threat, Joe, just might be a threat … How do you think it'll react to someone who has two canisters of live hemorrhagic smallpox virus?"

"As they should react: Thank you, Doctor Lessart. You have been most helpful. We'll take it from here."

"It's not that simple. I've been around Homeland Security ever since it started in 2003. I spend a lot of my time talking with its people; in my business, I have to. And the more I do, the more certain I am there is something seriously wrong with the organization."

"Anything specific?"

"Only the feeling you get when you're talking to someone, the one which tells you they know things they really, really don't want you to know. And I've been getting it a lot, almost always with the politicals. I don't know why yet, but I'm working on it."

"And then?"

"One, stay away from Homeland Security. Two, find another way to deal with those canisters."

"Now you're worrying me, Skylar. Give me a minute. I need to think."

Joe went over to the window. He had seen Skylar Rafiki's instincts at work; they had saved Hydra Research from the legion of hackers and crooks determined to steal the company's secrets, secrets worth billions.

He turned back to Rafiki. "Do you remember Jon Mironov?"

"One of your senior researchers, yes I do. The North Koreans were blackmailing him to hand over Hydra's research data."

"They were, and you picked. The data to support your call only came later ... Is that how you feel about Homeland Security's politicals?"

"It is how I feel, Joe. And, before you ask, I have a small team working to find out what those Homeland Security politicals don't want me to know."

"Let me talk with André. I'll let you know what we decide to do."

"Do it ... But there's something else you need to think about. I know how Washington works. If you tell Homeland Security, Defense will find out about those canisters inside a week ... and don't tell me it won't. It's no secret Defense has more moles inside Homeland Security than the Chinese and Russians put together."

"Maybe it does, but so what?" Joe said.

"Defense took a great deal of trouble to keep the *Maroku Maru*'s cargo a secret. Don't assume it'll just shrug its shoulders and say no problem when the secret comes out."

"Oh, come on!" Joe protested. "If there was a cover-up, it happened eighty years ago. Nobody cares anymore what went on back then. Besides, the people involved are all dead."

"Bureaucracies don't die nor do they forget, especially if something is vital to this country's security, which those canisters are."

"And what's Defense going to do about it? Last time I checked, Defense and Homeland Security were on the same side."

Rafiki laughed. "They haven't been for years. Before you know it, there'll be the mother of all turf wars and the whole thing will spin out of control heading godknows where. And we can't afford it, not with canisters which could kill millions."

Joe's head sagged. "Why is everything so damn hard? All André and I want to do is go diving, for chrissakes."

"Are you a praying man?" Skylar said.

"Hell, no."

"If you're thinking of starting a fight between Defense and Homeland Security, this might be time to become one."

—9—

Joe walked back out to the deck of his apartment, beers in hand. He tossed one to André and fell on a lounger. "We can't keep talking about this. We have to make a decision."

"The lawyers said Homeland Security can arrest us if we don't tell them about a threat, any threat, to America's security," André said. "Knowing my luck, they probably will. So, go call Klara. Let Homeland Security sort it out, and I don't care if that starts a turf war with Defense, I really don't."

"Oh, dear god," Joe said. André wasn't a brave man, and it showed; he'd said the same thing every time Joe had him cornered. "Listen to me," he went on. "You agreed Indonesia would never allow the US Navy to put a salvage ship over the *Maroku Maru* without knowing why first. And, even then it might refuse to cooperate; godknows where the canisters will end up then."

"Well, yes I did, but—"

"And we also agreed telling Indonesia was the same as telling China."

André's face was tight with misery, stress. "We did."

"Which means the decision isn't about covering our asses with Homeland Security. It's whether we trust China with the safety of the human race. Do you?"

André shook his head.

"I don't either. Nobody does, not since COVID-19. So, stop fighting me on this. Homeland Security cannot solve the problem. Only we can."

"But what if the Indonesians find out? Do you have any idea how bad Indonesian prisons are?"

"Listen to me, André. The only people I trust to do the right thing are you and me. Let's find those canisters. When we do, we get rid of them. If we can't find them, nobody will. And, if it gets too difficult or too dangerous or the Indonesians become a problem, we stop and rethink."

"Skylar said there'd been a cover-up by the US Navy. Have you thought about that?"

"For fuck's sake!" Joe snapped. "Nobody cares what happened eighty years ago, nobody. Come on. What have we got to lose?"

André threw his hands up. "Okay, okay! We'll do it your way."

Joe leapt from his lounger to plant a kiss on André's forehead. "I knew you'd agree. I'll go tell Rikki to get the *Sophie Scholl* ready to go."

—10—

Joe and Andre had searched the *Maroku Maru* until exhaustion threatened to overwhelm them. Day after day, inch by inch, they had fumbled through a blizzard of silt searching staterooms, workshops, storerooms, passageways, access trunks, machinery rooms, fuel and water tanks, a thin orange line their only guide out of the chaotic steel maze and back to the surface and safety.

After three weeks, stress and fatigue had forced them to take a break. Now Joe and Andre watched from the starboard waist as Omar eased the *Sophie Scholl* alongside Manokwari's wharf. A group of uniformed military personnel waited for them. Assault rifles in hand, faces impassive, their eyes were unreadable behind mirrored sunglasses.

Joe put a hand on André's arm. "Why's the army here?"

"Not army, police. Though they behave more like paramilitaries here in West Papua. The locals hate them."

"All secured," Omar called down from the bridge wing as the grumbling of the *Sophie Scholl*'s main engines died away.

"Come on," André said. "Grab your passport and we'll go meet them."

●●●

"The police didn't seem very happy," Joe said.

"Why would they?" André said. "Most of West Papua is a war zone. Ever since Vietnam signed its mutual-defense treaty with Papua New Guinea, the Free Papua movement has hit the Indonesian military hard."

He glanced up as Omar came in. "What's up, captain?"

"The people here are nervous. Big attack on Jayapura airport last night. Bad fighting. Many killed. They say Vietnamese soldiers there also."

"Are we safe here?"

"Police say yes; they guard the wharf. But we do not stay long. Food, dive gas, and spares for the ship come in the afternoon. Fuel tanker with diesel and bensin come tomorrow morning. Then we go."

André got to his feet, grinning at Joe. "Yay! I can see my cousin, Satri. My mother will be happy."

Joe smiled back. No matter where they went in Indonesia, André seemed to have relatives. "Have fun, and don't be late back."

"Yes, dad," André said over his shoulder.

•••

Two hours later, the second officer stuck his head around the door. "Sorry to interrupt."

Joe was happy to be diverted. The task of working out where they had searched inside the *Maroku Maru* was mind-numbing. "No problem."

"A government man here to see you."

"He wants me? Not the captain?"

"He say André or you."

"Well, I guess I'd better see him then. I'll be in the saloon in five."

"I take him."

•••

The Indonesian extended his hand. "Doctor Lessart. I am Hutomo Hardjoprajitno, but please call me Tommy."

"Welcome aboard the *Sophie Scholl*, Tommy," Joe said, shaking hands. "Please, have a seat. And call me Joe. Tea? Coffee? Something cold?"

"Tea, please," Tommy said.

When the niceties were over, Joe said, "The second officer said you were from the government."

Tommy handed a laminated card to Joe. "I am with BIN, Badan Intelijen Negara. You would say State Intelligence Agency in English."

Joe studied the card before passing it back. "I've never spoken to anyone from BIN before. How can I help you?"

"The fishermen say your ship was in the Lendari Gulf for many days," Tommy said. "BIN want to understand more what you do."

"This is an Indonesian-registered vessel, with an Indonesian crew, and we have all the necessary permits from the Ministry of Home Affairs. Do you need to see them?"

"Those I have seen. They say you are surveying. So, let me ask: surveying for what?"

"Wrecks. We want to make films about the interesting ones."

"Ah, films," Tommy said. "Like on Discovery or National Geographic?"

"As long as the wrecks still look like ships, yes. The viewers are not interested in piles of broken metal."

"I enjoy these channels ... Did you find these interesting wrecks?"

"Yes, four so far."

"Do you know the names?"

"Not yet. The Japanese lost thousands of ships during World War 2, and the records are not complete."

"Perhaps you take from the wrecks? To sell?"

Joe hated looters with a passion. His voice hardened. "You may not understand what we do, Tommy, but that does not permit you to insult me. I never have and never will steal from a ship. It dishonors the men who died, brave men doing their duty. Our job is to tell the story of those ships, of their crews, ordinary people like you and me. To record, not to take. Why would I destroy those ships to make money?"

Tommy inclined his head. "I am sorry. I should not have said. I apologize."

"There is no need; I'm sure it is a misunderstanding."

"You say you want to tell their story, like detectives with cold cases."

"Detectives of history, except these cases are like ice."

"The officers of BIN are detectives, but we do not care about the crimes people have committed. Those things are for the police. We are interested in crimes people think about."

Joe frowned. "So why would BIN care about us?"

"We are interested in everybody. One of your crew say to a fisherman one wreck is the *Maroku Maru.*"

Joe's chest tightened. Not for one second would any of the *Sophie Scholl*'s crew have said anything of the sort. But, if not them, then how did Tommy know the name?

"We have found one freighter," he said, "but not the Japanese records to confirm its identity. I'm sorry, Tommy, but we can't be sure of anything, not yet."

Tommy's eyes narrowed a fraction. Joe was sure he was not buying.

"Ships have names," Tommy said. "On the front and the back, like our ferries. Your ship has. Why do you not find those names?"

"Warships don't have names on their hulls. And all those ships out there were Imperial Japanese Navy ships."

"I am good judge of people, doctor," Tommy said. "I think one wreck is the *Maroku Maru*, and you think it is too."

"I hope so, but it might not be."

Tommy wrote in a small notebook, tore the page out and gave it to Joe. "If it is, please tell BIN first. Call this number. They expect you."

"Of course ... But why is BIN interested in it?"

"Not your concern, doctor. Now, may I see your ship? It is not something we see in Manokwari before."

"Of course."

•••

Joe was watching cylinders of helium and oxygen come aboard when André appeared on the jetty. He was glad his best friend had gone ashore. Never give André Tanadi a secret, a friend had said, and how right she was. BIN would have had him spilling his guts inside five minutes.

After a chat with the ever-present POLRI troopers, André bounced up the gangway.

Joe said, "You missed the man from BIN. Mister Hutomo Hardjopra ... Hadroj ... He said to call him Tommy."

André frowned. "BIN? Shit. What did he want?"

"A chat and a tour of the ship. I will tell you all about it over a beer. Let's go inside."

"No, out here. Tell me what happened."

•••

"Something's wrong," said André. "None of our crew would tell a passing fisherman we were diving on the *Maroku Maru*. They all understand how important what we're doing is."

"And Skylar Rafiki would never talk to BIN. Apart from her, nobody else knows."

"You didn't tell Tommy we've found the *Maroku Maru*, right?"

"I don't think so," Joe said.

"Why did he give up and leave then? That is not BIN's style. They are like terriers. Once the teeth sink in, they never let go.... Did Tommy stay with you while you were showing him the ship?"

"You sound paranoid."

"Never a bad thing if you're Hokkien Chinese in Indonesia," André said, "not after half-a-million of us were butchered in '65 and '66 ... Come on. Answer the question."

Joe thought for a moment. "Yes, he did ... Oh, wait, no, he didn't. We were on the bridge when Tommy had to make a call. I went out to the bridge wing until he was done. He was five minutes or so, and no, I didn't pay him any attention. Come on, André! What's bothering you?"

"How does Tommy confirm we've found the *Maroku Maru*?"

"He can't, not unless we tell him ... Oh, the sonofabitch! He's left a bug behind, hasn't he?"

"I would have. Why do you think we're standing out here?"

"Shit, shit, shit!" Joe muttered. "I am so dumb."

André laughed. "Lucky for you I am paranoid. Come on, let's go see if I'm right."

●●●

Joe pointed at the saloon's television screen. "That's the audio bug you found at the back of the bridge; all Tommy had to do was plug it in. It uses the ship's power cables to connect to the satcomm box, which then uploads the audio files to a Kyrgyzstani server every hour or so. I emailed the IP address to Skylar; she might be able to find out who it belongs to."

André frowned. "Tommy is taking way too much interest in us. I think we should use the bug to make him think him we're done with the *Maroku Maru*; we just have to make sure nobody ever mentions its name. And we do our diving at night, but only when the weather's so bad BIN's drones can't see what we're up to."

"BIN has drones which can get out so far?"

André laughed. "For sure. Nothing but the best from China."

"I didn't know ... Why don't we put the ROV to work on the escorts during the day? That should encourage Tommy to think we're done with the *Maroku Maru*."

We do. And let's confuse things a bit more. Remember Andrew Fock?"

"The underwater medicine guy?" Joe said. "Yeah, I do. We chat now and again."

"I'll give him a call to tell him about the *Sophie Scholl*, then let slip we've pushed the envelope a bit. Knowing Andrew, he'll tell me how dumb we are and to lay off for a while. I will say yes, good advice, thanks, we'll do that."

Joe laughed. "And Tommy will hear every word you say, because he is listening to every cellphone call you make."

A broad smile spread across André's face. "There are some advantages being in a country with zero interest in civil liberties."

—11—

The wind gusted out of the southwest, throwing up short, sharp seas battered by endless rain squalls. Now and again a hazy moon broke through jagged rents in the clouds scudding past.

The night was foul. A terrible night for diving. A night when the watchers would see nothing.

Joe was exhausted. He checked his watch. He should go. He went aft to the *Sophie Scholl*'s stern and down the ladder into the chase boat.

•••

The current fought them all the way down. As Joe reached the welcome shelter of the *Maroku Maru*'s superstructure, he was breathing hard, always a bad start to any dive.

"Let's get—"

Skrrrcchhh! The harsh sound of metal grating on metal.

"What was that?" André said. "Don't tell me the wreck's collapsing."

An icy hand squeezed Joe's heart; five minutes later and they would have been deep inside. Two of his friends had been killed by steel falling off wrecks. "I wouldn't th—"

Skrrraaaacchhh!

"It came from the bows, Joe. This wreck isn't safe anymore. It's collapsing. We—"

Skrrraaaacchhh!

"That's no collapse. What the hell is going on?"

"No idea, so let's find out … And best we turn our lights off. Come on."

André took hold of Joe's harness. "Hold on. I have a bad feeling about this."

"Don't go all wobbly on me, not now. We'll just take a peek."

Joe did not wait for an answer. He swam towards the bows. Abreast Number-1 hold, he stopped. The water up ahead pulsed with a faint light. "A strobe! Has somebody else put divers on this wreck?"

"How could they?" André said. "We're the only dive ship around ... I don't like this, I really don't, Joe ... Can we go?"

"Not yet. We need to check. Follow me."

They swam over the port side and went forward until the ship's stem loomed up, a vertical black slash cut out of water backlit by the strobe. Joe spotted a dark shape; it pitched and rolled as it fought the current ripping around the *Maroku Maru*'s bows. He could hear the whine of its thrusters rising and falling as it fought to keep station.

"What is that?" Joe asked.

"It looks like one of those things the SEALs use. Swimmer delivery vehicle, I think they call them. Come on, Joe, enough. Let's go, please."

"One second. I want to see what they do first."

They waited as the vehicle settled into position tucked behind the ship's bows, out of the current.

The strobe fired, lighting up a small shape as it dropped from the vehicle. Joe thought his heart had stopped; he was looking at a diver.

"Now we should go."

●●●

"I've checked on the 'net," André said. "What we saw was a Combat Support Submersible, CSS for short. It carries six SEALs and deploys from a modified Virginia-class nuke. Only the US Navy has them."

Joe felt like a complete idiot. "And there was me thinking they would have to put a salvage ship over the wreck to get the canisters back ... I'm sorry, André. You were right. We should have told Homeland Security."

"It's too late ... But why are SEALs on the wreck?"

"Same reason we are: looking for the canisters."

"Impossible. How did the SEALs find out about the *Maroku Maru*?"

"No idea, but they did."

They sat staring at the screen in silence.

Then it came to Joe. "Hold on. Skylar said there was a cover-up. And there was, except nobody destroyed the records. They were stored somewhere in the Pentagon, with people watching over them to make sure the *Maroku Maru* and its cargo stayed a secret. I think the watchers set tripwires to warn them someone was sniffing around."

"What are you talking about?"

"Tripwires; questions which trigger an alarm, questions only a diver who had dived the wrecks would know to ask."

"Oh, shit, Joe. We gave Skylar the serial number of the four-inch gun. When she went through the records to see which submarine it had been mounted on, the watchers knew *Orca* wasn't a secret anymore."

Joe rubbed his eyes; he felt old. "We've been played. When the watchers send Tommy to talk with us, I told him we didn't know if we'd found the *Maroku Maru*. He thought I was lying; I could tell."

"And Tommy updates the watchers, who start panicking because we've found the *Maroku Maru*."

"No," said Joe. "They start panicking because they think we might find the canisters and open them."

"You can't blame them. Too many of us divers have a shocking reputation for looting wrecks."

"True ... Anyway, they can't risk it, so they send the SEALs in a CSS to find them first .... And there was me worrying about drones and satellites," Joe went on. "Now we have a nuke and SEALs, along with BIN, Tommy, drones, and the watchers. The only positive news is they have no idea we're after the canisters."

André's face had turned gray. "I think we should get the hell out until things quieten down."

Joe shook his head. "If we do, there's every chance the SEALs will find the canisters. And what happens then? Would the virus be destroyed? Will the US government decide to keep it, just in case it's ever needed? Or would some corrupt asshole sell it to the Russians or the Chinese or, god help us all, the North Koreans?"

"I don't know."

"Neither do I, which is why I'm not going to take any risks. And nothing changes one simple fact: The only people I really trust to find and destroy the virus are you and me. We have to finish this."

André said nothing. He looked miserable.

"We'll keep going," Joe went on. "If we find the US Navy on the wreck, we'll abort and come back the next night. No submersible can stay on task forever."

"I still don't like it."

Joe took André's massive paw of a hand; it trembled, another reminder that, for all his size, André was not the bravest person he had ever met. "Sometimes you have to do the right thing," he said, "and putting those canisters somewhere they can't be found while we work out how to destroy them is what's right."

Silence, then André whispered, "Fine. We'll do it."

"We'll be careful. The bastards won't see us as long as we stick to the plan and keep our eyes open. The moment there are any problems, we will leave and fast, I promise."

A reluctant nod from André.

The big man looked like death.

—12—

Another filthy night. Only GPS and some instinct of Solly's which juggled wind, waves, and current had let him drop them right on top of the small buoy they had left sitting over the wreck.

As he left surface, Joe knew he could not do this much longer.

Too many dives. Too much bottom time. Too much decompression.

Even taking one day off after six diving on the wreck hadn't helped: The dull ache in his right shoulder had sharpened into stabs of pain, his vision was blurred, and his lungs crackled as they protested their over-long exposure to high-pressure oxygen.

And, early on, too many aborted dives because the SEALs were already on the wreck. Now the navy seemed to be taking an extended break, but there was always a chance they would be back.

In the end, he and André had to acknowledge their limits. They would give the wreck twelve more dives. If they hadn't found the canisters of smallpox virus by then, they would abandon the search and tell Homeland Security the whole story.

Even if they risked being arrested.

The downline took Joe to the navigation deck behind the wheelhouse. At least the current had gone, though the visibility was still poor. He went forward, leaving André to check the US Navy had not messed with their lift-bags. Hidden inside a locker, they'd take the canisters to the surface.

He swam around the funnel, past the clutter of exhaust vents, and into the wheelhouse. He could see across the forward holds to the fo'c's'le, searching for the faint pulses of light from the strobe the SEALs used to find their way back to the CSS's access lock.

Nothing.

Joe decided not to go forward to make certain the SEALs had taken the day off. There was no need; the visibility was good enough for him to see their strobes if they hadn't.

Joe headed aft and down into Number-4 hold. Hundreds of men had drowned here when *Orca*'s torpedoes hit; the massive space was a Golgotha of bleached bones and skulls, grinning up from the silt.

The *Maroku Maru* was more death house than wreck.

Five decks down from the navigation deck, he found the door he was looking for. André's line waited for him.

Joe flicked his helmet light on and swam inside. The line led through a lobby, then on along a passageway through a labyrinth of crew spaces, storerooms, offices, and machinery rooms, the deck below him a mess of silt, broken metal, skulls, and bones.

André hovered outside the first compartment for the day, peering in. He eased himself back as Joe arrived. "It's horrible in there."

Claustrophobia clawed at Joe. But he had to go in; it was his day to do the searching. He clipped the jump line to his belt and drifted inside. André was right; the conditions were atrocious. Silt lay in an undulating blanket of orange-brown over a tangle of debris pierced by spears of metal and bundles of wire. With one hand on the bulkhead, Joe started to sift through the debris, a painful process with one hand, the visibility reduced to zero as the fine, rust-brown silt bloomed into fog.

His rummaging turned up small buttons and buckles. Then boot soles. Lots of them. "Nothing there," he said when he had searched the compartment. "It's a clothing store."

Joe backed out and moved on to the next compartment, a long way inside the wreck. His life depended on André and a thin line of white cord, the only way he could ever find his way out. A fallen panel or tangle of wire could trap him, and he did not carry cylinders of backup gas if his rebreather failed, an insane but necessary risk.

That would only slow things down, they had decided, and time was not on their side.

The fourth compartment was worse than any of the other spaces he had searched; a jumble of boxes, corroded into shards of metal filled the space. Sharp shards, to which his lacerated hands bore witness. The work was slow and dangerous; it ended when his helmet bumped into the outboard bulkhead, unseen in the murk. He checked the opposite side. More boxes, but not so many, easier to search through. Then his left hand hit something hard. Rounded. Smooth. He worked his fingers around the object, tracing the shape of a handle, then another. "André! I've got something."

"Tell me something I want to hear."

"Wait on." Joe put his mask right up against the canister and scrubbed a patch clean. "It looks like a brass cylinder, about six or seven feet long, round ends. Hold on .... Yes, I can lift it. It feels about twenty pounds negative which means it's still full of air ... There's a second one, right next to it ... also intact. Sounds like what we came for?"

"I'd bet my life on it. We've got enough bottom time left to get them out, but we need to hustle."

"First one's coming your way now."

Joe heaved the canister out to André. He went back and dragged the second out amidst a swirling blizzard of silt.

Moving the first canister outside the wreck was brutal work. Obstructions unseen in the darkness—Joe tried not to think what they might be—snagged the handles as the canister churned through the silt like a small bulldozer. By the time they made it back to Number-4 hold, he was breathing hard; he tried not to think how much decompression he and André were racking up.

"Can you manage it from here?" André said when they were in the hold.

"Like I have a choice."

"I'll go back and start on the second, but don't be too long. This place is bugging me." The voice processor could not hide the stress in André's voice.

Joe clipped a line to the canister, inflated his wing to take its weight, and swam the uncooperative mass up to the navigation deck. Once there, he blew a marker buoy to the surface; it took a line, strobe, and low-power radio beacon with it. Next he secured a lift-bag to the canister and clipped it to the up-line. He made sure all was secure, cracked the air valve open a fraction and let the lift-bag fill. The moment it supported the canister's weight, he cracked the valve wide-open and the canister was torn from the deck to vanish into the darkness.

He hoped the boats up top were paying attention.

Joe swam back.

André appeared out of the swirling silt. "About time. I was about to call it quits."

"Don't tempt me. Come on, let's move this sonofabitch out."

The two of them maneuvered the canister along the passageway. It stopped with a jerk.

"Goddammed thing is caught," André said. "Help me shift it."

Joe turned around, one hand on the canister, the silt swirling brown in his helmet light. He found the problem. A thigh bone had jammed itself against one of the handles. "Lift it back your way a touch."

"Hold on ... It's free. Let's ... Hey! What the fuck? Someone's ... get off me ... The bastards are here. Go! Go!"

Joe turned, recoiling as a black shape, finned feet flailing, crashed into him out of the murk and then disappeared back the way it had come.

"André! André! Talk to me."

There was no answer. But Joe knew what had happened.

Running on pure adrenaline now, he bulldozed the second canister down the passageway and out to the hold before swimming it up to the navigation deck, working fast to attach the lift bag to take it to the surface.

The instant the second cylinder was on its way, he started back, then stopped, lungs heaving as they tried to flush out the carbon dioxide flooding his system. The SEALs had caught André. Joe knew there was nothing he could do to rescue him. He had to leave; if he did not, he would end dead or a prisoner.

Joe found his knife. He grabbed the up-line and slashed it free, letting what little current there was drift him away from the wreck and out into black water. His mind was a confused mess: horror at the thought of what lay in store for André; guilt he had escaped.

•••

Joe surfaced after hours of decompression, relieved to find the boats waiting for him. Solly and Arif pulled off Joe's gear and dragged him inboard. Exhausted, he slumped to the deck, shaking with cold.

Solly pressed a flask of hot soup into one hand, an oxygen mask in the other. "Where is André?"

Joe gulped down the soup. Its warmth brought life and energy back to his body. "The US Navy's got him," he said, slipping the oxygen mask over his mouth and turning on the gas.

"Ai!" Solly said, shaking his head. "Bad."

The second chase boat came alongside. "Hey, boss. What happens?" Budi asked.

"The Americans have André," Joe said.

"Americans? How?"

"Later. We need to go. The canisters I sent up. Where are they?"

"I have them," Budi said. "Heavy. Very heavy."

"I'll take them with me in Chase-2. I want you take Chase-1 back to the ship. Tell Omar he'll be getting underway as soon as I return."

"Hey, boss!" Budi said. "One of us should help."

"No, Budi. And don't worry. I'll be fine. Prop the canisters up on the gunwale so I can tip them over the side on my own. And get me a reel of line."

Budi's face made it clear what he thought, but he did as asked without a word. When Chase-2 was ready to go, Joe climbed across. The canisters were massive; he wondered how he had ever got them off the wreck. He started the engines and jammed the throttles onto the stops. As the boat slapped and banged through the chop, his eyes flickered between compass and GPS screen, Chase-2's position a tiny red lozenge on the chart display.

He was alone with the canisters, heading for a sprawling patch amidst an ocean of sand.

He wondered how André was going.

He smiled. Probably boring the SEALs to death; how the man loved to talk. Before the interrogators even turned up, André would have told the SEALs everything he had been doing on the *Maroku Maru*.

Which meant only one thing: It would not be long before the US government came after him.

•••

Once in position, Joe tied lines to the handles of the canisters. Heaving first one and then the second over the side, he lowered them to the seabed. Holding them taut, he fixed their position in his GPS, tied the lines together, attached a weight, and threw them clear.

Joe watched them sink. Without the coordinates in his GPS, nobody would ever find those canisters. No fisherman would risk his nets over such foul ground; any sonar returns from the canisters would be pinpricks amidst the chaotic clutter sent back by rocks which stretched for miles in all directions.

Their location was a secret, a secret only one person on earth now knew.

An ugly dawn slashed red streaks through dark, rushing clouds as Joe restarted the engines and raced back to the *Sophie Scholl* to refuel and collect his stuff.

•••

Joe slowed Chase-2 to look back.

A shaft of sunlight had broken through the thick monsoonal clouds. It picked out the *Sophie Scholl*—a brilliant patch of white against dirty gray sky—as it headed for Semarang.

It near broke him to see it go. Without him. Without André.

He settled the chase boat on course for Sorong, two hundred miles to the south-southwest. Weather permitting and running on one engine to save fuel, he should be there around midnight and on the first ferry out before midday

—13—

Shimmering in the morning heat, Makassar's ferry wharf was a mass of humanity, some fighting to get aboard the Surabaya ferry, some fighting to disembark, some just gawking idlers, all bathed in clouds of diesel smoke from the trucks laboring up the ramp onto the vehicle deck.

Joe wasn't concerned about the people. BIN would have agents there, for sure, but he'd never know who they were. His interest was in the pole-mounted surveillance cameras, one of China's gifts to Indonesia, a gift which pushed the country even further down the road to dictatorship. André had told him the identity-recognition software that came with the cameras could identify a tall *orang asing* wearing a hat and sunglasses in less than a second.

If BIN found him then Tommy would know. And so would the US government.

He did his best to confuse things. Joining an extended family, the adults all with large cloth-wrapped bundles on their heads, he shuffled his way through the throng, head down and broad-brimmed hat pulled over his face. Once aboard the *Ratu Makassar*, he found—to his surprise—he had the cabin he had paid for; best of all the air conditioning worked.

Throwing himself on the bunk, he pulled out a battered cellphone—ten dollars from a market stall in Pulau Anjani complete with an untraceable SIM card—and punched in Rikki Tengarran's number.

The *Sophie Scholl*'s manager was the only person in Indonesia who could help him now.

"Hallo?" the man said.

"Jangan mengatakan apa-apa. Cari phone baru. Hubungi saya di nomor ini," Joe said and cut the call, hoping Rikki could understand his mangled Indonesian. *Don't say anything. Find another phone. Call me back on this number.*

Anxious minutes passed before Joe's cellphone rang. "No names," Joe said before Rikki could speak. "I'll be—"

"Wait," Rikki said. "Our friends have disappeared. We have heard nothing. We are all very worried."

Shock left Joe struggling to speak for a moment. "We need to meet. I'll call to tell you when to expect me."

"Where are you?"

"Best I don't say. Wait for my call. Got to go. Don't worry. We'll find them."

"Please. They are family."

Joe cut the call.

He had no doubts what had happened: The US Navy—who else?—must have intercepted the *Sophie Scholl*, even though he had told the captain to switch off the automatic identification system tracking the ship's position.

Tommy must have left another GPS tracker somewhere onboard, the sonofabitch.

Not that it mattered how the SEALs had done it. They had taken André, his ship, and his crew.

And he would be next.

•••

The *Ratu Makassar*'s second officer yawned as he slipped out of his chair and went to the back of the bridge to put on the kettle.

"Hey, Janni. Kamu ingin teh?" he said to the helmsman. *Hey, Janni! You want some tea?*

No answer.

He turned to find himself looking down the barrel of a pistol held by a helmeted figure dressed in black. Beyond him, a second figure, shapeless in the dim light from the bridge screens, had a pistol jammed into the helmsman's neck.

Do what I say, and you will be fine, the figure said. *If you don't, I will kill you both. Understood?*

The man's Bahasa betrayed him; he was not Indonesian born.

Yes, yes, the second officer said, his voice shaking. *Please don't hurt me.*

•••

Sleep brought nightmares. Darkness. Broken steel. Impenetrable silt. Trapped in a maze. No way out. No hope of rescue. Out of gas. Death.

Joe awoke with a start, clammy with sweat, shaking with fear. He checked the time. Just past two. Another thirteen hours and the ferry would be alongside in Surabaya. Joe could only hope paying one of the truck drivers to smuggle him ashore would get him past BIN.

Its agents would be waiting for him. Joe was sure of it.

He sat up. Something felt wrong... Something was wrong; the engines had gone quiet.

He peered out of his scuttle. The ship's sidelight reflected green off the sea; he could see the ship was slowing. But why? In every ferry master's world, the timetable was god. Something must have happened to make the *Ratu Makassar* reduce speed.

Joe was not taking any chances. Ferry disasters were a regular feature of Indonesian life. If there was a problem, he would not be sitting around surrounded by panic-stricken passengers waiting for the crew to tell everyone what to do.

He went out onto the upper deck. No smoke. No flames. No list on the ship. No screams. No flustered crew. All promising signs everything was well with the *Ratu Makassar*. He picked a path through a carpet of sleeping bodies and looked over the rail.

An ice-cold hand clutched his guts. It took an effort not to panic.

Two inflatables were alongside the ferry. Black-suited figures were coming aboard. SEALs; they had to be.

And they were here for him.

Unless …

Joe sprinted back to his cabin. Into a waterproof pouch went his cellphone, passport, and money; his backpack took the rest of his stuff along with all the water he could find. He grabbed two lifejackets from their locker on the bulkhead and ran for the stern, lifting more bottles of water from their sleeping owners as he went before slipping behind a reel of a mooring rope.

He took a look. Helmeted figures in jumpsuits had appeared from the passenger saloon. In a line, they were working their way through the mass of sleeping bodies towards the stern, their torches splashing light around as they scanned faces.

Joe knew would not miss him.

He glanced over the stern. The ship's wake twisted away in the darkness through choppy seas flecked white. He hesitated.

But anything was better than being taken by the men in black.

He packed away the stolen water, donned one lifejacket, tied the other to his waist-strap, and slipped on the backpack.

Careful to keep the reel between him and the searchers, he slid over the guardrail, paused to take a breath, and jumped into the wash from the ship's propellers. Rolling over, he looked up at the *Ratu Makassar*'s stern towering overhead.

The searchers only had to glance over the rail and they would see him. He started to swim, a desperate, thrashing race to get away that only stopped when common-sense took back control.

He turned around.

Still no figures.

Taking a breath, he tried to dive down, but he forgotten the life-jackets. For a moment, he thought of throwing them away, then decided not to. He needed them to stay afloat long enough for some passing boat to pick him up. Resigned to his fate, he lay paid and stared at the sky.

It was a beautiful night, so dark the stars hung in extravagant splashes of pin-prick brilliance.

The sheer number of passengers saved him. Indonesian ferries invariably carried more passengers than they should; the *Ratu Makassar* had been no exception. With scores of faces to check, many rolled up in blankets against the wind, it was more than five minutes before Joe glimpsed movement around the ship's stern, by then four hundred yards away.

But Joe had seen his share of special-forces movies; the searchers would have night-vision goggles. He had to stay low and wet, relying on the broken, choppy waves to keep him hidden.

He put his head down, but his thumping heart was burning oxygen fast. Too soon, he had to lift his head to breathe. The figures were still there.

Again and again and again, Joe went under, stopping only when the ferry had dwindled to a distant point of light.

He swung around.

Apart from the *Ratu Makassar*'s stern light, the world around him was black.

He was alone.

He pulled his GPS from the backpack. He turned it on, relieved when the map showed a cluster of islands twenty-five miles to the southwest: the Kangean Islands, an archipelago fifty miles across. He checked the wind. Blowing a steady ten or so knots right towards the islands, it should generate a surface current that would take him right to the beach. If not, the Kangeans were large enough to support hundreds of fishing boats. One of them would come his way.

Surely?

By now, the last of the adrenaline had seeped away. He let his head fall back against the collar of the lifejacket and closed his eyes.

•••

Joe awoke to a dawn blazing gold and red, the sun striking shards of light off an empty ocean. The wind had fallen away, leaving him drifting on a long, glassy swell. He cursed his stupidity. The chances of being spotted were slim enough without letting a rescuer sail past while he snored his head off. Telling himself to do better, he took a sip of water and looked around.

There were no fishing boats. No ships. No birds. Nothing except ocean.

But the news from the GPS was good. As he'd hoped, the current was taking him towards the Kangean archipelago, now three welcome miles closer.

He would try his cell; he might be close enough to land to get a signal. He pulled the waterproof pouch from his backpack around and extracted the phone, his water-logged fingers fat and clumsy.

The cellphone was off. He stabbed the power button.

Nothing.

He tried second time. And a third.

Still nothing. His cellphone, charged when he had ripped it from its charging cable, was dead. Joe lifted his head and screamed.

For a moment, he thought about activating his EPIRB rescue beacon. But only for a moment. Even if the Indonesians rescued him, the US authorities would see an EPIRB activation close to where the SEALs had intercepted the *Ratu Makassar*.

A simple online check would confirm that the EPIRB was registered to the *Sophie Scholl*.

He would leave the beacon until death had its hands around his throat.

•••

The sun burned through his sunscreen. Joe could feel his face burning and his lips cracking.

Still no boats.

Mid-afternoon, the GPS beeped, a warning that the current had turned south; he was now no longer heading right for the Kangeans, the spine of the largest island now a broad, brown smudge across the horizon. If the current kept turning, he would miss land. His free ride was over. He had to start swimming. He took a long drink of water and settled in a slow, rhythmical, breaststroke.

By dusk, Joe had closed the gap to only five miles. But one of the locals would not be handing him a cold beer any time soon.

The current had swung hard left; now it was taking him parallel to the beach towards the arc of small islands at the eastern end of the Kangean archipelago. He did not like to think where it would go from there. Probably south into the Bali Sea, not a good place to be.

On the upside, the current had slowed. With land still close, he might have a chance. Ignoring the burning ache in his over-worked shoulders and chest, he started swimming again.

By midnight, he had clawed his way to within two miles of Pulau Paliat, the second largest island of the archipelago. Lights studded the shoreline. He could see the boats he had gambled his life on. The fishermen had them pulled well up the beach. They would not be anywhere any time soon.

Within an hour, the current had picked up again. Relentless, it swept him towards the last island between him and the Bali Sea. It lay seven miles ahead, separated from him by a cluster of small cays.

If the current held, he still had a chance.

He kept swimming. An hour later, he had nothing left. He was finished, too exhausted to continue. He had to rest, his life entrusted to the Fates.

His head fell back; within seconds, he was asleep.

•••

Joe woke with a start, his mind fogged by fatigue. His shoulders and arms burned. His whole upper body ached. He checked the sea around him; nothing but a white glare. He squinted through salt-encrusted eyes at the GPS. As best he could tell, he was drifting north, back the way he had come, towards a small island he must have passed in the night.

An island the GPS told him was only two miles away.

Two miles. He could do that, he told himself.

He forced himself to start swimming again, the complaints from his body ignored.

Keep going … keep going … keep going, he chanted under his breath.

Until he could not, defeated by the current's casual cruelty. It would push him off track, sometimes left, sometimes right, sometimes full circle, sometimes—worst of all—backwards. With less than a mile left between him and land, he could swim no more. He looked around for boats; even if they were there, he knew he'd never see them, the world around him now reduced to a vague blur by glare and salt.

The time had come to call for help, no matter the consequences; if he did not, he would not live to see another day.

With the white and wrinkled hands of a corpse, he found his EPIRB. He fumbled for the pin to activate.

Hei! Kita melihat anda, kami datang … Kami datang!

A man's voice, but the words made no sense. Not that they needed to. Joe let the beacon slip, lifted a hand, and waved.

—14—

"... and a fisherman arrived, hauled me out of the water, fixed me up, and put me on a boat to Sumenep. Two buses later, here I am."

Joe was checking the hotel lobby while he talked. If the SEALs could find him on a ferry, they would have no trouble tracking him down here. "We're okay here?" he said.

Rikki Tengarran leaned forward. "See those guys by the door? My boys. Outside? Two off-duty police with guns. Out back, same. Over us? Drones, like BIN and police have. But my ones are better than the drones China gives to my government. I also have people watching the cellphone traffic. Why do I do this? Because, after Sukarno, I do not trust the government to keep me safe from my enemies. Nobody will bother us, I promise."

"I apologize. I underestimated you."

Tengarran smiled. "Many people do. Now, the ones who take André and the crew, who are they?"

"The American government, but..." Joe's voice trailed off.

Tengarran put a hand on Joe's arm. "I cannot help if you keep secrets."

"No, it's not that. I'm confused. Here's the thing, Rikki. What has happened is crazy. The submersible, the SEALs, hijacking the *Sophie Scholl*, armed men boarding my ferry. It is all so ... extreme. The US government doesn't work like that."

Tengarran gave Joe a twisted smile. "You think? All governments are dirty. Yours as well; it has done many, many terrible things. And it does not treat Indonesia well."

"It doesn't, but all it needed was a video call from someone senior in Homeland Security to tell us they knew everything, make an appeal to our patriotic instincts, and so on. If we refused to cooperate, they just had to threaten us, and André would have told them everything we'd discovered."

Tengarran laughed. "He is not brave ... but you are not telling why they do this."

Joe longed to tell all he knew, to share the load. But he just shook his head. "All I can say is there was something in the *Maroku Maru* people want. Saying any more would put you at risk, so please don't ask."

"Okay ... What will you do now?"

"I need to get back to the United States, but I can't."

Tengarran seemed puzzled. "Why not? You are American."

"The minute I book a flight, American government will arrest me as soon as I step on US soil."

"Ah, sorry. Sorry; I am not smart ... You need a quiet way to go home. Let me talk to some people." Tengarran handed Joe a cellphone. "I will text you on this. I will arrange a room. Here you are safe."

•••

Tengarran's text hauled Joe out of a deep sleep. He dressed and hurried down to the lobby.

Tengarran waved a hand at the cadaverous man sitting beside him, his face pinched. "Please sit. This is Captain Hartanoeh. He is one of PT Ekspres Kontainer's senior officers. He takes ships to America. He can help you."

"This is what we do, Doctor Lessart," Hartanoeh said. "Five days from now..."

—15—

Captain Hartanoeh stepped into Joe's stateroom. He appeared anxious. The only man Joe had seen during the long crossing across the Pacific always did.

"Thirty minutes, you can go," Hartanoeh asked. "You don't want to stop this?"

"No, captain, I don't." Joe said. "How's the weather?"

"Wind northwest fifteen knots, choppy seas half a meter, visibility good. Engine room say water is thirteen degrees Celsius."

Joe grimaced. A touch over fifty-five Fahrenheit. That was cold. "I can handle it," he said, not at all sure he could.

Hartanoeh took Joe's hand in both of his. "My prayers are with you, Doctor Lessart," he said, his voice soft. "Please find our people."

Joe was both surprised and touched. "I will, captain, I will."

Hartanoeh turned and left. Joe knew he had misjudged the man; Hartanoeh wasn't doing this just for the money. That was part of it, of course, but loyalty to the clan, the same commitment André felt, had played its part too.

He pulled on a semi-dry wetsuit, then hood, boots, and gloves. Next came the scooter. Old and battered, Rikki Tengarran had not found anything better. He turned it on; five green lights on the battery status display, and the propeller burst into life when he blipped the throttle.

A final check of his backpack, fins, and mask. He was ready.

The minutes ran off.

He pushed open his stateroom door, unlocked for the first time in the voyage across the Pacific. The cross-passage to the port waist was clear. Joe was outside in seconds and heading for the stern.

A line was there, as Hartanoeh had promised. Joe secured it to the guardrail and tossed the end over the side. The drop into the wake was a long one; the *Ekspres Super* was a huge ship.

He hesitated.

But Joe knew he had to go on with it; the lives of André and the *Sophie Scholl*'s crew depended on him. He searched for any boats and drones.

Nothing close.

Mask in place and GPS switched on, he lowered the scooter over the side and let it hang on the end of a lanyard secured to his belt. He clambered over the rail, an awkward, clumsy process not helped by the scooter's awkward bulk. Wrapping his legs around the rope, he slid down the steel cliff that was the ship's stern, and slid into the sea, tumbling in the wash from the *Ekspres Super*'s enormous propeller. He struggled upright, jammed his fins on, pulled the scooter in, then scanned all around once more. Still nothing. He let the scooter pull him away from the ship through short, broken seas that sluiced icy water over his head.

To stay invisible, Joe forced as much of his body below the surface as he could. Masking his heat signature was another matter. Wearing the thickest hood Rikki Tengarran could find, he hoped repeated drenching by cold seawater would help him blend in. Even so, his head would always be warmer than the ocean; the military-grade infra-red cameras carried by Homeland Security drones might be able to detect such a tiny difference in temperature.

He spotted a red anti-collision light. A drone was angling in to cross the *Ekspres Super*'s wake.

Joe took a deep breath. Pitching forward, he let the scooter take him down, staying deep until the blood thundered in his ears, until his lungs burned, until he could no longer ignore his body's demands for air. He throttled back the scooter and drifted to the surface, gulping air down as he searched for the drone. He found it, turning to make a second pass.

The drone closed in. Joe went under.

The drone was running away down the ship's wake when he surfaced. He drifted until it turned back, submerging as it approached.

The drone forced him under six more times before its controller back in Long Beach must have decided the *Ekspres Super* was clean and took the drone off.

Joe gunned the scooter away, punching into the chop.

He was beginning to think his run in to Cabrillo Beach would not be the ordeal he had expected when, without warning, the scooter shut down leaving him floundering in the waves. It was dead, and no amount of button pushing and swearing would bring it back to life. He gave up and unclipped the scooter. He shoved it away, then turned on his back, his legs moving up and down, up down, driving him towards land, glad of the endless hours he spent training for just this eventuality.

The GPS told him he had five miles left to run. He did the math. He would make it with less than an hour of darkness left. If he cramped up or the current got worse or the drone reappeared, he would not reach the beach before the keep-fit fanatics appeared for their morning workout.

Not that he had much choice; he had to push on. The *Ekspres Super* was not coming back for him. If he gave up, the coastguard would pick him up. Or he would drown. Or something sleek and toothy would mistake him for a seal.

Unless hypothermia killed him first.

He left all that to fate and settled into the swim, scanning for boats and drones in between watching the GPS to make sure he stayed on track and ahead of schedule.

•••

Joe's fins touched the seabed. After hours of labor, his legs refused to let him stand, so he gave up and let the waves bump him the last few yards to the shore. Once well aground, he rolled over to check the beach.

He was hours behind schedule. Dawn was fifty minutes away. But Cabrillo Beach was empty, and the houses flanking its western side were still dark.

Frozen fingers fumbled fins, mask, and hood free. He tossed them away. Forcing his legs back to work, he stumbled out of the water.

This was the moment of maximum risk.

It would only take one early riser to spot a black-suited figure appearing from the water to have every security agency in Los Angeles on their way with enough firepower to take out a battalion of terrorists.

His thighs protesting the effort, he staggered up the beach. Once in the trees, he collapsed. Five minutes passed before he could move. But Joe could not sit around. He could not afford to be seen.

Ten minutes later, he was in dry clothes and heading into San Pedro.

—16—

Joe sat on the sidewalk. Dressed in an old army jacket over black t-shirt, blue jeans, battered boots, topped with a black cap, his hair was pulled back into a stubby ponytail, his face sporting a ratty beard.

He looked like a SoCal dope-smoker gone off the rails.

His friends would not recognize him.

For days, he had zigzagged eastwards across the continent in a bewildering sequence of buses and trains, the experience made worse by anxiety and stress that had left his face gaunt and eyes sunk deep in their sockets.

But he had made it to Washington without being picked up by America's vast, sprawling security machine. Not that trading the tired anonymity of America's bus and train lines for the paranoia of Washington was easy.

Joe tried not to keep checking his watch. Homeless bums were not clock-watchers. They had time to burn; their job was to sit motionless looking miserable.

Which was not difficult. Joe had never felt so disheartened, so alone.

He wanted to run.

Skylar Rafiki emerged from her office an hour later. Coffee time; Joe had shared many with her.

He dropped his head, another homeless vet with a begging bowl, empty save for a single five-dollar bill, a cry for help handwritten on the piece of cardboard:

US MARINE VET
WOUNDED IN BALTIC WAR

NO JOB   NO HOME   NO $$$ PLEASE HELP

Like everyone else who had rushed past that morning, Rafiki was making the reflexive move towards the gutter when Joe lifted his head. She glanced at him. Her eyes widened in surprise. She slowed a fraction, unsure of herself.

Joe kept his voice low. "Skylar!" he said. "It's me, Joe. Keep moving. Have your coffee. Meet me at Meridian Hill Park when you can. I'll wait on the corner of 16th St North West and Euclid. It's life or death. Don't stand me up."

Rafiki slowed a fraction. "I won't, but stay clear of me," she whispered. "And turn off everything except Bluetooth. We'll use FireChat."

Rafiki walked on without another word, a master class in Washingtonian contempt for bums down on their luck. Joe waited until she was long gone, rewarded for his patience with twenty dollars from a tourist. He got to his feet, pocketed his money, stowed bowl and sign in his backpack, and shuffled off to the metro.

Just another vet, tossed onto the streets by a nation without enough money to care.

●●●

"...which is why I think something weird is going on," Joe said.

"I guessed that the moment I saw you. Is this all about those canisters?"

"It has to be. Listen, Skylar. I'm sorry to drag you into this, but I have nobody else to talk to."

"Lucky me. Do you need my help to find your ship?"

"Yes, along with André and the crew. I want them back."

Silence.

Joe glanced at Rafiki. She sat on a bench fifty feet away. Like almost everyone else in the park, she had her phone to her ear.

"I agree with you," Rafiki said at last. "It does feel all wrong. Tasking Avenger drones to whack a bunch of terrorists is one thing, but sending a nuclear submarine and SEALs into Indonesian waters? Talk about risky; I can't think of a better way to piss off the Indonesians."

"No kidding. But why would the president risk that?"

"That's what I can't work out … You'll need to leave this with me. Go do your vet-begging thing but be back here tomorrow evening, after eight. You will find an old Nokia cellphone in a bag taped under this bench. Pull it off and try not to be obvious about it."

"Got it."

"The Nokia is Russian and illegal; don't wave it around. It only does calls and text; no data. I'm the only one who can call you."

"Wouldn't a burner be easier?"

"No. Thanks to the Open Crypt Act, any device accessing a US network must use encryption the NSA can break, or it won't work. The Nokia makes a new call using a new e-SIM and hardware profile every ten seconds. With thousands of active calls going on around you, that makes it almost impossible for the NSA to track what's being said."

"Isn't this all a bit extreme?"

"Not as extreme as ending up dead."

"You must work in dangerous places, Skylar."

"Sometimes. How much money do you have?"

"Two grand, give or take," Joe said.

"I'll leave you a no-name cash-card with ten k on it and a number. Multiply it by five to get the PIN... One last thing, and this is important: If anyone is forcing you to make a call, slip the words 'super tired' in as soon as you can. I'll do the same."

"Super tired?" Joe muttered. "That won't be hard."

All he wanted to do was find somewhere safe and sleep for a week.

Joe watched Rafiki leave. The woman must be more worried than she had let on. He was usually the one giving her money.

—17—

Without anything better to do, Joe unfolded the sheet of paper and started to read.

As well as the Nokia, Rafiki had left him an idiot's guide telling him how not to let himself get caught. Reading it did nothing for his confidence. It only reminded him that he was a rank amateur playing a game without knowing the rules against experienced players who did.

He was alone. Vulnerable. And very frightened.

The Nokia rang. He swung his legs off the worst bed he had ever slept on.

"Hi," Joe said.

"How are you? "

"Paranoid."

"Paranoids live longer in this business. Okay, I have made some progress. NAVSPECWARCOM—the US Navy's Special Warfare Command—had operational control of the SEAL team you came up against. Its submersible was deployed from the USS *Shark*. I've accounted for the other CSS-capable SSN's. One's off Norway, the other's in the Mediterranean."

"I still can't work out why the president authorized an operation like that? All she had to do was give us a call."

"One of the reasons I don't think she had anything to do with it," Rafiki said. "But there's another. The president's number one foreign-policy priority is pushing China out of southeast Asia, starting with Indonesia. That's why she sent the vice president to Jakarta. There's no way she would approve an operation that risked derailing all that."

"Does that mean someone senior inside NAVSPECWARCOM ordered the mission?" Joe asked.

"We will never know. NAVSPECWARCOM's operational security is very tight … You know, the more I think about what happened, the more I'm beginning to think it must be part of a bigger conspiracy."

"You sound like one of those Deep State nutjobs, Skylar. And it can't be much of a conspiracy if everyone knows about it."

"I am not everyone."

Joe could not miss the acid in Rafiki's voice. "Sorry," he said. "That was not what I meant. So why a conspiracy?"

"Remember when I gave you Doctor Sato's interrogation report?"

"Yes, I do, when I met with you in the Westin. You talked me out of going to talk with Homeland Security because you thought something wasn't right with them."

"A problem I have been working on ever since," Rafiki said. "And my sources say I was right to be concerned."

"Sources? What? Like gossip?"

"Much better than that. People talk for a lot of reasons: affairs going well, affairs gone wrong, alcohol, drugs, resentment, revenge, envy, hate. They all encourage people to say more than they should."

"And did they?"

"They did. They pointed me to a think-tank called Mobilizing America."

"They sent me a newsletter once. Nasty bunch; virulently anti-Chinese."

"That's them. Very powerful. Very influential. And very well-funded. I persuaded one of Mobilizing America's staffers—don't ask me how; it was pretty ugly—to give me a list of its members. Turns out most of them work for Homeland Security and Defense."

"So what? That's not illegal, is it?"

"Not at all," Rafiki said. "But that list gave me my targets, and three of them all told me the same thing: Mobilizing America is cover for an extremist conspiracy whose members believe the United States isn't doing enough to challenge China and never will."

"What does this network want?"

"To keep America the world's most powerful nation by destroying China."

"A bunch of seat-polishers in Washington is going to destroy China?" Joe protested. "Come on! That's ridiculous!"

"That was my initial reaction too, but it bugged me enough to have two of my brightest analysts wargame how a rogue element inside the US government could neutralize China. If the answer was it couldn't— which is what I expected—that meant Mobilizing America was just cover for another bunch of alt-right blah-blah-blah wannabes who posed no real threat to China or anyone else. Godknows, there are plenty of those assholes around.

"But I was wrong. It is feasible. Forget suitcase nukes. Forget chemical weapons. All you need is a virus that's highly lethal, very infectious, spreads through the air, and has an infection-to-symptom lag long enough to allow it to spread undetected."

"That sounds like COVID-19."

"It does, apart from the lethality," Rafiki said. "But a weaponized virus needs a reliable vaccine, one your enemies don't have. If you have all that, then delivery is easy. People with aerosols are enough to get the virus started in China's largest cities; the virus does the rest, especially if you time the attack for Chinese New Year. Within six months, the virus would have engulfed China, killing hundreds of millions and bringing the country to its knees. It would take a century to recover.

Joe's chest tightened as his mind filled with images of the streets of China littered with the dead and dying. "You know what? 5524, the strain of hemorrhagic smallpox developed by Unit 731, sounds to me like the perfect bioweapon."

"And the Japanese had a vaccine. If China was my target, I'd want it as an option. And the people who sent the SEALs to the *Maroku Maru* weren't thinking of the good of humankind, that's for damn sure."

Heart hammering, Joe started to hyper-ventilate, "This is getting out of hand. I'm sorry, but this is too big for me. If I can't take it to Homeland Security, I'll take it to the FBI."

"No, you can't. This conspiracy is real, I'm sure of it. Its people could be anywhere. It only takes one of them to find out what you've uncovered, and we're both dead."

"But—"

"No buts. We cannot afford to make any mistakes, Joe."

"Sorry. So, what do I do?"

"I can't prove any of what I've just said. We must have hard evidence before we talk to anyone. That means finding your ship and crew; if we can, we can prove the hijacking did take place."

"Makes sense, but we still don't know where it is."

"Remember we talked about where the hijackers might have taken the *Sophie Scholl*?" Rafiki said.

"Yeah, I do," Joe replied. "I picked the Philippines: close, good relations with the US, and doing its best to keep out the Chinese."

"Well, it looks like you might be right. One of my contacts inside the Filipino Department of National Defense says there are rumors the CIA ran a successful operation to intercept an Indonesian boat smuggling Iranian gold into North Korea. Payment for ballistic-missile technology, apparently."

"Why wouldn't the Indonesians just fly it direct?"

"That's what they usually do, which is why I think the whole gold smuggling thing is bullshit. I have told my contact to talk with the National Intelligence Coordinating Agency staffer responsible for US/Filipino intelligence liaison. Thanks to a massive gambling problem, she needs cash, so I am hoping I can persuade her to find your ship. Listen, that's it from me; I must go. I will be in touch as soon as I have more."

—18—

A text from Rafiki.

Source confirms ship berthed Philippines SPECFOR base, Ambulong Island, Mindoro. No news of crew. Cannot do more without burning my sources so over to you. Have incurred substantial costs in this project. Need $500k to cover past and expected expenses but NOT repeat NOT paid from any account traceable back to you. Neither of us will last a week if it is. Advise when ready to transfer. Bank details follow.

Joe sat back, exhilarated.

Belatedly, he had realized something important: He might not need witness statements from André and the crew. The *Sophie Scholl* had a systems logger that recorded data from every system onboard: position, course, speed, main engine and generator settings, fuel consumption, power usage, ship motion in three axes, and much more. All that data ended up on two datastores; they would give him all the hard evidence he needed to support his story.

He had to get them off the *Sophie Scholl*, of course, but that was a problem for another day.

First, he had to find Rafiki's money without showing himself to Homeland Security. And the money she had asked for was only the start; things were about to get expensive.

•••

Joe had waited in the scrub at the top of a steep gully leading down to Black's Beach since midnight. But, with the new day only minutes away, it should not be long now.

It wasn't. Joe offered up a silent prayer of thanks, relieved to see Adam Kuprovic's commitment to his daily workout—the one thing that kept him sane in a world gone mad, he had told Joe—had not changed.

Head down, arms pumping and breathing hard, Adam labored up the cut, heading—as he always did—for Torrey Pines golf course before he turned back for home.

Twenty feet from where Joe waited, he stopped. "Come on, Joe!" he called out. "I know you're there."

Joe stood, brushing the sand from his body, his face flushed with embarrassment. "I was so careful," he muttered.

Adam ran a critical eye over a disheveled Joe. "Not careful enough. You think I do this run alone? No way; there are too many fruitcakes around, which is why I have drones and a security team to cover me. Lucky I recognized you; the guys wanted to call the cops ... I have to say, Joe, you do look a bit rough."

"It's been a long night... I know you're a busy man, so I'll get right to it. I appreciate we never got on, Adam, but I need your help."

Adam frowned. "You do know you're asking the wrong man?"

"I'm asking the only man who can help me. If you don't, nobody will."

"Guess what, Joe?" Adam said. "I really don't care; I'm only talking with you because I was curious. And I don't react well to emotional blackmail, so fuck off before I call the cops."

Not for the first time, Joe wanted to punch the arrogant, smug sonofabitch. He told himself to calm down; he needed Adam Kuprovic.

"I wasn't trying to blackmail you, Adam. I was just stating a fact. I'd not be here now if there was anyone else. And giving me what I need matters more than anything you've ever done."

Adam laughed. "Yeah, right... More important than the billion I made last week selling my stake in Jaskana CyberTech? I don't think so."

"This is not about money, Adam. I need fifteen minutes. If you're not convinced, fine. I'll walk away and you'll never see me again."

"Well, you have my attention, so I'll give you your minutes. But not here... How about the parking lot at Scripps Clinical Research? I can be there in an hour."

•••

"I'll accept you can't access your own money," Adam said, "even though you won't tell me why. But a ransom of two million dollars to get André back? That will not wash. Five minutes on Google would tell the dumbest kidnapper that the man's worth a shitload more than that... Come on, Joe. If you want my help, you need to be more open with me."

Joe swore under his breath; he had forgotten Adam's uncanny ability to pick a lie. "You're right and I'm sorry, but I'm in a real hole, one I didn't want to drag you into."

"Very thoughtful of you, but you still have to tell me what the money's for."

"It's not for ransoms. I need it to pay for two things: the people who are helping me find André, and his rescue when they do. But, please, don't ask me for any more detail. If I could tell you more, I would, but I can't."

Adam said nothing for a long time. Joe was sure he was going to be turned down.

But the man surprised him. "The money's yours. Want me to tell you why?"

"Yes, I would."

"We were never friends, but there was something about you I did like: You never bullshitted me, not once, and I don't think you're bullshitting me now. That was one of the reasons I risked my money in Hydra, a lot of money, even for me, and I'm giving you the money now. But don't think I'm getting soft. I'm not; I'm still a total asshole; you have to be in my business if you want to win."

Joe smiled. "Hopefully I'll warm to you ... But there is one thing. This business with André could get dangerous."

Adam waved a dismissive hand. "That does not bother me. I am very well protected. Just keep me posted so my team knows what to expect. Do you need some cash as well?"

"As long as it can't be traced back to you, please."

"That won't be a problem ... Meet me back here at three tomorrow with your account details. I'll have a promissory note for you to sign and a no-name cash-card to cover immediate expenses. Will a hundred k be enough?"

"Plenty, thanks. One more thing: I need to leave the US but I can't use my passport. Any ideas?"

"Can I ask why?"

Joe grinned. "The US government thinks I'm still overseas."

Adam grinned back; all his early hostility had vanished. He seemed to be enjoying himself.

"I won't ask how you managed to get back into the US," he said, "but I know someone who's been very helpful whenever things get, uh ... complicated. I'll check with him first, though; he's paranoid when it comes to security. Now, there is one last thing. Two Homeland Security agents came to see me a few months back. They were from Office of Intelligence and Analysis."

Joe's stomach flipped. "What? Why?"

"To see if I knew what you were doing. I said I hadn't seen you since Hydra, we weren't friends, we weren't working on anything together, and I had no plans to. They seemed disappointed, but, since I was telling the truth, they had to leave it at that. They said to call them if you ever got in touch."

"And will you?" Joe said.

"Hah!" Adam snorted. "Why would I? I wouldn't trust Homeland Security to bury a dead rat. I need to go. I'll see you back here, tomorrow at ten."

Joe waited until Adam was gone, still troubled. He had just trusted his life to a man he knew only from work, someone he'd never much liked and who liked him even less, someone Homeland Security knew he had links with.

He might just have had made the biggest mistake of his life.

But what else could he do?

He pulled out the Nokia. He needed a bank account.

And Rikki Tengarran was going to get him one.

—19—

After a strip-search and full body scan—embarrassing and invasive did not begin to describe them—followed by three hours in two changes of wheels wearing disposable coveralls and booties, a thick hood, and flexicuffs on wrists and ankles, Joe heard the door slide back. Hands cut him free, pulled off the hood, and helped him out.

Joe's escort ushered him into a small office and pushed him into a seat. A large man sat opposite behind a battered desk. Heavy lids hooded his eyes, eyes so dark they were almost black.

"I'm Freddie Kemani," the man said. "Welcome, Doctor Lessart."

"Nice to meet you, Freddie," Joe said.

"A mutual friend says you need my help."

"I need to leave the country, but I can't use my own passport. Homeland Security thinks I'm still overseas."

"Oh! Is that all?" Kemani said. "No problem … Shall we say thirty thousand dollars?"

Joe blinked. "Thirty thou? That sounds like an expensive forgery."

"Who said anything about a forgery?" Kemani protested. "No, no, no. You will borrow a genuine United States passport from a friend of mine. You won't have any problems. Once you are overseas, my friend will report the passport stolen. I tell you, the crime these days is a disgrace."

"What use is a borrowed passport? The photo will be wrong, for a start. And what about the biometrics?"

Kemani laughed and shook his head. "This fine country of ours is fast becoming a police state, doctor, but we're not quite there yet. Has Homeland Security ever fingerprinted you leaving the country? Or asked you to stand in front of a camera while it checks your identity?"

"On the way back in, yes, but not on the way out."

"Which is why you'll be fine. Besides, I have many friends; I will find one your height with a face so like yours nobody will ever question your identity. In fact, I guarantee it. I always take great care of my customers."

"You should, Freddie, given the money I keep giving you," Joe said, sliding Adam's cash card across the desk.

"The best always costs, doctor," Kemani said as he pulled out a terminal. Payment made, he handed a piece of paper across the desk. "Call that number on Friday to arrange pickup. And we will need to know the date of your flight out. The passport's only good for a week once you leave the US."

"Thanks, Freddie. I appreciate your help."

The man gave an airy wave, "No problem at all. I hope I can do more business with you. Now, the van is waiting to take you back. Please give my regards to our friend when you see him next."

Back in the van, searched again, hooded and flexicuffed, Joe enjoyed a moment's optimism.

He knew where the *Sophie Scholl* was. With the help of an old dive buddy, Matti Seppä, he would recover the datastores. Even if Rafiki couldn't find André and the crew, he should have the hard evidence he needed to convince the US Government to take him seriously.

Not that he had any idea how to get the datastores off the *Sophie Scholl* without getting himself shot by the Filipino army.

—20—

The flight from Los Angeles had given Joe plenty of time to produce a workable plan to get onboard the *Sophie Scholl* to liberate the ship's datastores.

By the time he reached Manila, all he'd produced was a delusional fantasy involving a man fast approaching middle age, a man with a talent for diving, a man whose military experience was limited to a failed attempt to become a marine.

A fantasy whose major flaw was its assumption the Filipinos would make things easy for him.

True, they were over-stretched, now the US had cut back its military support. But that did not mean the special-forces unit protecting the base was incompetent. Joe was sure it wasn't. It was dangerous, more than capable of killing him.

But he could not give up now. He owed it to André and the crew; besides, he didn't have any better ideas.

The banca scrunched onto the beach, the plank went down, and Joe headed for the resort's lobby.

"I'm Mister Lopez," he said to the young woman behind the reception desk.

"Welcome to Puerto Galera, Mister Lopez. We are expecting you."

"Thank you. Are there any messages for me?"

"I will check ... Yes, one," the receptionist said, handing Joe a slim FedEx envelope.

Checked in, he went to his room. The envelope held a Jeju Bank cashcard and a note from Rikki to say the bank account he had given Joe had received Adam's money.

A quick text to Rikki and he had the PIN.

He was solvent again.

He headed out.

•••

The heavy-set man looked up from the mess of papers on the desk in front of him. "Joe!" he said, jumping to his feet. "You never tell me you visit."

"It's hard to stay away, Matti. I love Puerto Galera," Joe said before a bear hug squeezed the air out of his lungs.

Matti Seppä let go. "It is too long, my friend."

"Sure is. How's the dive business?"

"Is good. People love PG's new wrecks."

"The family?" Joe asked.

"Maria is well. Twins make me very happy. Two years next month, can you believe this?"

"Where does the time go? One thing, though. I'm not Joe Lessart, not here in the Philippines. I am Enrico Lopez. Just go with it, Matti; I have my reasons."

Seppä's eyes narrowed. "What are you doing, Joe? And why do you not look so well?"

"It's been a rough few months, what with work and all."

"I read you and André sell your business to buy dive boat," Seppä said. "Is it coming here?"

"One day, but I need your help with a problem."

"Please, ask. I was almost killed if not for you."

"Oh, come on, Matti. What happened was no big deal."

"You risk life to bring me back from one hundred meters, my friend. One hundred meters! A big, big deal. I was dead without you. Tell me what you want."

"You still have that old British diving set? What was it called?"

"CDBA. Better than the crazy name the English give: Clearance Diver's Breathing Apparatus. What is that, eh?"

Joe smiled. "Do you still have it?"

"Of course. I dive with it a lot. I like it very much."

"I need to borrow it, rigged for attack swimming on oxygen."

"I have Dräger LAR-V," Seppä said. "Is better. More modern."

"I prefer CDBA. Older sure, but simple, rugged, reliable."

Seppä shrugged. "If you want. What else?"

"Is there anyone in San José I can hire a boat from? Someone who'll keep his mouth shut."

"What? No way, my friend. We take my *Alakdan*. Best banca in PG. Any more?"

"Two things. You can't tell anyone what I'm doing, not even Maria. And you can't ask any questions … Well, you can, but don't get pissed when I refuse to answer them."

Seppä shrugged. "Sure, Mister Lopez. What you want, you get."

"Thanks … And I'll tell you what this is all about first chance I can, I promise."

"You better. Now, when?"

"I want to do as many check dives as I can on CDBA over the next few days. Once you are sure I won't kill myself, I want to head down to San José to look around. How's that sound?"

"No problem. We start tomorrow. Beer?"

"I'd kill for one."

—21—

Alakdan slapped its way through a small sea, the only sound the flat growl from her inboard diesel.

Joe glanced at his GPS. They were rounding the southern end of Mindoro before turning north, leaving Ambulong to starboard. All being well, they would be alongside in San José an hour after sunrise.

Joe had long since given up trying to sleep. Borrowing dive gear and a boat was one thing; taking liberties with Filipino special forces was another. Things could go to shit and fast. This was risky, for him and for everyone else he involved.

Which meant he owed it to Matti to level with him ... up to a point. He poked the man with his foot.

Seppä rolled over, rubbed his eyes, and yawned. "Where are we?'

"We'll pass Ambulong in about twenty minutes ... Matti, we need to talk."

"Ah, right. But we have tea first."

"I need to tell you what's going on," Joe said when they had their mugs.

Seppä put an arm around Joe's shoulders. "No. Your business, not mine. I trust you."

"Thanks, but you need to understand the risks I'm asking you to take, so listen up. Ambulong Island has an army training base on it."

"Camp Sierra is not secret," Seppä said. "Was resort many years ago. Now special-operations base. You Americans trained Filipinos for counterterrorism. Not now. Not since cutbacks."

"Have you seen it?"

"I go past many times, but never close. The army dig channel into lagoon and build new wharf. People say base enough for four hundred men. All that is lagoon side; you cannot see from the ocean. Cost America many dollars ... But why you ask?"

"The US Navy hijacked the dive boat André and I bought. They berthed it at Camp Sierra."

Seppä's head snapped round. "Are you joking me?"

"No, I'm not. They kidnapped André and the crew as well. I've been looking for them ever since."

"But why? You just two rich guys with fancy dive boat."

"I'm sorry, I can't tell you. It'd be too dangerous for you and your family."

Seppä shook his head. "You swim in to see your boat is there. This is why you want CDBA. Am I right?"

"Yes, you are."

"You are fucking mad. Joe. Camp Sierra is special-forces base. You know this."

Joe laughed. "Probably, but I have to prove where the *Sophie Scholl* is and how it got there. To do that, I need the datastores from the ship's systems logger. They'll have all the raw GPS and ship systems data to prove somebody turned it around and sailed it to Camp Sierra."

"Take pictures from hill on other side," Seppä said. "Safe. Easy. Why not?"

"Pictures aren't enough. I need those datastores."

Seppä shook his head. "Base has guards with guns. Drones with cameras. Acoustic sensors for terrorists who swim in for attack. If they hear something, they drop grenades. I know this. I was Finland navy combat diver, remember?"

"I'm not facing the Finnish Navy."

"Mistake to think Filipino military is nothing, Joe. Not much money, sure. But very hard men. Go to police … Please."

"If I do, the bad guys will find out. I can't risk it."

"Shit!" Seppä said. "Are you drug smuggler now?"

"No, no. I'm not. Please don't push for more."

"I have to trust you a lot."

"You do. And some shit might come your way if things go wrong. If all this too much, say so. You have a wife and kids to think about; I have neither … Perhaps I should find another way; I'll understand."

Seppä said nothing for a long time. Then he said, "No problem. I do everything to help. I have to; you save my life that time. But you must have buddy to do this. Not alone."

"Stop right there, Matti. This is my fight, not yours. Besides, two divers are twice as obvious as one. I am the only one going in. Nobody else."

Seppä threw his hands up. "You are like fucking donkey. So, what is your plan for this?"

"Well, here's how I see it. The first thing…"

—22—

Joe and Seppä crested the ridge overlooking Camp Sierra. The crawl in had been a long, hot business, their progress slowed by heavy scrub and patrolling drones.

Joe slid his body the last few feet and looked down at the base.

He was not interested in the buildings. His focus was on the concrete wharf jutting out into the lagoon. Studded with light poles and all the paraphernalia of a working jetty, eight assault boats were tied up on the northern side. On the southern side sat a large, shapeless blob of grays, greens, blacks, and browns.

There was no sign of the *Sophie Scholl*.

Joe raised his binoculars. He could not work out what the blob was. He put his mouth to Seppä's ear. "Southern side of the wharf, the blobby thing. What is that?"

"Camouflage netting. We go closer. We see underneath."

"No way. This is risky enough. I'll take pictures. Maybe we can make sense of them on a computer."

•••

Joe turned to Seppä. "You were right. It is camouflage netting, but see those flecks of white showing through? That's my boat."

"I think, yes." Seppä's face was pale, anxious.

Joe knew why. "Relax. It'll be fine."

"I don't think that. Talk with Ramón."

"Why? What's the problem?"

"You talk with him. Hey, Ramón," Seppä called out, waving *Alakdan*'s deckhand forward.

•••

"What do you think?" Joe said as Ramón went aft.

"You will die," Seppä said, his voice flat. "Every night they are dropping grenades to kill divers."

Joe sat silent. Risking his life was the price he had to pay to save André and the crew.

And nothing Ramón could say would ever change anything.

"I'm sorry," he said at last, "but I'm doing this. I need those datastores."

Seppä was pleading now. "Please, Joe. We go to PG, see what other things we can do."

"I don't have any other options," Joe said.

His words hung in the long silence.

"Fuck you. You are stupid prick." Seppä's voice trembled.

Joe reached out and put a hand on the man's arm. "I'm sorry, Matti," he said, "but I have to do this …. Now, my nerves cannot take much more hanging around. The sooner I do this, the better. Tonight, around midnight, I reckon. Weather's fine, and there's no moon. Ramón says the current off Ambulong will be a steady half-knot going north. Conditions are almost perfect."

"If you want," Seppä said.

•••

Alakdan eased through the moonless night, its diesel burbling as the exhaust dipped below the water, a faint phosphorescence flickering in its wake. A light breeze ruffled the surface into a slight chop.

Joe tried to stretch out the cramps tangling up his guts.

"Luis check with night 'scope," Seppä said. "He say no drones, no boats outside. I think we start. You ready?"

Joe gave a nod. His mind was jumping across everything that could go wrong. The list was long; having grenades tossed at him sat right at the top. If Ramon was right, the army dropped between fifteen and thirty across the seaward approaches to the base most nights, some nights far more. Never none.

"On gas, clear bag first time," Seppä said.

Joe was about to put his nose clip on when his stomach rebelled. He twisted away and emptied his dinner over the side.

Seppä put a bottle of water to Joe's mouth. "Stop, please. I beg you. We find better way."

Joe emptied the bottle, took another from Ramón and emptied that too. "No, we won't ... Right, let's do this."

Nose clip on. Full facemask over hooded head. Tabs tight, mask snug on his face. Joe emptied the counter-lung on his chest. The bag, divers called it, two shots of gas refilled it. Now he was breathing pure oxygen to leach the nitrogen out of his system.

Seppä ran his hands over the CDBA's connections. "All tight, Joe. Now, gear check ... safety kit, torch, camera, knife, lines to tie off equipment, pressure-proof container for datastores in pouch, and swim board. Check?"

Joe had touched each item as Seppä rattled them off. He gave the okay.

"You are ready," Seppä said. "Now remember. Breathe slow. Breathe deep, or you die. Not below twenty-seven feet. Surface slow. And show only top of mask. You did good before; now do better."

The CDBA was the least of Joe's worries. It might look like something from the dawn of diving, but it was rugged, reliable, and simple to dive. The biggest risk was the Filipino army. If they started dropping grenades close to him, he would have more to worry about than a piece of antique British dive gear.

"Two minutes," Seppä said. "Clear bag second time ... All good. And still no patrol boats, no drones. You're ready."

Joe gave the okay. He glanced at the cluster of orange lights marking Camp Sierra's position; it seemed quiet. He found his swim board—a digital stopwatch, compass, and depth gauge mounted on small piece of wood with two slots as handgrips—and slipped into the water. It felt warm and silky.

Joe set his compass for the swim in as *Alakdan* grumbled away, then let himself sink, bleeding oxygen into his counter-lung to stop at twelve feet.

He held the swim board out, turned to face the camp, zeroed the stopwatch, and started to swim, blipping gas into the bag as his body burned oxygen.

Fifteen minutes in, he stopped and drifted upwards. Small bubbles dribbled from his mouth as he released the excess gas from his bag. Two feet below the surface, he stopped. A check all round: no lights, no sounds, no boats. He tilted his head back and eased to the surface. With only a fraction of his facemask above water, he looked all round. The lights from Camp Sierra streaked the sea in long daggers of orange. The channel into the lagoon lay off to his left, a black slash cut into the gray of the shore.

He left surface and swam on.

The seabed came up to meet him; there was enough light from the camp to see it, the sand a pale gray, rocks patches of black. He went left. The seabed soon started to bear right and steepen until it was almost vertical.

He was in the channel.

If there were sensors, this was where they would be. Long slow kicks took him into the lagoon. Still no boats, no grenades, nothing. Joe began to let himself think he might pull this off.

The bank turned again, sharp right. On he went, the loom of the wharf lights filling the water with an ethereal orange glow.

Joe ignored Seppä's advice and went deep. Better oxygen poisoning than a hand grenade.

A weed-infested pillar appeared.

Joe's heart thrashed at his chest. The men with guns and grenades were only feet above him. Men who would assume he was an Abu Sayyaf terrorist and kill him on sight.

He swam up the bank, staying under the wharf until a black shape appeared overhead and to his left.

He surfaced, the concrete slab of the wharf four feet overhead. He searched for surveillance cameras.

None.

And there was a thin strip of white between water and camouflage netting. The hull of the *Sophie Scholl*, Joe was sure of it. "You beautiful thing," he whispered.

He went under, leaving barely a ripple, surfacing inside the camouflage netting. Still no sign of activity. He pulled out the camera and steadied himself to shoot video of the ship's name splashed across the transom before dropping to the propellers.

Seppä had made Joe rehearse removing the CDBA underwater until he could do it without thinking. Now that practice paid off. Joe held his breath, closed the mouthpiece, removed the facemask, then slipped off the set, and secured it to a propeller shaft. He pulled himself along the underside of the ship to the boat ladder. There he tied off his fins. The nose clip he left in place; he would only lose it if he took it off.

Taking care not to disturb the netting, he climbed the ladder. Every second rung he paused to check for any signs of life.

Close to the top, he froze. Two shapes cradling guns ambled along the wharf. They radiated a casual competence. Lit from above, he could see them; they would never see him, not through the netting, not with their night vision burned out by the lights.

He hoped.

Joe forced himself to relax. They were not here for him.

The men moved on. Joe slipped over the gunwale and slid to the deck. For a minute, he lay there, lungs heaving. Dread, not exertion. Aware that time was risk, he crawled forward across the deck and into the welcoming gloom of the *Sophie Scholl*'s dive prep room. Now he could move fast: up a ladder, along a passageway, up another ladder into then through the saloon, and up a third ladder to the bridge.

He went to the systems logger and pulled open the cabinet, relieved to find the datastores still in their slots. Joe popped the slim metal boxes out and sealed them in the pressure-proof container on his belt.

He headed back to the stern. The wharf was empty. He scuttled to the gunwale, down the ladder, slid into the water, pulled on his fins, took a breath, and headed down to the A-bracket. With another word of thanks to Matti Seppä, he put his set on, dribbling gas in to clear the mask.

He took a minute to calm down, using the time to check around him. Still there was nothing to see but water, sand, and the piles supporting the wharf.

He should go.

Joe swam under the wharf and into deep water. At forty feet, he turned and headed for the channel and the open sea where Seppä and the *Alakdan* waited.

Fifty yards later, he angled up the bank. He had only reached twenty-five feet when a sudden metallic whine filled the water. He spun around to work out where the noise was coming. Everywhere was the answer, so he fled for the safety of the seabed, scrabbling to dig himself in.

It was a boat, that much was obvious. If the sensors protecting the base had detected him, that meant grenades.

Joe waited.

The sound of high-speed propellers peaked, then faded. The boat was in the channel, headed out.

Joe's heart slowed. The boat hadn't been looking for anyone around the wharf. The sensors must have missed him as he swam in; they should miss him on the way out. On the downside, the bastards might decide tonight was the night to carpet the seaward approaches to the base with grenades.

Luck would now decide whether he lived or died.

Joe forced himself off the bottom. When he reached the channel, he cut across to the opposite bank. Now he could head for open water; there the north-running tide would take him away from the base. The bank started its swing to the right; he was out of the channel. He swam on, counting his leg strokes, moving faster now as the current picked him up. When he reached four hundred, he turned for deep water.

The patrol boat was a distant buzz.

Joe allowed himself to hope.

Five minutes later, the buzz started to strengthen. Joe drove his legs harder, thigh muscles ablaze.

The buzz strengthened into a resonant whine. Louder and louder until Joe was sure it would pass directly overhead. He stopped, wrapping his arms around his head.

Pointless, he knew. But he had to do something.

A flat, metallic *crack. Crack! Crack! Crack! Crack! Crack!*

None close.

He started swimming again.

He had misjudged the distance. Tracking the boat as he swam was impossible. The noise of its propeller filled the water. It seemed to come from all directions at once.

Crack!

The explosion ripped the water apart, the shock wave hammering Joe's body.

That one was close.

His best chance of surviving was to get away fast. Fear drove him on.

Crack. Another grenade. Too far away to be a problem. Another ten minutes and he would be clear.

Crack! Crack! Crack!

Much closer. The shock made his ears ring.

Crack! Crack!

Further away. Joe could see no pattern to the boat's movements.

Crack! Crack! Crack!

Nowhere near.

Joe knew now the boat was tossing grenades at random; if the sensors had found him, he would be dead. But he wasn't; ten more minutes and he'd be safe.

He fled for the open ocean.

—23—

Joe called Skylar Rafiki. "Hey. It's me. How are you going?"

"My report's done. A friend is on her way to your hotel with it now. It's on a datastick; I will text you the password. Call me tomorrow. You have a decision to make."

"Terrific," Joe said, but the line was dead.

•••

Understandably, Rafiki had been coy about her sources, but, by Joe's rough estimate she must have mined well over a hundred. Some produced fragments: names, words, meetings, new relationships, a paragraph from a document or email. Some revealed gaps: absences unaccounted for, actions without obvious cause, meetings between people who had no reason to meet, firings for no reason, inexplicable transfers.

Information Rafiki had fed to her analysts with their computers and databases and internet search bots, questions referred to sources, answers found, analysis and models updated, conclusions drawn, tested, some accepted, some modified, some rejected.

To produce the report Joe was reading. One long on analysis and method but short on facts. Even so, it was an extraordinary document, one that told a coherent, compelling story.

A conspiracy existed.

It called itself the Revival.

Its goal was US global hegemony.

Five of America's richest families funded the conspiracy; the Gang of 5, Rafiki called them.

Homeland Security and NAVSPECWARCOM were its power bases.

It had also infiltrated the NSA, Defense, and the executive branch.

It had not infiltrated the FBI and CIA.

Conclusions Rafiki had admitted she could not prove. The report was littered with caveats: 'a normally reliable source says', 'our reasonable assessment', 'on the balance of probabilities', 'our view is', 'we estimate', and 'the available evidence indicates', and more from the same vein.

And now Joe faced a decision he'd rather not make.

Rafiki had been adamant: Joe needed a journalist with the credibility—and courage—to break the story. A strategy Joe hated, well aware just how exposed he would be when the story broke.

Not that he had any better options, given his flat-out refusal to have anything to do with the US government.

He kept telling himself to be brave, but it was hard, his nerves shredded by all he had been through.

He called Rafiki.

She did not sound happy. "Any idea what time it is over here?"

Joe knew; it was three in the morning back in Washington. "Sorry, sorry." But he wasn't. He was afraid and desperate.

"Have you read the report?" Rafiki asked.

"I have ... I was hoping for something more concrete."

"You and me both, but the Revival's security is tight. We're lucky to get what we got. I'm sorry, but you have to get off your butt. The raw data from that logger is the only hard data that proves an American agency undertook an illegal operation. It's all we have to force the Revival into the open. But, to do that, you have to give the report to the media."

"Do I have to? Can't we find more evidence, something more solid?"

"No, we can't!" Rafiki snapped. "Why did you risk your life to get those datastores if all you are going to do is sit on your goddammed ass? You can't stop this madness unless you go public."

"But—"

"Listen to me, Joe. You think producing that report was easy? It wasn't, and I've made waves along the way. If the Revival notices them, then I am dead. You too. Our only chance of getting out of this mess alive is to blow it apart. And the sooner we do that, the longer the two of us are going to live."

"Fine, fine," Joe muttered. "I'll do it."

"Finally. I have shortlisted three names: Heifetz, New York Times; Trujillo, CNN; Grujic, Washington Post. They're the best investigative journalists in the US, all strong on security issues."

"Grujic? My girlfriend dumped me for him."

"Ah, okay … Would you have a problem if we went with him?"

"Me? No. Grujic? Probably not. Klara? Definitely."

"Why would that be a problem? We're interested in Grujic, not your ex-girlfriend. Why don't I sound out all three out to gauge their interest?"

"Will they be interested?"

"They should be," Rafiki said. "We have three huge stories behind the hijacking of your ship. First is the Revival; what it is, who's behind it, what do they want, and how do they plan to get it? Second, Homeland Security, the FBI, and the CIA; how come they don't seem to be doing anything to stop the conspiracy? Third, Vandergraaf and her administration; what do they know and when did they know it? Let me tell you, Joe, this is the stuff of Pulitzers. I'll let you know what they say."

"Do that. Any luck getting me a passport? Much as I love the Philippines, I need to get back to the States."

"Still working on it. My go-to person in Manila got himself arrested for credit-card fraud. Be patient. I'll be in touch when I have something for you."

"Okay."

Joe cut the call, found himself a beer, and collapsed into a chair.

He had made progress, yes. He had dumped the canisters of virus where nobody could find them. He had found the *Sophie Scholl*. He had the datastores from the systems logger to prove his ship had been hijacked.

But would it be enough?

He wondered if André and the crew were still alive.

—24—

"So Grujic's our man?" Joe asked.

"He is, though he did seem nervous. Not that I'm surprised. He's made a lot of enemies in Washington without adding the Revival to the list."

"Can't we use one of the other two?"

"Heifetz is investigating the CIA. Trujillo wanted to take it, but he says CNN's new management would never let him. Not visual enough for them; they like stories full of stuff exploding and so on. He said that's code for 'We don't do serious journalism anymore'."

"Let's find someone else. I'd rather not use Grujic."

"We don't have a lot of choice," Rafiki said. "Thanks to all the fake-news merchants, there aren't too many credible investigative journalists around and even fewer media companies willing to back them. I'm afraid it's Grujic or nobody. So, yes or no?"

"Yes. What else can I say?"

"He'll do the job, don't worry."

"Should I give Grujic a call? You know, just to say hello?"

"No. We wait until he's ready to talk. Until then, you stay right away from him, you hear?"

"Will do."

"Now let's talk about your return to the States," Rafiki went on. "Unless you fancy another swim, a Filipino passport is your only option. I'll text you the name of someone in Manila. She can supply the real thing, but it will cost. You don't look very Filipino; she will have to forge all the backup documentation and pay someone to upload your details into the citizens' registry."

Joe grimaced. "That still won't get me into the US."

"For chrissakes, Joe! We have talked about this. The Filipino passport will get you into Mexico without alerting Homeland Security. That's it! You'll use your own passport to cross back into the US."

"The Revival will nail me," Joe said.

"No, it won't. As long as the Revival's people inside Homeland Security haven't red-flagged you, you won't get stopped. All you need is an agent who's too tired to check for Mexican entry and exit stamps in your US passport."

"I can't believe you want me to risk my life on an agent not doing her job properly. Come on! I'm up against guys who can stop a ferry eight thousand miles from the US. I won't do it, Skylar. You have to find a better way."

"There isn't one. How many times do I have to say it?"

"But—"

"Enough, Joe! Red-flagging raises too many questions. Who flagged you? Why? Who authorized it? Where is the case file? What's the plan if you are arrested? Who in management gets told? Who interrogates you? Where? Will there be any political blow-back? And all that does is create a situation the Revival can't manage. It can't risk the exposure; they have to deal with you on their terms, not Homeland Security's. You'll be able to cross without a problem."

"I think I'd rather stay here."

"Oh, dear god," Rafiki said. "I've told you why you have to come home. You are Grujic's only witness. He has to interview you, face-to-face. Skype or Zoom or whatever will not do and you know it. And you can't stop the Revival without taking risks. You know that too."

"Yeah, I do. Sorry … Send me the contact details for the passport person. And watch yourself. I don't trust Grujic; he might not be the man you think he is."

Rafiki laughed. "Is that jealousy, by any chance? Listen, you don't need to worry about me. I have been in this game a long time. I can keep myself safe."

—25—

Anxious as he was, Joe still felt for the border-control agent; the woman's face was gray with fatigue. At the end of the busiest night of the week, she would have been on duty for hours, the pressure relentless to process new arrivals, fast.

The agent slid Joe's passport into the scanner, took his fingerprints, and photographed his face. Seconds later, she handed the passport back, welcomed him home, and was calling the next in line before Joe realized he was free to go.

Almost euphoric, he walked past the locals waiting for friends and relatives to exit the Paso del Norte border crossing. Once outside he turned right on East 6th Avenue.

The car Skylar had promised him—neither too old nor too new— waited for him on South Campbell next to Armijo Park, its tag tucked above the driver's side rear wheel.

•••

Sixteen days. Three thousand miles. Eight changes of clothes. Thirteen cheap motels. One car. Five buses. Four trains.

And now Joe was in Charlottesville waiting for the next bus to Washington.

Hunched against a bitter northerly, he stood with the Nokia to his ear, waiting for Rafiki to pick up. The call rang out, as it had done ever since their last call a week earlier.

He was worried. Washington was the Revival's town, not his. He was the outsider. Without Skylar Rafiki to hold his hand, he would have no friends, no contacts, nobody he could trust. He doubted he'd last a week.

For a moment, he considered calling Klara. Then he dismissed the idea. 'Fuck off' were her last words to him; she would hang up the instant she heard his voice.

Besides, Rafiki had told him—repeatedly—to stay away from everyone he knew.

In the end, he caught the bus. He could not think of anything better to do. He would try Rafiki again when he got closer.

Maybe she'd been busy on something else.

•••

Joe sat nursing a mug of coffee. Twice he had called Rafiki. Twice the call had rung out. He tried not to think why she did not answer.

He was out of options. He had to ignore Skylar's advice. He would call Klara. They might have parted on bad terms, but she was the only person he trusted to arrange a meeting with Grujic.

Besides, what other choice did he have?

He made the call.

The phone rang and rang. Joe was about to hang up when Klara answered.

"Hi Klara. It's me, Joe."

"Joe? Joe? Is that you? Where are you?"

"I'm in town, having a coffee. Sorry, I don't have much time. I need to speak with Cal. Is he there?"

Klara's voice crumpled. Through sobs, she said, "He's disappeared. We were supposed meet two days ago, but he didn't show. Now he's not answering his cell."

"Any idea what he was doing?"

"Working on a story, same as always. He was meeting with someone senior from Homeland Security."

"Did he give you a name?" Joe asked.

"I never asked. And I should have, Joe, I should have!"

"Why was he meeting this person?"

"To get information on a government project he was investigating," Klara said.

"Any idea what the project was?"

"No. Like I said, he kept things to himself."

"Have you told the police?"

"Jesus, Joe!" Klara snapped. "Of course. I am not an idiot."

"Sorry, sorry. What did they say?"

"None of the hospitals have admitted anyone fitting his description ... Or ... well, you know."

"That's something, Klara. At least he is still out there somewhere. Is there anything I can do?

"We should meet. We've had our differences, but I need your help. Please, Joe."

A flicker of doubt. Joe ignored it. He could trust Klara. "I'm in a coffee shop, the Wydown. 14th Street Northwest."

"I'll find it. Thirty minutes. Don't move."

"I won't."

"See you soon... Oh, Joe! I am so sorry," Klara said.

The call cut out. Joe wondered why Klara was saying sorry. She had nothing to apologize for.

He gave up trying to work Klara out and ordered another coffee to fill the time. He sat, staring at the people passing by, but seeing nothing. He still had not found André and the crew. Rafiki was not answering her phone. Grujic had vanished. Klara was a wreck. Hell, he was too.

Everything was turning to shit.

But Klara should know someone who could help, someone they could trust; her connections had to be better than his. If not, he would leave Washington and rethink the whole business.

"Doctor Lessart?" a voice behind him.

Without thinking, Joe turned. A man loomed over him. Too late, he said, "Sorry, who were you after?"

The man flashed an ID card. All Joe could read was 'FBI' in fat blue letters. "I'm Special Agent Fernandez, FBI, Doctor Lessart. Please come with us."

Joe jumped up and shoved the man away. "Hey! I'm not Doctor Lessart."

The two men flanking Fernandez grabbed Joe, spun him around, hustled him out to an unmarked white van, and threw him in. Joe had no time to break the fall; his face slammed into the floor. The men climbed in after him, the door slammed shut, and the van took off.

Joe spat blood as he rolled on his back. "What the hell are you doing?"

The men ignored him. With brutal efficiency, they flipped Joe back over and cable-tied his wrists. A prick of pain in his left hip.

Seconds later, Joe was unconscious.

•••

"Hey, shithead! Wake up!"

Joe's head jerked back as the hood was ripped off. He opened his eyes, then wished he hadn't. The lights were bright.

"You took your time," the voice said. Joe squinted at the man standing over him. A man in ski mask, gloves, and disposable blue overalls looked down at him. "Drink this."

A hand put a beaker with an oversize straw to his mouth. Joe drained the beaker dry. "Where am I? he croaked. "Who are you?"

The man left without a word. The door closed behind him with a solid click.

Joe had never been arrested, but he was sure the FBI did not allow suspects to be treated like this. No, these people worked for the Revival.

He cursed his stupidity. Skylar had told him to stay away from everyone he knew. And what had he done? Arrange a meeting with Klara, and she had betrayed him.

And things were about to get a whole lot worse. Thanks to André, the Revival would know they had found the canisters of smallpox virus. And the SEALs would have confirmed the canisters weren't in the wreck.

The Revival had kidnapped him because it needed those canisters. Joe's bowels cramped at the thought of what that meant. He had no illusions. He would tell them, and then, as soon as they had found the canisters, they would kill him.

He had to get out.

But how?

Cable ties secured his ankles and wrists to the chair. Bolts secured the chair to the floor behind a small table, a second chair opposite. The room's plywood walls had no windows, the floor no openings save for a small drain by his feet. Two lights, a speaker, and a camera were set into the ceiling, all too high to reach. Heavy mesh protected them. The door had no handle. It looked a tight fit.

He heaved and squirmed, testing his restraints.

A voice boomed overhead. "For chrissakes, doctor, stop it. You are wasting energy. That chair isn't going anywhere, and neither are you."

•••

Joe started as the door crashed back. Three men in ski masks, gloves and overalls walked in.

"Who are you?" Joe asked.

One of the three took the seat across the table.

"I want a name," Joe added. "I'm not saying another word until you tell me your name."

"You can call me Matt," the man sat opposite said. "May I call you Joe?"

"Call me what you like. Who are those two?"

"Brad is the small one, Jan's the big mother. Now, how about something to eat and a mug of coffee…"

Hunger overcame fear. Joe's mouth watered.

"…And a shower and clean clothes? Would you like that?"

"Yes, I would," Joe said. He stank of stale piss.

"The guys will fix you up."

•••

Joe pushed his plate away and belched. He felt better, not that anything had changed.

Matt wanted the canisters.

He did not want to tell Matt where they were.

He was a dead man.

The door banged open. Brad and Jan appeared. Without a word, they cable-tied his legs and wrists to the chair.

Matt followed a moment later, folder in hand. "Feeling better?"

"I was until you turned up, you scumbag."

"Some advice, doctor, the last I'll give you: It'll pay you to be polite. Right, let's start. Your dive ship, what is it called?"

"Oh, for fuck's sake!" Joe shouted. "You already know. Just tell me what you want."

Matt's eyes narrowed through the slits in the ski mask. "I'll play your game. What do I want?"

Joe shook his head. "You tell me ... please."

"Two canisters of hemorrhagic smallpox virus."

Joe did his best to seem surprised. "What canisters? My specialty is the influenza virus. As for smallpox, everybody knows the last samples are held in two secure labs in the US and Russia. But I'm sure the Russians will give you some if you ask nicely."

Matt opened the folder. "I have a file note here with a summary of Skylar Rafiki's interrogation. Let's see ... Hmm, she was a hard woman. Brave too. It took my guys ten days to break her."

Guilt overcame Joe. "You bastards!" he shouted.

Matt shrugged. "Yup, we sure are. She said you discussed the canisters and their contents with her."

"You're lying."

Matt gave a theatrical sigh. "Joe, Joe, Joe," he said, shaking his head. "André told us you took the canisters off the ship. Rafiki said the same."

"Now I know you're lying. André doesn't know what happened down there. How could he? He was too busy fighting off the SEALs. And why would I tell Rafiki something that didn't happen?"

"Where are the canisters?"

Joe said nothing for a moment, his mouth fixed into a stubborn line. "Where's Klara?"

Matt sighed. "Come on, Joe. This is not about her."

Anger, remorse, frustration. "She has no part in this. Let her go and I'll tell you everything."

Matt looked at Joe the way a rattlesnake sized up a rabbit. "I'm not doing deals with you. Where are the canisters of hemorrhagic smallpox virus?"

"What canisters?" said Joe.

Matt sat back. He waved Brad and Jan forward. "I have had enough of this. You have had your chance. It's time you found out how unpleasant things can get. Go for it, guys."

The two men stepped forward, cut the cable-ties, and lifted Joe from the chair. The blood rushed back to his feet and hands; numbness gave way to agony.

The men hustled him out, down the corridor, and into another room, empty except for a plank of wood about three feet wide resting on sawhorses, two buckets full of water, and a thick towel.

"This is where we hurt people who won't answer my questions. When Brad and Jan have finished, you'll be answering mine. You are nothing exceptional, Doctor Lessart. Not like Skylar Rafiki, and we still broke her."

"Fuck you," Joe mumbled as the men laid him face up on the board, secured his legs and arms, and placed the towel over his face.

Joe tried to drag air deep into his lungs, but the water was already soaking through the towel, running cold across his face. It did not stop, but the air did. Unable to purge carbon-dioxide, his lungs screamed for relief. His body arched to give his body the fresh air it needed, but there was only water. An involuntary spasm slammed his larynx shut; what little air he drew through the water-soaked towel never made it to his lungs, leaving him thrashing his legs and arms in mindless panic.

The men ripped off the towel, released his arms and pulled him upright. Joe's chest heaved, trying to claw air back into his lungs, but nothing happened.

Fists battered his back. The spasm gave way, and Joe's larynx relaxed. Air rushed in and out. The panic faded, and Joe allowed himself to believe he would live.

Matt leaned over. "Was that fun, Joe? We call it dry drowning. You're a diver; I'm sure you've heard of it."

Joe stared at his torturer. "You animal." His voice was a broken rasp.

"We can do this forever. You can't. Tell me where those canisters are."

The temptation to say 'yes' clawed at Joe's resolve. "I'm not saying anything until you let everyone go."

Matt shook his head. "Again, boys, and I don't care how much fuss he puts up. Make the sonofabitch suffer this time."

Brad and Jan forced Joe back down, tied his hands, and placed the towel over his head. Water splashed down.

The first time was a nightmare. The second was much worse; Joe knew what was coming.

His body was deep into crisis before the towel came off. His lungs were empty, his larynx had snapped tight, and carbon dioxide had saturated his system, bringing nausea, headache, the urge to vomit, pain, and panic in an unholy cocktail of suffering.

Pain flayed his chest, his lungs protesting the insults inflicted on them.

His vital organs were shutting down, diverting precious oxygen to his brain.

This time, Death had him cradled in its arms before the towel came off. Again, Brad and Jan pounded his back, but he was further gone this time. An eternity later, his larynx reopened. A rasping, gasping, choking, spluttering heave as his lungs fought for air.

When Joe was breathing again, the men dumped him on the floor. Half-conscious, his head lolled slack-jawed, his mouth open, lips frothing with blood and sputum.

Matt leaned over him. "What do you think, boys? One more time?"

"I think so," Brad said. "He's an awkward sonofabitch."

"No, please … I'll tell you." Joe's voice was a feeble whisper.

"Not so tough now, eh?" Matt said. "Take him back."

The two men returned Joe to the room with the chairs and table. They did not bother to tie him down. Joe knew why; he did not have the strength to flatten a roach.

"Did you and André find the canisters?" Matt asked.

"Yes, we did." Joe's voice was a rasping croak.

"After the SEALs captured André, what did you do with them?"

"I left them on the *Maroku Maru*."

Matt leaned across the table. "Don't lie to me, Joe. Tell me the truth, or I will waterboard you until your heart explodes. You understand me?"

"Yes, yes, yes. Believe me, I left the canisters on the ship. I'm not Superman; they were too heavy for me on my own."

"You're lying. The SEALs were watching you. They saw you drag those two canisters out of the wreck."

"Bullshit!" Joe said. "Do you have any idea what the diving is like on that ship? Do you?"

"I'm not a diver, so why don't you tell me?"

"The silt in Number-4 hold is a foot deep; it's like dirty, red talcum powder. I brought a ton of it out with me. The SEALs would have seen nothing, trust me. They were too busy dealing with André to pay me any attention."

Matt laughed. "They were busy all right. André put two of them in hospital."

Joe wanted to cheer. "Well done, André."

"But the SEALs did see you ... well, their cameras did."

"More lies. There were no cameras. We would have spotted them."

"Except you didn't. The SEALs rigged them up to cover every door into that ship. Little black boxes, smaller than my hand with fiber-optic cables running back to an uplink. They recorded every time you went in and every time you came out."

Joe tried to conceal his shock. Like a man peeling an onion one layer at a time, Matt was stripping his lies away. "The silt remember?" he said. "There's no camera built that can see through that stuff."

"The canisters. Where did you leave them?"

"You know what? The SEALs screwed up the whole business. Why didn't they kidnap us both and do the searching themselves?"

"The mission commander wanted to, but her boss said no. Even SEALs have their limits, and she'd already lost two early on."

"Wow! This just gets better and better. I thought SEALs were invincible."

"Some of them seem to think so, I'm afraid. They're not, though. One slashed his arm open on a piece of steel. Another drowned; she was caught inside when she lost her line. She never made it out."

Joe felt a surge of compassion for the anonymous SEAL. It had happened to him inside the *Repulse* off Singapore, in a compartment called Barry's Quiet Place after the first diver to get trapped there. Hunting for a way out had been the worst hour of his life.

Until now.

"The SEALs said you were competent divers," Matt went on, "so the Navy decided to use you as extra searchers. The moment you found the canisters, they would take them and you."

Joe felt like an idiot. He tried not to think about all the precious bottom time he had frittered away looking for the SEALs while they were sitting back in their fancy submersible, warm and dry, laughing their asses off as he and André did their best to get killed. "What a shit plan. I escaped, and you don't have the canisters."

Matt laughed. "Oh, too harsh. No, they didn't have too many other options. And there was a lot of pressure on them; the bosses were worried the Indonesians might turn up and start poking around. Their navy's a lot better than people give them credit for, and so is their satellite surveillance, thanks to those Chinese sonsofbitches. They'd have spotted the CSS if a malfunction forced it to surface ... something it has a habit of doing, I'm sorry to say."

Joe folded his arms, a smirk of triumph on his face. "So, despite all their fancy gear, the SEALs still made a mess of it. And those cameras missed the only thing that mattered: what I did with the canisters."

"Answer my questions, or I'll hand you back to Brad and Jan. Only this time I will let them waterboard you for as long as they like. Your choice."

Joe let the silence drag on. As Matt turned to Brad, he said, "Fine. I'll tell you."

He paused. The lies he was about to tell had to be right. Staying alive depended on it.

"Come on, come on. We don't have all day," said Matt.

"After we found the canisters..."

•••

"… and then I dragged the canisters aft to Number-5 Hold and lifted them to the weather deck. That nearly killed me; they were damn heavy. I left them there, on the starboard side, so the lift-bags wouldn't get tangled in the Sampson posts when we blew them to the surface."

Matt's eyes were glazing over. The man did not have a clue what Joe was talking about. He was no more a seaman than he was a diver.

"This is all very interesting, but how about answering the question? You say the canisters were there, but the SEALs have searched the entire ship, and they're not. So, where are they?"

"If they're not where I left them, I don't know … In the hold? On the seabed? Yeah, probably on the seabed. There were days when the current was strong enough to pick them up and take them away; it is very exposed. They won't be far, though... a couple of klicks, four or five if the current was really bad and got them rolling along the seabed," Joe added, happy to rub the SEALs' faces in their failures.

Joe could see this was beyond Matt; the man needed someone who understood the problems of wreck diving.

Matt stood and left the room. A few minutes later, he was back with a tablet. He placed it on the table, handed Joe a stylus, and pointed at the screen. "That's a schematic of the ship's upper deck. Mark where you left the canisters."

Joe marked a cross on the starboard waist next to Number-5 hold. "The first one was here. If it's gone, the current must have taken it. You can see how open it is."

"The other one?

Joe put a question mark beside the first cross. "This is where I was aiming for, but I might have dropped it along the way. Like I said, I had carbon dioxide poisoning; the canisters were heavy; the SEALS had kidnapped André; I was alone and in a lot of trouble ... I thought ... No, I knew for sure I was about to die."

"What a hero," Matt said. He took the tablet back. Then, without a word, he left.

An age later, he returned.

"I've talked with the people responsible for searching the *Maroku Maru*. They think you might be telling the truth."

"Why are you so surprised? I am telling the truth."

"Whereas I'm sure you're not," Matt said as he waved Brad and Jan forward. The men hauled Joe to his feet, holding him by the arms. Matt's open hand smashed into Joe's face, then a second and third, brutal blows that split the skin around his mouth and left eye.

Matt leaned in. "I have been interrogating shitheads like you for years," he whispered. "I can smell a liar."

"I'm not lying," Joe rasped, spitting blood.

"We'll see ... But, before I go, I want you to understand something. If what you have told me is crap—which it is—we will waterboard you five times before we talk again. Five times, and no amount of blubbering from you will stop that. Now, would you like to change anything?"

"Why would I?" Joe mumbled. "Somewhere around there you'll find those canisters."

"We both know you're lying. Care to guess what happens to liars?"

"I'm telling you the truth."

"Last chance ... Come on, Joe ... No? Well then, if that is what you want. But just to remind you what happens when you refuse to cooperate, the boys are going to show you how bad waterboarding can get."

"Please, no," Joe said, his voice shaking. "You promised."

"I don't think I did. All yours, boys."

—26—

Joe had lost track of time.

No watch. No clock. No windows. No day. No night. No rhythm to the hours. Meals at random. The occasional waterboarding. He slept, dozed, or daydreamed.

The door banged open. Brad and Jan ambled in. Joe cringed.

"Oh, boy," Jan said, yanking Joe to his feet, "you have really fucked up now. Guess what happens now?"

Joe shook his head. But he knew.

The two men hustled him down the corridor to the room with the board and buckets. The waterboarding room.

Matt stood, waiting. His eyes glittered through the slit in his mask. "Well, doctor. Are you ready for another session?"

"But why?"

"Because you lied to me. I've heard back from the SEALs on the *Maroku Maru*. There is no sign of those canisters, not anywhere on the ship, not in the hold, not on the seabed within five klicks of the wreck, nowhere. And, believe me, they have looked."

"I left them there. I did, I promise."

"No, you didn't. And that makes you a lying sack of shit." Matt turned to Jan. "What do we do to liars?"

"We hurt them, boss."

Matt turned back. "You think waterboarding is bad, Joe? Well, wait until you see what else my boys can do when I let them loose. They will make you regret the day—"

The door banged open. A man in a ski mask burst in. Joe had not seen him before. "Boss! Message from Jackpot; the state police are on their way from Elkins. One vehicle with a couple of troopers."

"What?" Matt snapped. "How?"

"Jackpot says one of the neighbors called the terrorist hot-line; he said we seemed suspicious. The state police aren't taking the man seriously; they're only responding to keep him quiet. He calls in a lot."

"I said this whole bullshit cabin-in-the-woods thing was a mistake. Did Jackpot say which way they're coming in?"

"Through Oak Flat and Fort Seybert."

Matt put his face to Joe's. "Don't think this is over, doctor. So you've something to look forward to, I'll have the boys waterboard you as soon as we're at the next safe house ... Okay, everyone. You know what to do."

The men hauled Joe away to a tired, worn room with a pair of lounges, a table covered in the remains of a meal, chairs, a TV, a small kitchen off to one side.

"Clothes on," Brad snapped, tossing a bag at Joe, "and make it quick."

When Joe was dressed, Brad sat him on a lounge, jammed a hood over his head, and secured his hands and ankles with cable-ties. "Do not move, asshole."

"What's happening?" Joe said. "Come on, tell me."

Matt ignored him. "Get him out of here. And make sure you have all his stuff .... Take the SUV, and be careful. The trail is all iced up."

"Yes, boss."

Hands grabbed Joe and took him outside—the cold was bitter— heaved him into the SUV and covered him with what felt like a blanket.

"I'll be watching you," Brad said. "If you move, I will blow a hole in your gut. Understood?"

"Yes, yes," Joe said. The man sounded rattled. Joe wondered why. Matt's team ought to be able to handle two state troopers.

The door slammed, the engine started, and Brad gunned the SUV away, tires fighting for traction.

'Be careful,' had been Matt's order. But Brad had not listened. Even stuck in the trunk, Joe could feel the man hammering the SUV to its limits.

Fifteen minutes in, Brad cornered hard. Too hard. The SUV drifted to one side and slammed to a stop amidst the shriek of torn metal, the impact driving Joe into the side of the SUV.

Joe lay, dazed and hurting; nothing seemed broken. Over the clicking of the engine as it cooled, he could hear a soft sound, rising and falling.

Brad's voice was a strangled whimper. "Help me, please. Help me."

Joe kicked the blanket off and scrabbled the bag off his head. He looked around. In front, Brad was slumped over the wheel.

Joe knew this was the only chance he was going to get.

He clawed his way into the back seat, pushed the door open, and tumbled out into the snow. He bunny-hopped around to the driver's side. An uprooted tree had stopped the SUV from going over the edge. To unblock the trail, the road crew had cut its branches back to points sharp as blades; the impact had driven one into the door.

Which explained the whimpering from Brad.

Joe went around to the passenger door, opened it, and wriggled his way in. Brad pawed at the branch in the left side of his stomach. He was wasting his time; he would never move it.

"If you want me to help you," Joe said, "I need a knife."

Brad's voice was a croak. "My belt ... right side."

Joe found a small jackknife. He pressed it into Brad's hand. "Get these cable-ties off me. Come on, come on!"

With hands and ankles free, Joe put the shift into park, and restarted the engine.

"What are you doing?" Brad mumbled. "Get me a medic. I'm dying here."

Joe ignored him. He pulled Brad's feet off the pedals, jammed his foot on the brake, and put the shift into reverse.

"This is going to hurt, my man, so hold on."

Joe lifted his foot off the brake and stamped on the gas.

The SUV jumped backwards, ripping the branch clean out of Brad's body. The screech of tortured metal could not drown the man's agonized shrieks.

Joe stopped the SUV. He heaved Brad over to the passenger seat, ignoring yet more screams. Pads cut from the blanket patched Brad's wound.

"Keep the pressure on if you don't want to bleed out," he said as took the wheel and eased the SUV back to the trail, ignoring Brad's whimpering.

Ten minutes later, he came to a T-junction. US-33, the sign said; left for Harrisonburg, Virginia.

Joe did not stop, gunning the SUV around, relieved to be off the treacherous forest trail and back on blacktop.

"Listen up, Brad," he said, "I'm giving you two options. Answer my questions, and I will find a hospital in Harrisonburg for you. Don't talk, and I'll dump you in the snow, and you will die. Your pick."

Brad shook his head. He was gray faced. Sweaty. The man was in shock.

"Answer my questions, Brad, or you'll be dead inside fifteen minutes. See al that snow and ice? That means it's cold out there."

"What do you want?"

"Why is Matt so interested in me? And who is he?"

"Mike Anderson's his name," Brad said; his voice was weak, shaking. "But that's all I know. I just do what he tells me. Never says why …. too dangerous to ask questions."

"Dangerous? How?"

"He's messed up … crystal meth mostly. He goes crazy, swearing, kicking stuff. He shot one of the guys in the leg one time, no reason … Ah, sweet Jesus, that hurts … I can't do this anymore."

Joe braked hard. The SUV skidded to a stop that sent Brad into the dash, screaming, hands clutching the wound in his side. "Listen! Keep talking, and you might live. Don't, and you will die. Did Anderson ever tell you what all this is about? Come on! He must have said something."

"One time, he started blubbering. Never seen him so bad. He'd hit the meth hard … I've done lots of terrible shit, but at least I was working for the government. But it would never do what he was talking about."

"Which is what?"

"China. America's worst enemy, he said. The bosses were going to send the Chinese to hell … all gone. No more China. No more Chinese."

"What? Like killing them all?"

"Sounded like it to me … I feel like shit."

"You should have chosen a different line of work, my friend," Joe said, tapping the brakes to remind Brad of his options. "Did you believe what he was saying?"

"Fuck yes! It came from the heart, man. Meth heads are fucking crazy, but they tell how they see it."

"Did Anderson say anything else?"

Brad's face was twisted with pain. "Can't you go any faster?" he mumbled, head sagging.

"Hey! Stay with me!" Joe shouted. "Anderson; what did he say?"

"Uh ... Mexico. He was going to Mexico," Brad said.

"Where?"

"Valle de something ... Banda maybe ... Not sure."

"This Banda place. What happens there?"

"No idea ... Cohen runs it ... No, Cojen ... Can't remember. Anderson said ... full of people in white coats ... evil people."

"Any names?"

"No way," Brad said. "If I started ... questions ... He's a killer ... I just ... I don't..."

Brad's voice drifted into silence.

Joe knew he'd not get any more from the man.

"Let's find you a hospital," Joe said, wondering if he had left it too late. Not that he cared too much.

He was going to find Brad's Banda place. He had a feeling he knew what the evil white coats were up to.

•••

Joe stuffed a credit card from Brad's wallet into the man's pocket. "Get out! Take a right up ahead; the hospital will be right in front of you."

"I'll never make it."

Joe reached over and pushed the door open. "Surprise yourself."

"You'd better hope we never meet again," Brad snarled.

Joe lost it. With one savage kick, he slammed the man out of the SUV. "Best you start walking, sport," he shouted over the screaming the man's brutal exit had triggered.

He closed the door, hung a U-turn, and accelerated away. He checked the mirror. Brad was stumbling down the road, hands clamped to the wound in his side.

Joe could see the blood seeping past the man's fingers. A lot of blood. He tried to care. He failed.

Ten miles later, Joe turned the SUV off the road and stopped, throwing the door open an instant before he vomited, convulsive heaves that racked an already battered body.

When there was nothing left to throw up, he looked around the SUV, hoping to find water and Kleenex. Instead he found two backpacks sat in the foot well of the back seats.

And one was his.

"I'll be damned," he said, wiping his mouth on his sleeve.

He opened it. Not a thing was missing: spare clothes, cash-card, two passports, even Rafiki's Nokia and its charger. It was all there.

Joe turned on the Nokia, then shut it down and put in his pocket. Who would he call? The Revival had taken most of the people who could help him. Only three remained: Adam Kuprovic, Freddie Kemani, and Matti Seppä, and he would not drag any of them into his nightmare until he had worked out what to do next.

Anger surged. Fuck the Revival; he would have to find a way to stop it. But, as fast as it had come, the anger faded. One man against a criminal conspiracy planning to destroy China? He shook his head. Talk about ludicrous.

But he was smart. There had to be a way.

—27—

The Nashville bus pulled over for a comfort stop. Joe stepped out and powered up the Nokia to call Matti Seppä.

The man took a while to answer Joe's call. "Hell, man! Where have you been?"

"Later. Any luck finding the guys?"

"Army guy I know hears talk of tall 'Asian-looking' Amerikano. Prisoner in army camp in Mindanao. I am checking this, but not easy. Mindanao is bad place; Abu Sayyaf is problem."

"Don't take any risks. All I need is information."

"I do not worry about Abu Sayyaf."

Seppä's gung-ho tone was unsettling. Joe had caused enough collateral damage; he could not let anyone hurt the man or his family. "Hey!" he said. "Listen to me. Do not go anywhere near Mindanao. Send somebody else. And I mean it, Matti, you hear me?"

"You sound like my mama. But I stay away. Promise."

Joe thought the man sounded relieved; all the bravado had vanished. "A promise I expect you to keep, Matti. I'll call you in a week."

Joe cut the call, relieved. He was a one step closer to finding André and the crew.

Relief gave way to anger. Anger at the Revival for what they had done: to him, to Klara, to Grujic, to Rafiki, to Omar, Solly and the rest of the *Sophie Scholl*'s crew …. and, most of all to André.

He had to stop hoping others would deal with the cancer in America's heart. That task was his now.

And he could think of no better place to start than Anderson's evil people in white coats.

Joe called Adam's burner cellphone.

"Yes? Who is this?" Adam said.

"It's me. I need another couple of mill. Same arrangements, and soon. I'll sign the papers when I can; until then, trust me."

"You're making me nervous."

"Don't go all floppy on me now, Adam. It's only money."

"It'll be in the account in an hour. Anything else?"

"No. We're done."

Joe hung up, then called Kemani.

—28—

Kemani sat, silent, inscrutable, a finger tapping his lips.

"Getting you in and out of Mexico?" he said at last. "I can do that. But have you been trained to carry out covert surveillance and kidnapping operations?"

Joe shrugged. "No, but how hard can it be? And I'm sure you can arrange a gun in case things get difficult."

"Ah, yes, how hard can it be … The words of someone who understands nothing. Listen to me, Doctor Lessart. Valle de Banderas and Puerto Vallarta are dangerous places ever since the Venganza cartel took over Jalisco. One mistake, and you're dead. And you won't die easily; they are cruel people."

"I'll take a gun."

"The Venganza carry assault rifles," Kemani said, "which they've been trained to use."

"So, find me some people who can keep me safe. Come on, Freddie! Help me here."

"Let me see … I think Max Beharry is the man you need. He is one of my people; ex-special forces, a very competent man. He will not go with you, but—"

"Hold on!" Joe said. "Why not?"

"When he came to work for me, he said no foreign jobs, non-negotiable. But, don't worry. He will make sure you don't make too many stupid mistakes. But you will need someone to help you in Puerto Vallarta; trying to do this on your own is a very bad idea. Give me a second."

Kemani extracted a black notebook from the drawer of his desk. He skimmed through it, then stopped to run his finger down a page.

"I have two people who can help. They were Jalisco State Police officers until the Venganza took over; they are experienced and reliable. They will do their best to make sure nobody troubles you."

"Fine. How much?"

Kemani smiled, bent his head, and started to scribble on a piece of paper, mumbling to himself. He spun the paper around for Joe to read.

The price was outrageous, but Joe was too tired to argue. "I'll transfer the money to your account."

"Thank you. And please do not get yourself killed, Joe. A dead client is bad for my reputation."

—29—

A woman in her forties, Joana Serdán was one of the two ex-cops Kemani had lined up for Joe. She had told him the two-day hike in to Cogent's laboratory outside Valle de Banderas would be a bastard.

She was only half-right.

Joe wiped sweat from his eyes and cursed everything about this godforsaken place: terrain, drones, heat, humidity, bugs, thorns, aching legs, exhaustion, thirst. Just being here.

Times like this, he was glad he had never become a marine.

Joe lay in the bushes on a bluff. A building the size of two football pitches side-by-side dominated the compound below. He knew a serious laboratory complex when he saw one: single level, no windows, one entrance facing the gate next to a loading dock, its roof cluttered with air-con units. And surveillance cameras. Lots of them. Out back stood a lattice mast with microwave antennae, satellite dishes, and a cluster of smaller whip aerials, all connected to thick black cables running into a junction box mounted at its base.

Two rows of huts flanked the laboratory. On the left, stores, workshops, and plant; Joe could hear the flat growl of diesel generators from one. Another sported a tall chimney; the bio-hazmat incinerator. On the right, accommodation huts and a canteen. A game of soccer was underway in front of one, the players all young men, fit and wiry. Venganza foot-soldiers, Joe thought.

Two razor-wire fences topped with floodlights and surveillance cameras secured the compound. Laser tripwires screened the rough ground outside, whilst a pair of drones zigzagged over the complex.

The road from Valle de Banderas emerged from woods to the south. Once through a chicane of concrete pipes to slow incoming vehicles, it entered the compound through gates flanked by a sand-bagged security post complete with a pintle-mounted heavy machine gun.

What concerned Joe was the number of armed men around. He had counted thirty. Serdán had said the well-fed ones giving the orders would be Americans or Russians; Joe had seen four of those so far. If he added the men off-watch and out patrolling, he reckoned the laboratory's security force was a hundred strong.

And then there were the laboratory staff, the evil people in white coats that had so upset Anderson. Joe had given up trying to count them; they all looked the same.

A quick look at his watch. Behind schedule. He was an idiot. Hanging around rubbernecking was a sure way to get caught.

Five minutes later, he had placed a surveillance camera in position and was on his way out, unreeling a fiber-optic cable—so thin it was all but invisible—as he went.

A thousand anxious yards later, he reached the cellphone he had taped to a tree on his way in along with a small solar panel to keep it charged. He connected the cable, relieved to see the phone and camera talking.

Now he had to get out without one of the roving patrols catching him. He had seen three on the way in; they hadn't been hard to avoid. They made a lot of noise.

He moved off, stopping only when he came to a rock-strewn gully. Dangerous places, Max Beharry had said, perfect for ambushes.

Satisfied it was safe to cross, Joe was about to move on when his earphone beeped. Long before he'd have heard it, one of Beharry's gadgets had detected the buzz of an inbound drone. He backed under a small tree, sank to the ground, and froze.

This drone was slow to leave. When it did, Joe was about to stand when a movement high on the opposite bank caught his eye, a flicker which came and went, a shape that changed amongst the thousands drawn by rocks and vegetation, by sun and shade, by leaves and branches.

Joe stared across the gully. A glint of metal. His brain resolved the angular shape of an assault rifle. Then a camo-creamed face. And another. Two men in mottled camouflage uniforms were moving into the shade of a sprawling tree.

If he had tried to cross a few minutes later they'd have been waiting for him, an amateur with a pistol facing two professionals with automatic weapons.

Terrible odds.

Twenty minutes passed. Still the two men had not moved. Sunset was close. Joe could not wait any longer; he did not need Beharry to tell him crossing hostile ground at night would be difficult and dangerous.

The two men might only be forty yards away, but he had to move.

One tiny step at a time, he was easing back when his ears caught a sound, something alien amidst the susurrus of wind through forest canopy.

A boot-broken twig? A kicked rock? Joe wasn't sure. But it sounded close.

Had he been spotted? Were the two men there to ambush him? The urge to run was almost irresistible.

He forced himself to calm down. If he ran, he was dead.

"Just a goat, boss." A voice from across the creek, soft but audible in the pre-dusk quiet. A local. "It's nothing."

"Did not sound like goat." A Russian. "Come from left of big tree, this side of gully."

Joe let himself breathe again. Whatever the men were looking for was nowhere near him.

"Come on, boss. Chill. Lots of goats here."

"Yeah, but I call in ... Alfa-one, Six-six. Possible contact, Charlie-seven-one ... Roger, we check. Six-six out ... Let's move, Pablito. I follow creek, you stay thirty right. Go slow. If goat, we shoot it."

"Sure, boss."

Joe's mind's eye worked out the men's path. They would be moving along the opposite bank, down the gully, away from him.

He should go.

He had started to move back when a burst of gunfire shattered the quiet. He flinched but did not stop. Another burst. Joe took advantage of the racket to pick up the pace. More bursts. Shouts of laughter.

Two bored men taking out their frustration on a goat.

•••

Joe climbed the outside stairs to his cramped room above a small café south of the Rio Cuale. He opened his laptop and connected with the camera.

The Cogent compound appeared, the image sharp in the harsh glare of floodlights. He started the download, collapsed on his bed, and fell asleep.

—30—

After days watching video from the camera above the compound, Joe was certain he had found the person running Cogent's laboratory: a woman in her late-forties, bleached blond hair cut shoulder-length, always in a white coat.

Blondie, he'd tagged her.

Three or four times a day, she shared a cigarette with a well-muscled man with buzz-cut white hair; the Colonel, Joe called him. The man always wore a green t-shirt and camouflage trousers bloused into high-laced jump boots, a pistol in a thigh holster. He seemed to be the head of security; when he wasn't talking with Blondie, he spent much of his time haranguing the armed men protecting the compound.

The Colonel was a dangerous man. Joe wasn't going anywhere near him.

Which made Blondie his target.

•••

As they had done every night for two weeks, Joe and Serdán were parked up back from the road into Puerta Vallarta, a mile from the walled compound that housed Blondie and her laboratory staff, its gate covered by another of Joe's cameras.

Around seven, a vehicle left the compound and turned for Puerto Vallarta.

Joe froze the image on his tablet. "Blondie's in the first van with six more people. The Colonel's not with her .... No Russians or Americans, only lab staff ... and we have one SUV with four Venganza. I think that's it for tonight, Joana."

"Yes. We go."

Serdán eased the car in behind the convoy. "You will meet Esteban when we find where they eat," she said.

Thirty minutes later, taillights flared red as the convoy pulled over. As they drove past, Cogent staffers were leaving the van.

"They go to River Café or Oscar's," Serdán said. "Let me call Esteban."

A flurry of Spanish. "He will wait at River bridge," Serdán said.

She pulled over to let Joe out. "Go left then three hundred meters," she said. "River bridge is on left. I wait at Calle Encino and Matamoros. Any problem you text."

Joe and Serdán had watched several of the Cogent staffers' nights out. They were always long, boozy affairs; he was sure tonight would be no different. He took a deep breath No need to rush.

He made himself slow down.

Esteban Orejon, a short, heavy man, was waiting for him.

"Blondie is eating at the River Café or Oscar's. You ready?"

Orejon nodded. "Sure."

Joe slung his jacket over his arm and went to do what Max Beharry had said was one if the hardest things anyone could do: abduct someone from a public place without screwing it up.

•••

Joe pulled his hat down over his face and idled past Isla Cuale's shops and market stalls, relieved to see so few tourists. A crowd would have made what he planned to do impossible. Not that he was surprised it was so quiet. Tourists did not come to Puerto Vallarta the way they used to;

nobody liked being shaken down by gun-toting Venganza punks. None of whom were around, thankfully.

He strolled past the River Café.

A glance inside confirmed Orejon's report. If the wine bottles cluttering their table were any guide, Blondie and her people planned a heavy night, the Venganzans too. Their table was even more crowded.

Nobody expected trouble.

Orejon waited for him under the bridge carrying the highway north.

"Blondie is drinking plenty vino," Orejon said. "She will use restroom. If nobody come with her, we are okay."

"Cameras?"

"Two outside. They do not see the restroom. Now we walk to beach and back around. Then wait until Blondie comes out. Do like we practice, no problem."

Joe hoped Orejon was right.

Deep into the evening, Blondie tottered to the restrooms, back beside the restaurant. She was drunk. Alone. Vulnerable.

Joe let himself hope. Isla Cuale was deserted, its shops and stalls long closed. Orejon pointed to the restroom as Blondie went inside. They went over to wait.

Finally, Blondie reappeared. As she stopped to fiddle with her handbag, Orejon stepped in. He jammed his gun into her back and put a hand across her mouth as Joe grabbed her left arm, pushing her behind a shuttered kiosk.

"Unless you do what we say," Joe whispered into her ear, "we will kill you. Nod if you understand."

The woman trembled. She hesitated, then nodded.

"We will let go of you now. If you make any sound or try to escape, my friend will shoot you. He's right behind you; he cannot miss. Understood?"

Another nod.

"Now," Joe went on, "I'll put my arm around your shoulders, just two lovers having fun. We'll go to my car, get in, and drive away. When we've talked, I'll bring you back here to be with your friends. You will never see either of us again, I promise. Understand?"

The woman bobbed her head.

Ten minutes later, Serdán drove them out of town. Blondie was in back, hooded, wrists bandaged and cable-tied. Another Max Beharry maxim: Never leave marks on the target unless you mean to.

Joe sat beside the woman; shock was setting in. She was shaking.

He made no attempt to comfort her. Make the target feel isolated and vulnerable, Beharry had told him.

Well out of Puerto Vallarta, Serdán turned down a dirt track. She drove on for a few miles, then pulled off into the scrub and stopped.

Joe slipped on a black ski mask, opened the door, and pulled Blondie after him. Once Serdán had reversed the car back, he took off Blondie's hood. Her face was ashen in the headlights. Her eyes hunted left and right in terror.

"Walk over to the tree," Joe said, "then turn and sit down."

"Why? What will you do?"

"Just talk. You'll be fine."

The woman hesitated for a moment before doing as she was told. Once she was on the ground, Joe bandaged and then cable-tied her ankles. "Don't move."

He walked back to the car and retrieved the camera bag, tripod, and battery-powered light. The woman stared, wide-eyed, as he set them up.

He signaled Serdán to turn off the headlights, then squatted next to the woman.

"What's your name?" Joe asked.

Blondie just stared at him.

"This must be terrifying, I know, but I won't hurt you. Now, take a deep breath ... and another ... Better?"

"Yes."

"I have some questions. When you have answered them, when I'm sure you have told me the truth, then this is all over, and we will take you back."

He stepped back to turn on the light and start the camera. "Now, what's your name?"

"Marina Pavel, Doctor Marina Pavel. I am biochemist."

"And where are you from, Marina?"

"Poltava, in Ukraine. But I've lived in the States for twenty years."

"And who do you work for?"

"Cogent Biotech. I am the director of the Valle de Banderas research laboratory."

"Who's your boss?"

"Ah ... I..."

"Come on, all I need is a name. Where's the harm?"

Pavel shook her head. Tears flowed down her cheeks and her shoulders shook. "None, I suppose," she whispered, "but I can't."

Joe's gut tightened; he had hoped the woman would not be difficult. He pointed at Orejon. "See him?"

"Yes."

"His name is Joko. The Venganza couldn't handle him, so now he works for me. Why? Because he does whatever I tell him, no questions asked. And he really likes hurting people."

"You're just trying to frighten me."

The sweat beading on Pavel's face told Joe he had succeeded. "I hope I am, because you have two options here. Either you answer my questions, or I will let Joko hurt you more than you've ever been hurt before."

"You wouldn't do that."

Joe waved Orejon over. "She's all yours, Joko. But don't hurt her too much. She's no use to me dead."

"Yes, boss."

Orejon pulled a scarf from one pocket, a small bottle of water from another. He secured the scarf across Pavel's mouth and nose. The woman was trembling.

Joie put his face up to Pavel's. "Now you'll find out what death feels like, Marina ... unless you answer my questions."

Pavel shook her head.

Joe stepped back. "Do it, Joko."

He took Pavel's wrists as Orejon poured water on the scarf. Within seconds, the woman's body was shaking as she fought to breathe. But she couldn't. Shaking turned to thrashing, her head whipping side to side.

Orejon waited for thirty seconds, unmoving. Then he pulled the scarf off.

Pavel dragged the air back into her lungs, her chest heaving as she purged carbon-dioxide from her body in a series of rasping, choking breaths.

"Not much fun, eh?" Joe said. "But I did warn you."

"You bastard!" Pavel croaked.

"Are you going to talk now ... No?" Joe turned to Orejon. "One more time. But this time make her suffer."

As the man reached for the scarf, Pavel whispered, "No, please. No! I'll tell you."

Joe waved Orejon back. "So, who is your boss?"

"Tom Mapathi."

"That was easy. And Tom works for Cogent?"

"No. He's never said. He comes down every few months, but we do most of our business by email."

"Tell me what you do."

"I run the laboratory. We are ... No, I can't do this. You don't understand. They'll hurt me if I tell you anything. Maybe kill me."

"Nobody's going to kill you, Marina," Joe said. "I'll make sure you can explain why you went off."

"How?"

"Do you like men? Physically, I mean."

Pavel stared at Joe, open-mouthed. "Are you talking about sex?"

"Yes, I am."

"With the right man, of course," Pavel said, her voice tight with anger. "I'm not dead yet ... But never with you, you bastard."

"What a shame ... Now, listen to me. If anybody asks, you will say you went to the washroom, met a man, a fine-looking man. You talked. You were very drunk, he was funny, you liked him, he liked you, you went for a walk, one thing led to another, and I don't think you will need to say any more. Everyone will understand people like you sometimes go a bit wild. And why not? It's natural."

Pavel shook her head. "Nothing with Kernow is ever simple," she said. "He hates it when someone goes off without checking with the security people. We thought he would kill Frankie after he disappeared for the night with some tourist woman."

Joe took a chance. "Kernow; he's your security chief, right? A tall man, lots of muscles, white hair cut short, ex-military, always carries a pistol?"

"Yes, he is. I hate him. He always talking about whose ass he wants to kick next. He thinks people call him Bruce the Ass-Kicker, but nobody does. He's a pig."

"Why?"

"He treats the Venganza like dirt. I know they're not good people, but some are only boys; he beats them just because he can. And he's always coming into the labs, hassling the staff, asking questions though he has no idea how a lab works. And all my emails to Tom have to go through him; it's irritating, but Kernow says it's more secure. He's a bad man; if he thinks I've said something I shouldn't, he will hurt me."

"Not if you stick your story," Joe said.

"I wish I could believe that."

"You can. Now, tell me what you are doing out back of Valle de Banderas."

"I can't talk about that," Pavel said. "And I won't, no matter what your man does to me."

"I guess that makes it my turn," Joe said.

He reached into a pocket, pulled out his pistol., and screwed on a stubby silencer. He had hoped he would not need it; he didn't think he could shoot Pavel.

"Are you doing this job for the money, Marina?" Joe asked.

"A ton of money," Pavel said, looking away from the gun. "Why else would I come to such a shithole to work with scum like Kernow?"

"He can't be as bad as Anderson."

"He's way worse," Pavel said. "Three weeks ago, he killed a Russian for stealing a laptop from the lab. Shot him, like a dog … The Venganza cheered. They hate the Russians."

"Does everyone feel the same way ... about working for Cogent, I mean?" Joe asked.

"God, yes. Without the money, none of us would be here."

"Here doing what?"

Silence, then Pavel said, "I cannot say."

"There's something I have to tell you, Marina. This is not about what we can do to hurt you, not anymore. We're past that."

"Let me go then."

Joe put the pistol to Pavel's face. "Only when you have answered my questions ... and I will kill you if you don't." He pointed to one side. "We'll bury you over there; you can watch Joko dig your grave ... Better to answer my questions, and then we can all go home."

Pavel pulled back, her face hardening into defiance. "You wouldn't kill me."

Joe brushed Pavel's lips with the muzzle of his pistol. "You sure about that?"

Silence.

A *whump* as Joe fired a shot past Pavel's head. "Joko," he called out. "Get the shovel. Looks like you're going to have to dig—"

"No, please!" Pavel shouted. The fight had drained from her face. "Ask your questions. I'm screwed either way."

Joe pulled the gun away and let himself breathe again. "I asked what you do."

"I manage the laboratory and its staff, mostly virologists and lab technicians. Their job is to work out how to mass-produce live viruses."

"Using biovats?"

Pavel nodded. "Yes. Angström 340s."

"Nice, but I've always thought Karstellar's are better."

"Oh! You understand these things?"

"I'm a biochemist, like you … What progress have you made?"

"We have finalized our production protocols," Pavel said. "Our vats can make enough virus to fill two dispensers every day. We've proved that using a range of harmless viruses."

"Dispensers?"

"Like aerosol cans of sunscreen. Just one can infect ten thousand targets, even more in a crowded city like New York."

The woman was smiling. Joe's heart hardened. She was proud of the job she was doing.

"Let's be clear here. Are you saying the Valle de Banderas facility can turn out enough virus each day to kill twenty thousand people?"

"With the right virus, yes."

"Where's it going to be used?"

"China," Pavel said. "Where else?"

"Why China?"

"I didn't vote for her, but President Vandergraaf was dead right when she said China is the biggest threat the United States faces. And she said so, many times. Everyone here thinks they are doing what our president wants."

"You think she wants to kill hundreds of millions of innocent people?"

"If that's what it takes to defeat China, yes."

Joe had to stop for a moment. Pavel sounded like someone discussing a new kitchen. "Do you have the right virus yet, the one which will be used against China?"

"No, not here. The bioweapons people back in the States haven't supplied us with a weaponized virus yet. When they do, we will start production."

Joe tried to conceal his shock. "You said 'back in the States'. Where?"

Pavel shook her head. "I don't know."

Joe pulled his gun out again. "But you do, don't you, Marina?"

Pavel stared at him. "Yes, I do ... NBACC handles virus and vaccine development. It's part of Homeland Security, based at Fort Detrick."

"NBACC? The National Biodefense Analysis and Countermeasures Center?"

"Yes."

"But NBACC's a Federal agency. How is this even possible? What if somebody found out?"

"Hah!" Pavel snorted. "Homeland Security is a circus: all shouting and confusion. Do this. No, wait, do that! Okay, now do something different. The senior people are all too busy playing politics to know what's going on. Let me tell you something: It's not hard to bury a black bioweapons project underneath a genuine NBACC program."

"Wait on. Are you saying the United States is developing viruses?"

"They have to so we won't be caught out if China, Russia, or whoever deploys a new bioweapon," Pavel said. "The United States will have its countermeasures, all ready to go."

"Was NBACC developing the virus you need anyway?'

"No. All NBACC's viruses are disabled. The one we need must be live; release it and millions will die ... which is the whole point, of course."

Joe was appalled: ingenious, yet so simple. "How far has NBACC got?"

"Ask them. My job is virus production, not development."

Joe lifted the gun. "No more lies, Marina, so answer my questions ... No? Joko, get over here. I want you to hold the bitch still while I shoot her in the gut. Then you can start digging."

Pavel's brief flash of defiance vanished as Orejon strode over, shovel in hand. "No! I'll tell you."

Joe waved Orejon back. "You won't get another chance, Marina. Has NBACC produced an effective bioweapons-grade virus?"

"No, not yet. They've working on Sin Nombre—a pulmonary hantavirus—but it's turning out to be too unstable. And they are having a lot of trouble producing a vaccine; the human trials in Chad were a disaster. Tom thinks they'll have to find an alternative."

"I'd agree. They should go for Doctor Sato's hemorrhagic smallpox virus. Strain 5524, I think it's called. The Japanese did a great job; I think it would make the perfect bioweapon."

What little color was left drained from Pavel's face. "Who told you about 5524?" she whispered.

Joe knew he had broken the woman. "A friend, Marina ... Now, let's assume you have the right virus. What happens then?"

"We start mass production at Valle de Banderas," Pavel said. "Even if NBACC has to drop Sin Nombre and go to Strain 5524, Tom says that will be next year."

"What about a vaccine?"

"A company called Carbonel will manufacture it in Panama; construction's already started on the production plant. But that shouldn't be a problem, not with the new genomic and other tools we have now. If the Japanese could develop one back in 1943, so can we."

Joe had heard enough. "One last thing. I want the full names of everyone you work with. Senior or junior, it doesn't matter."

Pavel never hesitated. She reeled off a lengthy list of names. Joe could see she had given up.

"I can't remember any more," Pavel said at last.

"Fine, Marina. Let's go through your cover story, and then we'll drop you back in town."

•••

It took hours before Pavel had her cover story sorted. Not that Joe cared. Pavel should be able to handle Bruce the Ass-Kicker as long as he didn't tie her to a tree and wave a pistol in her face.

Right now, all Joe cared about was getting out of Puerto Vallarta before the Venganza came looking for him.

"I think we're done, Marina," said Joe at last. "We'll show you the room where we spent the night. And it might help if you left something personal."

Pavel leaned forward and spit at him. "How about my knickers? That should be enough to convince Kernow I'm a drunken slut."

"Calm down, Marina; your necklace will do. Then you can catch a cab home."

"No need," Pavel said. "They'll be waiting for me at the café. They always wait."

"This isn't the first time?"

"For me, yes. Not for the others, though. What we do is not much fun. You know something? I used to love Mexico. I hate it now."

Joe handed her a bottle of rum. "I can't think why. Now, before we go, take a swig of this, a big one. And let some spill down your front."

Pavel spluttered as the alcohol hit her throat.

"Right, we're done. Unless you want to end up dead, stick to your cover story."

"I intend to," Pavel whispered. "Kernow will shoot me if I don't."

•••

Two weeks after Joe had fled Puerto Vallarta, he was back in the United States, dirty, sweat-stained, and aching all over.

Even escorted by two of Kemani's men, crossing the border had been brutal. Sixty long, hard miles through the Sonoran Desert, across broken rocks, scree, and drifted sand, terrain that sucked the energy from legs and lungs, their already slow progress interrupted by drones forcing them to find cover. The nights were no better, cold nights spent jammed into narrow clefts of rock, under overhangs, or in dusty little caves hidden from yet more drones and their infrared cameras.

But, for all that, the pain had been worth it. He had the camera with Pavel's confession. If it didn't convince America it had a problem, nothing would.

The helicopter came in fast and low. It flared hard and settled on the ground. Joe's guides hustled him onboard. A minute later, the helicopter lifted off amidst a storm of dust and fled north.

—31—

Joe called Seppä.

"Any progress with your project down south?" he asked.

"No," Seppä said. "Listen. I know you are my friend and you save my ass, but I must stop. Two guys came last week. Locals. Army intelligence, they said, but no ID. They say to stop asking questions. If not, they hurt my family."

"Jesus! The bastards ... Listen, Matti. Do what they say. Back off. It'll be fine."

"You sure?" Seppä said.

"Yes, so keep your head down .... No, take the family away, somewhere far away. Can you do that?"

"Finland is safe. I have no family there anymore."

"I'll put thirty k in your account to cover the costs."

"No, you don't have—"

"Don't argue with me, Matti. Just do it."

"Okay, okay. We go tonight to Manila ... and thank you."

Joe cut the call, swearing long and hard.

Marti Seppä's visitors had been sent by the Revival. Who else could reach across the Pacific Ocean to lean on somebody so obscure?

Joe sensed the trap closing around him.

There would be no second chances. When the Revival found him, it would hand him back to Anderson, who would tear the location of the canisters out of him.

And then Anderson would kill him.

•••

Midnight was long gone.

Joe had given up trying to sleep. Not because of the bed or the traffic; in happier times, he could sleep through the Apocalypse. No, what troubled him was what to do next.

He knew what he should do: give everything to the FBI. But that risked talking to one of the Revival's people. If he did, he was dead.

He needed someone he could trust, someone with connections, someone to find the right people to talk to, people who could show him a way to defeat the Revival.

Adam Kuprovic was the obvious person. Even though he was no Washington insider, he was obscenely rich. And, if nothing else, the obscenely rich had connections.

Adam would know someone who could help, someone he trusted, somebody Joe could trust.

Something else persuaded Joe to go to Adam.

He had already entrusted his life to Adam. The man knew the account holding Joe's fighting fund. If he had passed that information on to the Revival, Joe knew he'd have been dead long since.

Yet here he was, in yet another shitty motel not four hundred yards from the ATM he had patronized three hours earlier.

Joe knew he was being careless, but he no longer had the energy to care. He had tested Adam. The man was his best hope. His only hope.

It was time to find out how much Adam Kuprovic was prepared to do.

—32—

"I hope you're here to pay back the money you owe me," Adam Kuprovic said as Joe sat down. "I don't like making unsecured loans to people who refuse to tell me what they're doing."

"Sorry to disappoint you, but no."

"Why are we here then? Is it to do with André's disappearance?"

Joe reached into his backpack and pulled out his tablet. "What I'm going to show you is much bigger than André. Watch this."

When the presentation had ended, Adam sat back. "What have you got yourself involved in, Joe? And Marina Pavel; was she telling the truth when she said China is the target?"

"She thought I was going to kill her if she lied to me, so yes."

"I talk with plenty of wealthy people. For years, too many of them have used their money to corrupt American politics. I can see some of them paying to reshape the world to make themselves even richer and more powerful."

"Which is what the Gang of 5 are doing. They're a bunch of uber-rich crazies who don't like the way things are. They get together to bitch about the way China's treating the US—"

"They should. The Dasslers lost billions when the Chinese government stole Sino-Dassler from them."

"My heart bleeds for them, Adam. Anyway, they agree things will get worse if China is not stopped. They decide to use their trillions to do that. Being crazies, they don't much care how they do it, and so the Revival is born with one simple goal: stop China."

"You have to wonder how America got so messed up they even thought they'd get away with it."

"I was so busy trying to make Hydra a success, I never stopped to think about what was happening here. I let all the corruption and lies and bullshit wash over me. I assumed we'd come to our senses and things would sort themselves out."

"Which they haven't," Adam said.

"No. And we're all going to pay ... Now, listen, enough navel gazing. Now that the Revival has pulled down what network I had, I need help. I was hoping you might have some ideas."

Adam was silent for a long time.

"Let me say something first," he said at last. "The Revival is an obscenity, and I will help you any way I can to make sure they are stopped ... And I think Miyuki Murata is the person you need. She is a retired marine brigadier general and was my company commander for a spell; we have stayed in touch ever since. She is chair of the Center for Arms Control and Non-Proliferation; it focuses on weapons of mass destruction. Since the Revival plans to use WMDs, she's the right woman to talk to. And the Center has a lot of connections in Washington."

"Hmm ... Her politics?"

"Lapsed Republican. She switched to New America when the GOP lost its way."

"What's she like as a person?"

"The most moral, upright, decent and honest human being I have ever known. I would trust her with my life."

"I trusted Klara with mine," Joe said, "and look how well that ended."

"Come on! She was coerced."

"I like to think so."

Joe paused. He wanted to say no to Adam's suggestion—he hated involving someone new, someone he did not know—but he was too tired to argue.

Besides, he had no better options.

"Alright, I'll meet with the general but make it somewhere a long way from Washington."

—33—

Brigadier General Miyuki Murata, United States Marine Corps, gazed out at the brilliant Las Vegas afternoon.

She turned from the window. She was a striking figure: tall and wiry, with iron-gray hair cut short, her African American mother's skin, her Japanese father's high cheekbones, and piercing brown eyes.

Eyes that made Joe feel like a wayward kid in front of the school principal.

"The information you've given me confirms rumors we've heard that America is back in the biological warfare business," Murata said. "The last president told me he had not authorized any bioweapon programs. He also said none of NBACC's work contravened the Biological and Toxin Weapons Convention of 1972. And, much as I disliked the man, I believed him; he does not do lying well."

"He doesn't," Adam said, "which makes you wonder how he was ever elected."

Murata laughed. "Quite. And what he told us was backed up by people we trust inside NBACC ... not that there are too many of them."

"But what about black projects?" Joe said. "They only exist so they can be denied."

"You have a point. All I can say is we found no evidence of any."

"What do we do then? China just gets stronger and more aggressive. The US has given up challenging them in the South China Sea. Apart from Vietnam, the countries of southeast Asia are Chinese colonies in all but name, thanks to bribery and debt slavery. The Revival must move soon. And we do too, if we're to have any chance of destroying this conspiracy."

"I agree ... Now, you won't like this, but I think you should talk with the FBI."

Joe shot to his feet to look Murata right in the face. "The FBI? No way will I trust them. We're talking about a conspiracy which has suborned senior officers in the US Navy, for chrissakes."

"The single most worrying thing in your report."

"No kidding! If the Revival can do that, what makes you think they would have any trouble infiltrating the FBI? I am sorry, but no. This is my life you're playing with here."

Murata put out a hand. "I understand, Joe, I do. But there are compelling reasons to go to the FBI."

"I can't think of any. My answer's still no."

"Hear her out," Adam said.

Joe put a hand up. "Sorry, general. Go on, please."

"What you've achieved is remarkable, but you cannot do any more on your own. You said so yourself. You need an organization with the resources, skills, and experience to take on a criminal conspiracy as capable as the Revival. And there is only one such organization: the FBI. You might not trust everyone in the FBI, but you must trust the organization to enforce the law. If it cannot, we have lost before we start ... And one more thing: Director Agnelli is a friend, and him I do trust."

Joe threw his hands up. "Oh, fine! Whatever was I worrying about?"

"Settle down," Adam snapped.

"Alright," Joe muttered, sour-faced, "we'll go to the FBI. But just you and me, general. The Revival doesn't know about Adam, and I want to keep it that way."

"Come on, Joe!" Adam protested. "It's time I got involved."

"You're no use to me dead, which you will be if the Revival finds out you're my banker. And I'm not being kind. I cannot do anything without money, and a dead banker's no use to me."

"Good to know," Adam muttered.

—34—

"…and thank you America."

Joe turned the television off. "Kill me now," he muttered.

"What's the problem, Doctor Lessart?"

Joe glanced over at Agent Benny Elias. "The mind-numbing tedium of it all, and yes, I am talking about The Ellen DeGeneres Show."

Elias grinned. "Hey! I love that woman."

Joe laughed. "Actually, so do I. No, I hate the political ads; all the lies and spin and bullshit. You need to be a moron to believe any of them. Tell you what, Benny, I might ask Director Agnelli to find me a better place. I am over this one. It sucks."

"I've seen worse."

Joe sighed. After months of stress, the comfort of being in a safe house guarded by FBI agents had worn off. More frustrating was the lack of progress. Director Agnelli had promised Joe he would organize a task force—all agents he could vouch for—to take down the Revival. Joe wondered what they had achieved all these weeks. "Any word on how much longer I'll be here?"

"The boss was seeing the ASAC this morning. I'll ask her."

"If you could. Another week in this place and I'll start eating the drapes. You want a coff—"

Three small canisters shattered the windows, bounced on the carpet, and exploded in flashes which seared Joe's eyeballs and turned his brain to mush. Dazed and disoriented, it took a while before he even realized Elias had crash-tackled him to the ground and was dragging him away. Around him, automatic gunfire was shredding the blinds and chopping the ceiling into a blizzard of falling plaster.

"...into the kitchen," Elias was shouting, pointing the way with his gun. "Let's go! Morrison's here with Kubic. Backup's on the way."

Joe needed no encouragement; being shot at was proving to be a bowel-twisting business. As he slithered to safety, Agent Morrison was heading the other way, pistol in hand. Elias hauled Joe into the kitchen, pulled the table over, and pushed him behind it. "Keep down and don't move!"

Wondering what had happened to the security Agnelli had promised, Joe lay flat on the floor with his head cradled in his arms as jackhammers tore the house apart.

Joe knew what had happened. As he had warned Murata, the Revival had penetrated the FBI. It would not be long before he was back with his old friend Anderson having a chat about canisters of live smallpox virus.

He flinched as a burst of gunfire chewed through the kitchen wall. The FBI agents were out-gunned and outnumbered. What use were handguns against automatic weapons? And where was the backup?

The attack's intensity grew. Elias shouted, "We need to move you out. Garage, now!"

"They'll kill us if we make a run for it."

"They will if we don't, so don't argue! Go!"

Joe scuttled after the agent as chunks of wall and ceiling showered down. Elias eased the door into the garage open. Sunlight lanced bright across the waiting SUV.

Elias grabbed Joe. "The garage door is open, so we're ... aarrggh, shiiiit!"

Joe swung around. The agent was sinking to his knees, a shoulder wound spewing blood.

A bloody hand thrust out the SUV's tag. "Go," Elias said. "Nothing you can do here ... Go ... somewhere safe. We'll find you."

Joe flinched as a burst of gunfire ripped the air apart overhead, chewing lumps out of the house. "No way. I'm not leaving you."

Elias did not respond, slumped to the floor, eyes closed. He was not going anywhere. Instinct drove Joe for the SUV. He tore the door open and dove across the seat, twisting his body to squeeze his legs under the wheel.

Joe peeked over the dash.

A battered van and two pickups were out front. Around them, men in ski masks poured automatic fire into the fast-disintegrating safe house, spent cartridge cases sparkling in the sun as they arced to ground.

They ignored the garage.

Joe punched the start button. The engine kicked into life. He slammed the transmission into drive, released the brake, and floored the gas pedal. With a shriek of tires, the SUV burst from the garage. Engine howling, it roared down the driveway, clipped the nearest pickup, and smashed it aside.

Joe swung the vehicle up the empty road and accelerated hard, tires screeching. He looked behind. Nobody was chasing him. He slowed. He could not run forever. He needed somewhere safe to hole up while he worked out what to do.

The FBI agents had never told him where the safe house was, and his hand was shaking so badly the SUV's nav system refused to cooperate. Hanging lefts and rights at random, he drove on until he reached a mall, massive, sprawling, anonymous. He swung parked up in a space behind an RV the size of a Greyhound bus. He switched off the engine and sat back, unable to move.

When he had recovered his composure, he sauntered into the mall, touching the Nokia in his pocket. One of his obsessions; he did every few minutes.

Two hours later, sporting yet another coat and hat, he ambled into his third mall. He had not spotted any watchers; he didn't expect to. The Revival could have drones overhead and people all around him; he'd never have seen them.

He found a café, bought a coffee, and took a seat. No longer adrenaline-urged to run, his spirits slumped. Once again, people he had trusted with his life had betrayed him. Once again, he was alone. Once again, he faced the question: What next?

If the Revival could find an FBI safe house, it would find him. How hard could it be? His blundering escape would have left a trail no amount of ducking in and out of malls could erase.

And, when the Revival did find him, an unmarked grave would be his only reward for giving up the canisters. He shivered as he imagined a shallow scrape, hidden in some patch of forest nobody would ever visit.

If he was going to die, he preferred to die fighting, not on his knees with the muzzle of Anderson's gun jammed against his skull. And he knew how to hurt the Revival where it most mattered.

Joe dug out the Nokia and called Adam's burner.

"The safe house was attacked," he said when Adam picked up. "I was right; the FBI's compromised."

"You are kidding me!"

"I wish. My minder was shot, but I got away in the confusion. We have to talk."

"Where?"

"I'll organize for you to be picked up at your place. They'll bring you to meet me. And don't go with them unless they give you the right codeword. Let's see ... Purple rain?"

"Purple rain. Got it."

Joe's next call was to Kemani.

The man was not happy. "Call me tomorrow, doctor. I do not do business this late."

"Shut the fuck up, Freddie. You want to make a shitload of money? Yes or no?"

"Yes, of course," Kemani said.

"Right, here's what I need, and I need it in a hurry. First—"

"Hold on. How do I know you'll pay?"

"You don't, but I will."

"I hope you understand what happens if you don't. I am not a man who—."

"You will get your goddammed money," Joe snarled, "so go shove all your mobster bullshit up your fat ass, you hear me?"

"All right, all right. Calm down. Tell me what you need."

•••

Adam strode into the all-nighter Kemani's team had taken Joe to and threw himself into a seat. "Tell you what, Joe," he said, wiping sweat from his face. "Those were the scariest people I've ever met."

Joe laughed at the pained look on Adam's face. "Which is the idea."

"Yeah ... Right, what's the story?"

"I need more money, a lot more."

"Well, there's a surprise. But I am your banker, so that shouldn't be a problem. What for this time?"

"Being blasted out of a safe house proves the FBI cannot be trusted, Adam, which is why I have decided I won't run, not anymore."

"What will you do?"

"I'm declaring war."

Adam grimaced. "War is an expensive business. How much will you need?'

"Not sure. Ten million? Twenty? Jeez, Adam! I don't know. Whatever it takes is how much I need."

"And why would I lend you so much?"

"Because you can afford it. Because I don't trust anybody else to. Because I will pay you back. And because those Revivalist scumbags will kill half humanity if you don't."

Adam grimaced. "You really like to ratchet up the pressure."

Joe leaned forward. "I do not have the time to beg. Just tell me you're good for what I need."

Adam thought for a moment. "I can't believe I'm saying this," he said, "but yes. I do have one condition, though."

"Which is?"

"I want to be part of whatever you're planning to do."

Joe stared at Adam. "If you're tired of making shitloads of money, fine, I don't care. But leave your mid-life crisis at home. You do not want to be part of this, trust me."

"Sorry, but I do."

"No, you do not. I could not be any deeper in the shit. The Revival has no idea you are financing everything I do. You're useless to me dead, and I need you, now more than ever."

Adam tapped the table. "If you want my money, that's a condition precedent. And it's non-negotiable."

Joe had watched Adam haggle his way through hours of negotiation. Pursed lips and narrowed eyes meant Adam Kuprovic was digging in for a fight.

Joe did not have the time to winkle him out of his foxhole. But the man had to understand what he was getting himself into.

"Any idea what waterboarding's like?" Joe asked.

Adam frowned. "Waterboarding? Uh, no … only what I have read."

"The Revival waterboarded me."

"You never told me. What is it like?"

"Like drowning in two inches of water. You can't breathe, your throat closes up, your heart beats so hard you think it's going to burst out of your chest, your lungs can't get any air no matter how hard you try, you're frightened, panicking. It's beyond horrific, Adam. Waterboarding is the perfect torture: no drugs, no physical violence, and no visible injuries if it's done right. That is its awful beauty: The scars are all in the mind, which is why some people argue it's not torture. Well, fuck them. It is. Do you understand what I'm saying?"

"I guess."

Joe could see Adam did not. How could he? "This is not a game; things will get a whole lot worse before this is over. This is war, and we are losing. Along the way, people will die, people like you and me. Now, you sure you want to be part of this?"

"No, I'm not."

"Then we're done."

Adam shook his head. "No, we're not. Just because I'm not sure doesn't mean I'm going to sit back and let you do this on your own."

"You won't be sitting back. You'll be providing the money."

"Oh, for chrissakes, Joe! I've so much money, I cannot spend it. All I do is sit around wondering how to make even more."

Joe shrugged. "Be like everyone else who with a mid-life crisis: play golf."

"I'm not that desperate. Come on, you said time was short, so stop wasting it. I'll pay the bills, but I want in."

Joe raised his hands in defeat. "Fine. Let's go meet with Mister Kemani."

"Ah, Freddie. I wondered if he'd organized my escort."

•••

Freddie Kemani pulled Adam into a hug. "Good to see you. It's been a while."

"You haven't changed, you old bloodsucker."

"And I never will," Kemani said, laughing.

He turned to Joe. "We need to talk about your account. A full security and cyber surveillance team plus drones, vans, and backup vehicles does not come cheap."

Adam put his hand on Joe's arm. "Tell me how much, and I'll have the money wired to any account you like."

A grin split Kemani's face. "This why I always I liked you, Adam."

"Crap, Freddie. You're a greedy prick, and I pay well."

Again, Kemani laughed. He opened a drawer, pulled out a file, copied a string of numbers on a piece of paper, and passed it to Adam. "This much, to this account please."

"Lichtenstein?" Adam said.

Kemani's grin broadened. "Aha! You know your SWIFT codes."

Adam returned the smile. "Years of practice."

Joe rolled his eyes. "Oh, please. Spare me the 'I love you as a brother' shit."

"Your friend is very rude," said Kemani.

Adam leaned forward. "Try working with the asshole," he whispered, but loud enough for Joe to hear. Kemani laughed.

"Oh, for chrissakes," Joe said. "Can we move on please?"

Kemani waved a hand. "Please."

"First, security, my security. I need a base, somewhere the Revival, FBI, CIA, and anyone else who wants a piece of my ass can't find me, somewhere with secure egress to a backup safe house."

"Not a problem. What else?"

"I want to…"

—35—

Hermann Márquez stared across the table from thick-lidded, brown eyes embedded deep in a hard, lined face. "You ask a lot, Doctor Lessart," the head of the Escorpiónes drug cartel said, "perhaps too much."

Joe shrugged. "I must apologize, Mister Márquez. We seem to have made a mistake."

"What mistake?"

"I hoped your organization could support our project. I also thought you wanted to destroy the Venganza cartel. But I was wrong. No problem; we will find another way."

Márquez let Joe's insults hang in the air for a moment. "You should think before you open your mouth."

"Perhaps I should. Perhaps your organization does have the resources we need. Perhaps you do want to destroy the Venganza as much as we do. Which makes me wonder why you think I'm asking for too much."

Márquez smiled, a fleeting curl of the lips. "We have what you need, and yes, I am always happy to hurt Venganza sewer rats."

"I am pleased to hear it."

"Don't be," Márquez said. "Now I have met you, I must question Mister Kemani's judgment. He said I could work with you. But I don't think so, What are you? Just another Yanqui cocksucker who thinks he can cross the border to tell us Mexican peasants what to do."

Adam cut in. "We're here to do business, Mister Márquez, to come to an arrangement which works for you and works for us."

Márquez ignored Adam. "I did not talk to you."

Adam took Joe's arm before he could respond. "Let me handle this." He looked at Márquez for a moment, then said, "We are businessmen and I don't care who you talked to or what they said. I'm talking to you now, so ..."

The men around the leader of the Escorpiónes drug cartel lifted their assault rifles.

"...please listen to what we propose. If what we say is of no interest to you, fine. We will leave and say nothing more about it."

Márquez leaned forward. "You see too many movies, Mister Kuprovic. Movies where the hero talks tough, the bad guy says what cojones you have, and then they are best buddies. But that is not how life is. I do not want to make you happy. You can live. You can die. I do not care. If I want, I kill you, here, now. Why? Because I hate Yanquis. Or because you make me angry. Or because my balls itch. And I do not worry if Freddie Kemani gets upset because my boys blow your brains out. Down here, he is dogshit under my shoe. And so are you."

Márquez leaned to one side and spit on the ground.

Adam stood. "We're wasting our time, Joe. Thank you for your time, Mister Márquez. It is much appreciated."

Joe's stomach had knotted tight. He wanted to slide under the table. With an effort, he got to his feet. Now the guns pointed right at him.

"Sit!" Márquez barked.

Adam did not waver. "I came to talk business. If we cannot do that, we will leave."

Márquez laughed. "Yes, you will ... dead."

"Perhaps, but how careless of you to walk away from the many millions of dollars we are prepared to pay for the services of your men."

Nobody moved.

Joe started to sweat, his heart galloping.

Márquez frowned. "Many millions? Mister Kemani said you would not pay more than ten."

"It is not his business to say that. We are asking a lot, and we expect to pay a price you're happy with. Am I right?" Adam said, turning to Joe.

"Er, yes. Of course," Joe muttered. He felt sick.

Márquez waved at his men to back off. "Please sit, both of you. I apologize if I did not explain so well. I do business with many Yanquis, and always it is the same. Please, Mister Márquez, we want five hundred kilos of la cocaína, but we only pay for four. They treat me like campesino selling tomatoes in the market and I should say yes, señor, of course, señor if that is what you want, señor. Every time it is the same. Todos son pendejos."

"Like I said, Mister Márquez, we are reasonable people and are happy to pay a reasonable price. You know what we want. Tell us what you want."

Not for one second did Márquez hesitate. "Thirty million, paid before I do anything."

"Twenty million," Adam said, no less fast. "One third up front, the rest on completion."

"Even old Russian helicopters are expensive, Mister Kuprovic. Twenty-five. Half up front."

Adam turned to Joe.

Joe nodded; he just wanted out.

"Deal," Adam said.

Márquez chuckled, and his face broke into a broad smile. "Hey! I like you guys. And I like to think about my Escorpiónes kicking the Venganza in the balls. Very much."

"I'm pleased to hear it," Joe said. And he meant it.

Márquez clapped his hands. "We should drink now to seal our agreement. Champagne? Yes, I think so."

•••

The SUV rolled out through the gates of Márquez's estancia past yet more men carrying assault rifles.

"Tell you what, Joe," Adam said. "I never want to see that place or that man ever again."

Joe nodded. "I liked his place, though. Beautiful gardens, but Hermann Márquez? No thanks."

"He makes me think lawyers and bankers might not be so bad. It's extraordinary how people like that flourish."

"What? Lawyers and bankers?"

Adam laughed. "No, people like Márquez."

"He is what he is because Americans like their coke too much. We've known for decades prohibition breeds corruption and violence; why are we surprised when Nixon's war on drugs floated scum like Hermann Márquez to the top?"

"Only the brutal survive, though the man has his hands full dealing with the Venganza. Word is they have his Escorpiónes on the back foot."

"You think he'll deliver?"

"Yes, I do. We're paying him to hurt his worst enemy, and he wants to humiliate the Venganza, more than he wants the money. Tell you what, Joe, I think Márquez is more trustworthy than some of the people I have done business with over the years."

Joe raised an eyebrow. "You mean it?"

"I do. When he says a deal's a deal, he means it."

"As a matter of honor?"

Adam shook his head "Something simpler. There is no formal framework within which to conduct business in Márquez's world: no laws, no police, no courts, no lawyers, no judges, no contracts. He creates his own framework by always meaning what he says and making sure everyone knows it. That creates trust; without it, nobody could do business with him."

"I hope you're right. We're about to give him an awful lot of our money."

"My money, Joe, my money."

"Until I pay it back, which I will."

They fell silent.

Joe had not enjoyed the visit to Monterrey, but at least he would not have to see Márquez again. Manuel Xipalli, a relaxed and friendly man with an air of quiet competence, would be running the operation Joe had planned.

But, much as Joe wanted to trust Xipalli, trust was something he had in short supply. What he wanted was Max Beharry, out of retirement and standing beside him, not shouting advice from across the US border.

But Beharry and Xipalli were not his only concerns. For no obvious reason, Kemani was beginning to worry him. He had proved reliable thus far, but that was no guarantee Joe could rely him in the future, not when all Kemani cared about was money.

But he did not know anyone else who could do what Kemani did.

Not Adam, even with his enormous wealth. He was plugged into a world illuminated by laws and contracts, lawyers and accountants, meetings and dinners, of manners and protocol, of governments and lobbyists.

Not the Feds. Homeland Security? The FBI? Defense? All compromised.

Not General Murata, the woman with the 'you can trust the FBI' strategy? He would never put his life in her hands again.

The media? Their craven pursuit of profit over truth made them part of the problem.

Joe had even considered approaching the Chinese; they did have the most to lose if the Revival succeeded. But dealing with the enemy of your enemy felt like a bad idea, given China hewed to one overarching principle: anything went, so long as it advantaged China.

It would see the Revival as a threat, of course. It would also see the Revival as an opportunity to damage the United States. China's political DNA would make sure of it. He could not risk talking to them.

Joe was out of options. Like it or not, he was saddled with a corruptible man. He hoped the Revival did not make Kemani a better offer.

Because Kemani would take it without a moment's thought.

—36—

Max Beharry rubbed a hand of aged teak across a skull covered in short gray stubble. "I'm sorry, but no. I will not come with you."

"If you want more money," Joe said, "I can fix that."

"Forget money. I have other reasons."

Joe knew he had underestimated Beharry; the man was more than a mercenary. "What if tell you everything I know? Then you can give your answer."

"Why?" Beharry said. "You already have my answer."

"You might change your mind when you know what the stakes are."

"I really doubt it, but I'll give you ten minutes anyway."

"Thank you. The best place to start is..."

•••

Joe stopped the presentation. "Now you can see why I need you."

"They waterboarded you?" Beharry said. "Holy shit."

"As in holy shit, yes?"

"Oh, no. My answer's the same. I won't do what you ask."

Joe wanted to scream. "Fine, but tell me why, Max. You owe me that much."

"I guess I do. All right then ... Did Freddie tell you I was ex-special forces?"

"Yeah, he did."

Beharry shook his head. "All spin. I was with the 101st Airborne. We were in Afghanistan, my third tour, embedded with the Afghani's 6th Commando Kandak—a battalion—in Helmand province.

"Towards the end of my tour, the Afghanis received intel on a cache of ordnance hidden in a madrassa, an Islamic school, in a town close to the Pakistan border. They mounted up, and we went off to find it, in trucks, of course. There were never enough choppers.

"Just as we entered the town, I shot a woman … No, she was a girl. Sixteen or seventeen. She was the first non-combatant I'd ever killed. A double-tap right between the eyes. Blue, they were. The most beautiful eyes I have ever seen. I remember them like it was last week."

Joe's eyes widened. "You just killed her?"

"I thought the Taliban had pegged her out so she'd be killed in the crossfire. The bastards did it all the time; every non-com death hurt us far more than it hurt them. I only spotted the box in her hands when I waved at her to stay down. I shot her as she triggered bombs which killed twenty-two Afghani soldiers. If I had done my job properly instead of worrying about her, I could have saved those Afghanis, men I liked, men I respected, men I had eaten with, men I had fought alongside."

"You can't blame yourself."

"I can, and I do; they died because of me. Anyway, it was over for me, so I mustered out first chance I got. I'm sorry, Joe, I can't come with you; my days as a soldier are over … I'm not the man I once was."

"You can be, by finding redemption."

"Redemption?" Beharry said. "What are you now? A fucking shrink? A priest? A discover-your-inner-power guru? I've seen them all. Trust me, they're bullshit."

"I'm just someone with a problem he can't handle without your help … But nothing can change what happened in Afghanistan. But you can redeem yourself by helping me defeat the Revival … If you turn your back on me, you're telling me those dead Afghan soldiers matter more than the billions of lives the Revival has put at risk. Think about it, Max; the dead or the living, guilt or redemption. Which is it to be?"

Beharry said nothing for a long time, his head down, fingers intertwined, hands working one against the other. The silence ran on and on. Then his head came up. "You are one persuasive sonofabitch ... I can't believe I'm saying this, but I'll do what you want."

—37—

"Now you've talked with Xipalli," Joe said, "what do you reckon?"

"He's a professional soldier," Beharry said. "His plans are solid, he has real-time surveillance in place, and the Escorpiónes have solid intelligence on the Venganza. As they should; they've been fighting them for long enough."

Adam frowned. "Won't the Venganza find out what we're planning?"

"I don't think operational security will be a problem. All the guys Xipalli's chosen are ex-army. He's keeping them isolated: no cellphones, no internet, no alcohol, no drugs, no socializing. All they do is train, train, train. Xipalli won't tell them what the target is until the day of the operation. And he's made sure they all know Márquez himself will come after them if they screw up."

"Can Xipalli pull this off?"

"He'll have three advantages: surprise, speed, and concentration of force. The plan's simple, his people will have rehearsed the operation, and his best guys will be where he needs them most. But on the day, who can tell? Shit always happens when the bullets start flying, but I think Xipalli can handle it."

"The moles inside the FBI must have told the Revival I'd found Cogent's laboratory. Surely the Venganza will have beefed up security?"

Beharry shook his head. "There's no sign of it. I did my own reconnaissance; what I saw was business as normal: Venganza thugs, sloppy and ill-disciplined being bossed around by American and Russians thugs. Nothing's changed since you did your own recon."

"Hold on," Adam said. "That makes no sense. The Valle de Banderas laboratory is critical to the Revival's plans."

"It makes sense if they don't expect an attack, and Xipalli is emphatic they don't. The US military is never going to cross the border into Mexico to kick Cogent's door down. The Mexican army and police won't either, not since the Venganza booted them out of Jalisco. That is why the Revival picked the place: close to the US, but untouchable, so they think. That's made them careless."

'Yeah, but—"

"Joe! Stop! As far as the Revival is concerned, it's just you. One man isn't a threat. And the fact the Revival hasn't asked the Venganza to tighten security proves it."

"Well, I hope you're right."

"We'll find out. Sorry, I need to go, so unless there's anything else … No? Okay, I'm out of here."

"I hate to think how we'd have managed without him," Adam said once Beharry had left.

●●●

Kemani waved the young woman forward. "This is Raffa. She'll brief you on what to search for … Adam, let's go next door. We need to talk about money."

"Paying the bills is what I do best, Freddie," Adam said as he followed Kemani out.

Joe stood, his hand out. "Hi, Raffa. I'm Doctor Lessart. Call me Joe. Do you have a second name?"

Raffa ignored Joe's hand and sat down. "Not one I am prepared to tell you, Doctor Lessart."

Joe felt two feet tall. "Oh, right."

"Let's start," Raffa went on. "Once you are inside the compound, you must recover any personal devices: cellphones, laptops, tablets along with any modems they're connected to. And these too ..."

Raffa brought up an image on her tablet.

"... if you can find them. Cogent's datastores are like this. They're made by IBM..."

Joe knew better than to ask how Raffa knew.

"... and store the laboratory's management and research data. They'll be rack-mounted in cabinets somewhere."

"Can you get the data from them?"

"It's possible. In my experience, the stronger the perimeter, the less secure the data inside. And Mister Kemani says the target is well defended."

"So the Venganza think. Anything else?"

Raffa closed her laptop and stood. "No. Tell Mister Kemani if you have questions. Goodbye, doctor."

—38—

The Airbus A320 accelerated down the runway and lifted into a steep climb out of Puerto Vallarta International.

The watcher tapped her cellphone.

Mortars mounted on flatbed trucks fired. Rounds arced skywards, hung for an instant, then plunged into the airport's taxiways and aprons. Impact fuses fired. Phosphorus payloads ignited on contact with air. Clouds of white smoke billowed across the apron and enveloped the terminal building, workers scattering in all directions.

Out front, motorbikes skidded to a stop. Their passengers unloaded stun and smoke grenades, fired sustained bursts of automatic fire into the terminal's façade, the attack triggering chaos as vehicles bulldozed each other aside trying to flee.

A minute after the first mortar round had exploded, the motorbikes vanished.

Xipalli's cameras had captured it all. He keyed his radio. *El Gordo, El Gordo.*

•••

The driver wrestled the ancient bus round a tight corner. He slammed on the brakes. An SUV blocked the road, its nose in the ditch. There was no way past the trees crowding the dirt road.

The driver smiled. Now he would not have to explain to the Yanqui bastards running the compound why he was running late.

A man trotted over, one hand out in apology, the other holding a submachine gun.

The driver opened the door. *What's the problem, boss?* he called out.

Blew a tire and ran off the road, the man said. *The Yanquis are sending a truck to pull me out. We won't be long. And we've told them you're held up.*

The driver shrugged. Like he gave a shit. He was reaching for his cigarettes when the man came up the steps, assault rifle held out, shouting, *Hands up! Up, where I can see them.*

Hands shot up amidst a chorus of wails and moans.

Quiet or I'll shoot you like dogs. Everyone off the bus, now! Take everything with you. And if anyone touches their cell, they're dead. Move it!

Men with assault rifles had emerged from the forest. They herded the passengers away.

•••

"Xipalli says the Venganza have taken the bait," Beharry said, starting the SUV. "They're on their way to the airport in force. His boys have the bus, so here we go … and no macho shit, guys."

Joe glanced at Adam. The man's face was a washed-out yellow; he hadn't enjoyed the wait either.

The bus ground past trailed by the trucks carrying the assault force.

"Our turn," Beharry said, tucking the SUV in behind the last truck. Its tailgate was down. It was loaded with men and jerrycans. The smell of diesel hung heavy in the morning air.

•••

The sniper—callsign Lancero—ran his 'scope over the gate's security post, manned by two Venganza in combat fatigues. One was inside leaning on the sandbags, yawning, a black-gloved hand resting on a heavy machine gun, smoke from the cigarette hanging out of his mouth uncoiling away in the still morning air. A second stood by the gate, cradling his assault rifle. Head down, he was busy kicking the dirt with a booted foot.

The men looked bored.

Standby, his spotter said. *El Gordo inbound.*

Lancero watched the bus rattle out from the trees, belching black smoke.

Not long now.

He settled his Barrett on its bipod and pulled the recoil pad into his shoulder, slowed his breathing down and put the 'scope on the Venganza behind the machine gun.

Thirty yards out, the bus juddered to a stop as its engine died. The driver climbed out. He shrugged, strolled around behind the bus, and then started to run.

Fire, Lancero's spotter whispered.

Lancero took a breath, held it, and squeezed the trigger.

The Barrett kicked, hard. Less than a second later, the half-inch round hit the man behind the machine gun in the chest, throwing him back.

The second sniper's shot followed an instant later. His Raufoss anti-materiel round hit the foot of the radio mast. Its incendiary/explosive charge ripped the junction box apart, the tungsten steel penetrator punching into one of the mast's steel legs.

An instant later, the bus erupted, sending flames skywards on a pillar of black smoke.

The force of the explosion knocked the second gate sentry into a crumpled heap on the dirt. Lancero put a round into him to make sure he stayed down.

The spotter called out, *Target. Alpha, one left, man, five hundred*.

Lancero found his next target—a man standing, stunned into immobility, one finger's width left of the gate at five hundred yards—and dropped him with a single shot.

Fifty yards to Lancero's right, the second sniper had destroyed the junction box; Cogent's compound was isolated. Now he put a stream of Raufoss rounds into the building housing the diesel generators. Amidst phlegmatic belches and clouds of steam, first one generator, and then the second, died.

The assault started in earnest.

Xipalli's first truck erupted from the trees. Moving fast, it charged past the shattered remains of the bus, swung away just short of the chicane, and plowed through the razor-wire fences, the rest of the assault close behind. Trailing torn wire, two trucks slid to a stop amidst clouds of dust, their noses jammed against the wall of the laboratory building either side of the entrance. Their side panels—ballistic shields, some still marked 'Policía Federal'—slid to the ground as the third stopped in front of the laboratory entrance.

The Escorpiónes piled out. Leaving the laboratory doors splintered wrecks, some headed inside. Some went left to neutralize the support huts. The rest went right, pouring heavy fire into the accommodation huts in disciplined bursts which felled Venganza foot-soldiers as they appeared, their attack joined by a pair of technical-mounted machine guns outside the wire, shredding huts and men in an orgy of indiscriminate brutality.

Beharry skidded the SUV to a stop beside the last truck, its crew busy carrying jerrycans of diesel into the laboratory.

Beharry, Joe, and Adam sprinted inside.

Inside the lights were off. Joe stumbled over something on the floor. He flicked on his headtorch. He recoiled as the beam settled on a body, eviscerated by sustained burst of gunfire. A young woman. Blood drenched her lab coat, and her mouth sagged open in surprise, eyes staring up at him in accusation.

One of Anderson's evil people.

Joe did not care. The white coats knew what they were here to do. They deserved to die.

"Move!" Beharry shouted.

Up ahead, Xipalli's men were working through the building. Room by room, they pulled out men and women and killed them with shots to the head.

He moved on down corridor to the laboratories, the floor slick with blood and littered with more white-coated bodies.

Joe ignored them; his focus was the labs. Adam would check everywhere else. He peered through a polycarbonate viewing port into the first lab. A placard on the door: **BIOHAZARD. BIOSAFETY LEVEL 4**.

"Max! I need this door open," Joe shouted.

"Is this place safe?"

"Ignore the sign. They only handle harmless viruses here."

"I hope you're right." Beharry waved Joe aside and stitched bullet holes around the handle. He stepped back and the kicked the door hard.

It did not move, not a millimeter.

"This pissant UMP's useless. Wait!"

He returned a moment later with two of Xipalli's men and pointed at the door. The men opened fire in sustained bursts from their timeworn AK-104s; their 7.62mm rounds had three times the kinetic energy of the UMP's. The door fell apart, the inner door following a moment later.

"Open up all the doors like this," Beharry shouted, waving the Escorpiónes away. "Go!"

Joe stepped inside. Only lab equipment on empty benches. "Nothing, Max. Next one."

They raced after the two Escorpiónes. Lab after lab after lab came up dry. Joe started to worry. They had to find something useful, or he would have nothing to show for the whole bloody exercise.

A hail of bullets opened the doors into the last lab. Joe sprinted in. But every benchtop was empty: no cellphones, no tablets, no laptops. Nothing.

Marina Pavel ran a tight ship.

"Time we went," Beharry said.

As Joe left the lab, he spotted the last door along the corridor. Its handwritten sign said, 'Department of Ass-Kicking'.

Ass-kicking. Why had that rang a bell? Joe forced himself to think through his adrenaline rush. Something Pavel had said ... Yes! The lab's security chief, Kernow. He wanted people to call him Bruce the Ass-Kicker. "We need to check in there," he shouted.

"No time," Beharry snapped. "We're running late. We have to go."

"Break it down .... Just do it!"

Beharry's boot kicked the door off its hinges. "If you're not out thirty seconds, I'll put a round up your ass."

A small, windowless office. A desk with a large monitor. One chair. Filing cabinet. Bookcase stuffed with folders. Whiteboard graffitied with indecipherable scribblings. Coffee machine. Small fridge.

And a laptop connected to a modem.

"Thank you!" Joe shouted as he ripped out the power cords and shoved computer and modem in his backpack. "I'm done!"

"Exit, now!" Beharry shouted as he pushed Joe ahead of him. "I'll tell Xipalli we're done ... Come on, Joe! Move!"

Joe ran, the air thick with the cloying smell of the diesel Xipalli's men were busy splashing everywhere. He stopped inside the entrance. Only now did he notice the sustained crackle of the firefight raging outside. The Venganza must be fighting back.

Adam arrived. He held out a matte-black datastore. It bore the IBM logo.

"Found twenty of these mothers and a bunch of cellphones," he said with a grin, stuffing it into a bulging backpack.

Beharry ducked outside. He was back in seconds. "The Venganza are getting their shit together; all the vehicles are toast. When I say go, you run like hell for the fence. Our rides will be there to extract us. Xipalli's people will cover us and then pull back. Got it?"

Joe and Adam nodded.

The Escorpiónes let fly, emptying whole magazines in single, sustained bursts. Xipalli's technicals—pickups mounting DShK heavy machine guns—opened fire from outside the compound, the heavy bass of their 12.7mm rounds underscoring the crackling buzz of the assault force's assault rifles and light machine guns.

And, above all the noise, Joe could hear the distinctive *thump-boom* of Xipalli's snipers.

"Go, go, go!" Beharry shouted.

Outside, the trucks and Beharry's SUV were well alight, flames and greasy black smoke swirling across Escorpiónes pouring fire into the Venganza.

Joe ran for the fence, jumping a body, a red brassard marking him as an Escorpióne. Bullets ripped the air around him as he ran, ducking, weaving, flinching. Puffs of dust leapt from the ground around him.

Rounds tore past his ears. One plucked at his sleeve. A second punched him in the back; Joe muttered a quick word of thanks to Beharry for insisting they wore body armor.

He was through the truck-torn gap in the razor-wire when a fist smashed his left leg out from beneath him. He gave a cry, twisted around, and collapsed in a tangle of limbs.

Pain flared.

He levered himself upright. His left leg draggled as he struggled to get away.

Adam grabbed him. "Max! Joe's hit!"

They hauled Joe away from the wire, heading for the road to meet the extraction vehicles. Joe's screams of pain as his leg bounced across the ground were ignored.

Beharry and Adam heaved Joe into the first vehicle. "Go!" Beharry shouted as he and Adam piled in.

The driver gunned the SUV away. Joe slumped back. His body trembled as shock and pain flushed the adrenaline from his system. He looked at his thigh. It was a bloody ruin. And it hurt.

Beharry propped Joe against the door and lifted his leg onto the seat. He cut the trouser leg away. "Stay with me, Joe, Adam! First aid kit! Now!"

Joe lifted his head, a crooked smile on his face. "Guess what, Max?" he mumbled, his words shock-slurred. "After all the time I spent on the firing range, I didn't use my gun, not once."

"Be happy," Beharry said. His fingers probed the bloody pulp in Joe's thigh. He grunted as he applied a wad of field dressings. "You're a lucky man. The round's missed the bone and the femoral artery."

Joe did not care. His mind was too full of images of Xipalli's men as they chopped laboratory workers down.

●●●

Lancero had always enjoyed killing Venganza, though killing foreigners was better. Yanquis were the best of all. Without their lust for drugs, there would be no Hermann Márquez, no Venganza, no Escorpiónes, no Americans and Russians, men turned into animals by Iraq and Afghanistan and Chechnya and all the other god-forgotten places their political masters had sent them to.

And Mexico might have been the proud, independent, rich nation it should have been.

Fucking Yanquis, he whispered as he dropped another.

Down in the compound, Venganza poured fire at the fast-retiring Escorpiónes. Xipalli's technicals persuaded them to think again, and resistance collapsed as men scrambled for cover wherever they could find it.

A pony-tailed blanco appeared, his arms waving as he harangued the Venganza to keep fighting. His AK-12 assault rifle marked him as a Russian.

Lancero put a clean shot into the man's chest sent him back, his mouth open in an 'oh' of surprise.

You should have stayed at home, you Russani pig.

A second man was kicking reluctant Venganza back to their feet. Also Russian, skinny, tattooed, bullpup A-91 in hand. Another shot, and he too fell. Lancero's next shot took out one of the few Venganza heading for the hole in the wire. The man pitched forward, hit the ground, face down, arms spread.

Our boys are all out, Lancero's observer said. *Time to go.*

Lancero had fired more rounds than he could count. His shoulder ached. He glanced over the compound as he broke down his rifle. Fingers of fire had broken through the walls of laboratory, the ground around it a shambles of bodies and flaming vehicles.

A thin line of gray caught the corner of his eye. A line which streaked from the sky and hit the center of the laboratory building.

Lancero's world flared white as a massive explosion had obliterated the compound and everything in it. Its blast wave ripped across the ground; stones torn from the ridge slashed the sniper's exposed skin.

Wiping the blood from the cuts, Lancero rose to his feet. *Madre de Dios! What did those bastards keep in there?* he said.

Who cares? his spotter said. *Let's get the hell out of here before those Venganza goatfuckers come after us.*

Lancero collected his gear and ran.

Behind him, a colossal column of smoke and flame boiled into the early morning sky.

●●●

Adam and Xipalli stood back as an ancient Mil Mi-17 helicopter unloaded the last of Xipalli's men airlifted out of Valle de Banderas.

"Nice job, captain," Adam said. "Your people did well."

"Thank you," Xipalli said. His eyes still glistened with excitement.

Adam passed a thick envelope over. "This is the mission bonus and the money for families of the men who were killed or wounded. Tell me if I have missed anyone. And if any of the wounded don't make it, I'll fix it."

"The families are happy to receive the money. Life without their men is always hard. How is Doctor Lessart?"

"He has a through-and-through in his left thigh. He lost a lot of blood, but he'll pull through. He is on my plane back to the States. Max went with him."

"Max is a fine soldier. But I must go. Señor Márquez wants me. He say he has another job for me."

"You take care now. And thanks."

Adam watched Xipalli leave, a decent man sucked into in the hurricane of corruption and violence the War on Drugs had inflicted on Mexico.

The man would need a miracle to survive Hermann Márquez.

—39—

Joe stared at the ceiling, and endless stream of images from the battle filling his mind.

The endless wait. The feeling of dread. Dry mouth. Sweaty hands. Heart hammering.

The SUV bucking and heaving like a wild thing as it charged through the wire and into the compound.

A bullet shattering the window beside him as the SUV skidded to a stop.

The familiar calm of a laboratory drowning in an orgy of gunfire and death.

The young lab technician on her back, mouth open, her life drained away into pools of blood.

His uncaring reaction.

His near panic when his search of the labs came up dry.

The rush of exhilaration when he found Bruce the Ass-Kicker's laptop.

The adrenaline-fueled run for safety. Frantic. Terrifying. Exhilarating.

The instant a Venganza bullet cut him down. Shock. Pain. Fear.

The compound exploding in a searing flash, bleaching all the color from the world.

The blast wave slamming the vehicle to one side.

The stream of Spanish profanities from the driver as he fought the SUV back onto the track.

Beharry hunched over his leg, packing the wound, shouting at the driver to go faster.

The Escorpiónes pouring into the LZ, their manic grins of triumph, guns stabbed skywards.

A huge bunch of red roses dropped on the chest of a dead Venganza.

The huge square of cardboard behind the man's head with the crudely scrawled words: 'Ten un diá maravillosa. Saludos, Hermann Márquez'.

The locals a blur of shocked faces and open mouths as the SUV raced past.

The stream of vehicles arriving at the landing zone with Xipalli's men, some jubilant, some grim-faced, some pinched in pain.

The medics loading him into a helicopter.

Questions in fractured English, questions his brain could not process.

The medic stripping Beharry's crude dressings off, cleaning the wound, applying new dressings.

Adam leaning over him, a bag of Hextend held high as the medic put a line into his arm.

More pain. Heart fluttering. Hard to breathe.

The clatter as the dilapidated helicopter lifted off, banking hard as it climbed away.

The moaning, mumbling, and crying of the wounded when the helicopter landed and shut down.

The quiet as hands loaded him into an SUV.

Beharry's quiet assurance he was on his way to hospital in the US. Hang in, Joe. You will be fine.

Blessed darkness.

•••

"Hey, Doctor Lessart. The doctor tells me the surgery went well, but I've gotta say you don't look so hot."

Joe opened his eyes. Kemani.

"You're supposed to comfort me, not tell it like it is."

"I always tell the truth; it's a weakness of mine … How's the leg?"

"The surgeon says I was lucky. The bullet missed the important bits. The muscle's not too happy, though."

"You'll be fine."

"Am I safe here?" Joe asked. "I keep wondering if a bunch of Revival thugs are going to pay me a bedside visit."

Kemani patted Joe's arm. "Relax. I have a full security detail with drones covering you. And a cyber-sec team watching the cellphone traffic in the area. The NSA aren't the only people who can crack the encryption, you know."

"Cyber-sec? Let me guess. Raffa?"

"Her people, yes. I have to protect my best customer."

Kemani's words did little to reassure. Joe knew he had hurt the Revival. They would be coming after him, and the quickest way to find him was to ask the man standing by his bed.

It would have no trouble finding the man, not with Hermann Márquez telling anyone who cared to listen how his Escorpiónes had kicked the Venganza cartel's ass.

"I spoke with Márquez," Kemani went on. "He is happy his guys killed so many Venganza. He thinks he can to take Jalisco from them before June. He said any time you need his help, just ask."

"I have met some awful people these last few months, Freddie, but he is the worst. I never want to see him again."

Kemani shrugged. "We work with the people we have to."

So true, thought Joe. "Talking of Raffa, how is she going?" he asked.

"Nothing to tell you. She is still trying to break in. It all takes time."

"Here's hoping. I have to see what's inside Kernow's laptop."

●●●

Once Kemani had left, Joe did the one thing he had sworn he would not do: He found his Nokia and dialed the Center for Arms Control and Non-Proliferation.

He would talk with Murata. For all the general's misplaced faith in the FBI, she was a soldier, she had connections, and Adam had vouched for her moral integrity.

With his trust in Freddie Kemani evaporating fast, he needed new allies.

—40—

Murata pulled a chair up to Joe's bed and sat down. "Director Agnelli told me you disappeared when your FBI safe house was shot up. Where have you been hiding all these weeks? You too, Adam. How come you haven't returned my calls?"

"We have been busy," Adam said.

"You could still have called." A hint of frost.

"Don't blame Adam," Joe said. "He wanted to, but I was too paranoid to let him."

"Hmm … What's with the leg?"

"I hope you like long stories, general," Joe said.

•••

"… and, as always, the problem is what we do now," Joe said. "My new best friend, Hermann Márquez, can get us all the muscle we need, but muscle won't help us now. Out problem is targets; apart from Carbonel's vaccine plant in Panama, we don't have any."

"And taking it out is not an option," Adam added.

Murata grimaced. "I wish it was," she said. "No, after what you did to Cogent's lab, the Revival will have so much security in place you'd need a full airborne assault to take out Carbonel."

"Any thoughts on what we do next, general?" Joe asked.

Adam held out a hand. "Hold on a second. I have a question for the general before we talk about the future. What went wrong with the FBI?"

Murata had the grace to look embarrassed. "Ah, yes ... I'm sorry, but I don't know. Director Agnelli keeps stonewalling me ... and yes, it is possible the Revival has suborned him too."

Possible? How about probable? But Joe let it go. 'So, what do we do now?"

His words dangled for a long time, unanswered.

Finally, Murata said, "The Revival is America's problem. There is only one person who can fix this: the president herself."

"You're kidding. Before you pick up the phone to call her or anyone else, let me remind you of something. The scientist from Valle de Banderas, the one I kidnapped, thought this went all the way to the top, implicating Vandergraaf, and Vice President Ramirez too. We'd be signing our own death warrants approaching them."

"You have a point, Joe," Murata conceded. "I only know Ramirez, and him I do not trust. When I worked on his campaign, I saw the real Ramirez: vain, egotistical, cruel, a man convinced he had a god-given right to be president. People like him are dangerous and unpredictable."

"He sounds like just the man the Revival would recruit," Joe said.

"He is. As for Vandergraaf, I don't know her at all, though my instincts say she's not as bad as Ramirez."

"Successful politicians learn early to hide their real personas," Joe said.

Adam put his hand up. "Hold it, guys. It doesn't matter what we think of Vandergraaf or Ramirez. Until we've ruled them out of the conspiracy, approaching them is too dangerous."

Murata's face twisted in frustration. "Sounds like we're stalled."

"I'm afraid we are," Joe said, "though things will change if our hacker can break into the laptop we recovered."

"You're hoping?" Murata said. "Is hope the best you've got?"

"I'm afraid it is, general."

Murata threw her arms up. "Goddammit! Okay, you win. I'll sit tight. Contact me when you've got past hoping."

"Will do, general."

Joe let the door close behind Murata. "Have we made the same mistake again?"

"The FBI is the problem," Adam said, "not Murata."

Joe lay back, exhausted. His injured leg was not to blame. It was the endless not-knowing, like a small kid racing home late at night, alone, frightened, wondering when—not if—the bogeyman would come roaring out of the night.

"You're very quiet," Adam said.

"Just thinking."

—41—

Joe stared into the mirror. His grandmother would not have recognized him: gaunt, hollow-eyed, his face hidden behind a thick black beard, hair streaked with gray. He had aged ten years since he and André had sold Hydra.

There was a tap on the door. "Joe? Freddie's here."

"Yeah, come on in," Joe said.

Freddie Kemani walked into the cabin and threw himself into a chair, Raffa close behind. "You remember Raffa, Joe?" he asked.

"Of course. Hi, Raffa. Good to see you again."

Raffa ignored him, sat down, and pulled out a tablet. She flipped it open. Her fingers flew across the keyboard.

"Let's get started," she said. "The cellphones you recovered had nothing of interest," she said, "but a brute-force attack got me into Mister Kernow's laptop. It was a personal machine and not well protected."

"But how?" Joe said. "Everything I've read says that's impossible."

Kemani put a hand on Raffa's arm before she could reply. "Doctor Lessart is my best client. Tell him why it is possible, my dear."

Raffa's lip curled. "It is possible when you have a million clones of Mapathi's machine accurate to the last chip, a full 3-D model of his face, his fingerprints, and every detail of his life, right down to the brand of toilet paper he prefers."

"Sorry ... I can see why this is costing me so much."

"The best is never cheap."

Joe smiled. "Something I've heard before. What about the datastores?"

"Not yet. Their security is tight; they were configured by Cogent's corporate IT people. But we will keep trying. Okay, let's look at Mister Kernow. He was the gateway between Marina Pavel, Cogent's laboratory manager, and Tom Mapathi. Any problem the people on site couldn't fix passed through his hands: laboratory issues, security, money, staff, the Venganza, everything."

"Which fits what Pavel told me. The people Mapathi talks to aren't just the problem-solvers, they run the show."

Kemani tapped the table. "Hold on a second, Joe. Don't you think it's time you told me what this 'show' of yours is all about?"

"No. Why would I?"

"When you came here, you were pretty zonked. You talked about a conspiracy called the Revival. And a smallpox attack on China. What's that about?"

Joe stared at Kemani for a moment, hard-eyed, then said, "I'm not as dumb as Raffa thinks. She's worked out what's going on, and she's told you."

Kemani's lips tightened. "Yes, she has, but you should have told me, rather than letting me find out for myself. Come on, Joe! An American conspiracy to attack China with bioweapons and you did not think to tell me?"

"I have been hunted by SEALs," snapped Joe. "I have had grenades dropped on me. I have been kidnapped. I have been waterboarded in between getting the shit kicked out of me. I have been in a car crash. I have been shot. I have been betrayed by the FBI. I'm being hunted by the biggest criminal conspiracy in human history. I don't trust anyone anymore. And when I go to sleep at night—if I do—I'm not sure I'll wake up alive."

He stood and leaned over Kemani.

"So, Mister Freddie Fucking Kemani, I do not care what you think. Your job is not to speculate. It is to deliver what I pay for, nothing more. So keep your damn mouth closed and my business private."

Kemani's face reddened. "I suggest—"

"Shut it!" Joe spit. "I appreciate what you've done for me, Freddie, but let's keep it in perspective. I have paid for everything, in cash, in full. I don't owe you anything, and I don't need you to tell me what to do."

"I think—"

"I haven't finished! How often have I heard you say all you care about is money? The minute someone makes you a better offer, you'll take it. Christ, Freddie! The Revival could buy you ten thousand times over, which is why I didn't tell you what the 'show' was about, all right?"

Joe slumped back into his seat.

Kemani glared at him. "The last person who talked like that, regretted it."

Joe waved the man's words away. "Go fuck yourself. I'm too tired to care."

"A lot's happened to you," Kemani said, "so I'll ignore what you've said. But I strongly advise you to watch what you say."

Joe leaned forward. "You think you frighten me?'

"I should."

"You don't come close. So, get your hand off your dick, and do what I pay you to do. And when the time comes to betray me to the Revival, take a minute to think what that will mean for me, for Raffa, for Max, for Adam, and for the millions of sad bastards out there."

The silence hung ugly in the air.

"We should move on," Kemani said at last, "but before we do, let me say this. I am a businessman. And yes, my principal interest is money, but if you think I would work with people prepared to murder millions of Chinese, you misjudge me. Freddie Kemani has his limits too."

Joe did not believe the man, not for one second. But he said, "Thank you, Freddie. I appreciate you telling me. And I apologize for what I said. I was out of line."

"You're under pressure, so let's forget it, shall we? Now, Raffa, where were we?"

●●●

"I'm done, Doctor Lessart. Here is a pen drive with all the data files from Kernow's laptop, plus the ones he thought he had deleted and everything I scraped from the websites he has accounts with. You'll also find Tom Mapathi's bio."

"Thanks, Raffa. Outstanding work."

The woman dismissed the compliment with the flick of a hand. "I'm done. I'll be outside, Mister Kemani."

"So, Joe," Kemani said when Raffa had left. "You happy?"

"Very. Raffa is a smart woman. Once I have read all the files, I can decide what to do next."

Kemani rose to his feet. "I'll wait to hear from you. One more thing, Joe. I meant what I said I would not deal with the Revival."

"Thank you, Freddie, I believe you."

"I'm not sure you do, but then I probably wouldn't believe me either. But you should. Oh, one more thing. The next safe house is ready. We'll move you tomorrow."

"Sure. Can Max come with me?"

"If he's happy to, I'm happy," Kemani said as he headed out the door. "Ask him."

Joe sat twirling the pen drive in his fingers long after Kemani had left. The man would sell his own mother if the price was right. He could not worry about it though. It wasn't like he had a conga line of Freddies to choose from.

He had to go back to Washington. But, before he returned to that snake-filled swamp, he needed to talk with Adam.

—42—

Adam sat back. "Raffa's a goddammed genius."

Joe winced as he tried to stretch cramp out of his damaged leg. "She is, but there is a problem. I have analyzed all Kernow's emails, and I cannot find any evidence to confirm Vandergraaf and Ramirez are part of the conspiracy. Or anyone else. Names never get mentioned."

"Why are you surprised?" Adam said. "Gatekeepers are there to make sure people like us don't find out. Have we got anything to link Mapathi to the Revival?"

"Nothing. He's a member of New America who worked for Ramirez and then for the Vandergraaf-Ramirez campaign, as did thousands of other people."

"Where is Mapathi now?"

"With a think tank in Washington, the 1945 Institute. It seems legit."

Adam thought for a while. "We need to go through everything Raffa took from the laptop again. And we ought to brief Murata on what we've got; she's not too happy with us leaving her out of the loop. Why don't I fix up a meeting in Washington, make it easy for her? We can take my plane."

"I agree we should go to Washington, though not to keep the general happy. This conspiracy began there, and where it must end. But no planes. Way too much security."

Adam rolled his eyes. "Oh, dear god. Please, not Amtrak. And no buses, either."

Joe laughed. "You're such a snob, Adam. No, I have something much better in mind: We rent an RV—there are millions of them on the road, so nobody will pay us any attention—and head for Washington. That will reduce the risk of the Revival finding us and give us time to go through the material from Kernow's laptop."

Adam buried his head in his hands. "I'm going to cross America in an RV. Kill me now."

"You're such a snob, Adam. Millions of Americans love RVs; I'm sure you will too ... I'll ask Max to talk with Freddie. They can organize security for us when we get there."

— 43—

Beharry was at the wheel of the RV as it headed across Texas.

Sat beside him, Joe was beyond frustrated. Kernow had sent Mapathi a ton of emails about problems affecting Cogent's operations in Valle de Banderas, problems which people on the ground could not resolve. Mapathi would have passed those emails on to someone senior enough to make things happen.

But he and Adam had found not one clue to the problem-solvers' identities; they could only see Mapathi's replies to Kernow's emails. When he got around to replying. Oftentimes he would take days, even with simple problems.

Joe wondered why.

But there were never any names. And, without them, his search for the people who ran the Revival had stalled.

He closed his eyes and put his head back.

•••

Joe woke with a start.

Beharry glanced at him. He grinned. "You snore, a lot."

"Sorry; I do when I'm stressed. When this is all over, I going to take a vacation, somewhere remote, somewhere cut-off from the rest of the world, no phones, no television, no emails, no…" He sat up. "No phones … Goddamn it! No phones!"

"What about them?" Beharry asked.

"Not sure," Joe replied, as he headed back to where he had left Adam, hunched over his tablet, muttering profanities.

●●●

"You're right, Joe," Adam said. "Mapathi does take a long time to respond to the problems Kernow sends him, even the simple ones. They shouldn't need days to resolve, but they do. Which is very odd, I agree. It's not how a conspiracy to take over the world should work."

"No, it's not. Take the requests for money." Joe pointed at his laptop's screen. "Here's one: Kernow asks for five grand to fix one of the diesel generators. Simple, right? Except Mapathi take eight days before he tells Kernow the money's on its way."

"Because the problem-solvers are out of town and cannot deal with anything until they get back?"

"It's the only explanation I can think of. If we can match the delays to the absences, I'm hoping we can see who Mapathi talks to."

"Jeezus! Is that even possible?"

"An analysis of the emails will give us the delays, right?'

"Right," Adam said.

"And, thanks to the Honesty in Government Act, all Federal employees put their diaries on-line, the president and her cabinet included. That will show us when people are away from home. The people whose absences match the delays are our prime suspects."

Adam grimaced. "One more time, Joe."

"The reason Mapathi takes a long time to fix some of Kernow's problems is because the problem-solver is out of town. What we have to do is see whose absence match up best with the delays. If we can, we will know who the problem-solvers are."

"Ah, okay. Got it now .... But you are making a lot of assumptions," he went. "Mapathi's problem-solvers being all Feds for one."

"I think most of them have to be. The Revival cannot do what it has done from outside government; people like you and me cannot deploy submarines and SEALs. And Marina Pavel's told us the Revival's people inside NBACC are weaponizing the virus to use against China. Which implicates Homeland Security."

"Hmm … I'll buy the Feds thing," Adam said, "but why can't they use burner phones to swap emails with Mapathi?"

Joe waved his battered Nokia at Adam. "I have this because the National Security Agency can listen to every conversation and read every email, message, and datafile sent from every mobile device using every US cellular and satellite network. No exceptions."

"Ah, yes. The Open Crypt Act. I forgot."

"Which was enacted after the Philadelphia bombings to ensure people using mobile devices have no secrets, the reason why Hydra used landlines through secure gateways. We never used cellphones for anything important. It was a pain, but we could not risk compromising our security."

"You did, I remember … and the Revival's people will have to do the same. It's the only way they can keep their secrets secret."

"And, if the conspirators are Feds," Joe said, "they can't use the landlines in Federal offices to communicate either. The NSA monitors those as well … I know I'm grabbing at flies here, but hardwired gateways with fixed internet connections, VPNs, and bullet-proof encryption are the only safe way the conspirators can talk with each other."

"Landlines they can't take with them when they're out of town," Adam said.

"Which is why Mapathi has to wait for his answers."

Adam grimaced. "Checking all those diaries is a huge job. We'll need a bunch of data scientists and statisticians, shit-hot ones. And access to a shitload of computing grunt to make sense of all the data."

Joe laughed, relief mostly. For the first time he sensed he might have found a way out of the Kernow-Mapathi email morass.

"We don't need anything, Adam. We have Raffa; if she can run a simulation with a million clones of Kernow's laptop, I don't think we'll have a problem. And, just in case my Fed employee theory turns out to be wrong, we'll have her broaden the search."

"Starting with Rafiki's list of psychotic multi-billionaires who think slaughtering half the human race is a fine idea. Come on, let's write the brief for Raffa."

—44—

"Adam!" Joe said. "Get your ass in here. Email from Raffa. Looks like she's delivered."

"Oh, thank god," Adam said as he slid onto the bench beside Joe. "Maybe now we can stop wandering around Virginia in this goddammed RV."

"Here's hoping," Joe said as Raffa's analysis came up on the RV's wall-mounted screen.

A table.

Hundreds of names in a column down one side.

A row of dates across the top.

Terabytes of data reduced to give a score to every Federal employee senior enough to make the decisions Kernow was asking Mapathi for.

Joe's fingers flashed across the keyboard. "The higher the score, the better the match between absences and email delays. I've sorted the table to put the people with the highest scores at the top. If my theory's correct, that's where we'll find our conspirators."

"This is scary," Adam said as he studied the first forty or so names. "If those are Mapathi's problem-solvers, we are screwed; we're looking at some big hitters. And the president and vice president are way too close to the top of the list. If they run the Revival, it's all over."

"Calm down, Adam. They're just possibilities at this stage. Now, the key to this is the diaries. Raffa says she will update them using sources she didn't want to talk about; she says government people aren't always as honest and open as they should be."

Adam laughed. "Well, hell! There's a surprise."

"And she's going to add in Skylar Rafiki's Gang of 5, the rich assholes who are financing the Revival," Joe said, ignoring a sudden stab of guilt; if Rafiki was dead, he was responsible.

"Is there any point? I'm an asshole with lots of money, and I take a lot of care to make sure what I do stays private, let me tell you."

"You, my friend, are deluded. Raffa is an expert at finding the rocks people like you hide their dirty little secrets under."

"Bugger. Okay, what now?"

"I don't like just sitting around waiting for Raffa to finish her analysis. Why don't we have a chat with Mapathi? What Raffa's given us is a bit rough, but it might be enough crack him open. Maybe he'll tell us who this Boss is."

"Shouldn't we talk to Murata first? She ought see what we've got."

Joe shook his head. "No, it's too early. Let's see what we can squeeze out of Mapathi first."

After a moment's thought, Adam said, "What the hell; at least we'll be doing something. But how can we kidnap Mapathi without being arrested?"

"Hmm ... Not sure. Washington's not Puerto Vallarta."

"Max Beharry!" Adam called out, and they both laughed.

—45—

The street was tree-lined and flanked by townhouses long since converted to offices, empty of all but scattered laggards on their way home.

It was time. After days watching Mapathi, he had turned out to be a man of routine. It was going-home time.

Beharry tapped Joe on the arm. "Okay, it's time. But don't rush it. All you have to do is stop the man; we'll do the rest. Any problems you can't handle, walk away."

Joe swallowed hard. Beharry had volunteered to grab Mapathi. Joe wondered why he had not taken the offer.

He stepped from the battered van into the heat and humidity of an early Washington summer. He pulled out his cellphone, put it to his ear, and started an animated one-sided conversation, right hand on the pistol in his pocket.

The front door of the 1945 Institute opened. Laughter splashed across the sidewalk. Joe's heart sank. Beharry instructions had been explicit: If anyone was with Mapathi, he must abort and try again another night.

The door closed. The laughter died. Mapathi appeared. He was alone. Joe let himself breathe again.

The man did not spare Joe a glance as he set off down the street. Joe set off after him. The street was empty. He pulled a ski mask down across his face and took out his gun.

"Hey Tom! Tom!" he called out when he was close.

Mapathi stopped and turned. "Oh, fuck!" he whispered when he saw Joe's gun.

"Oh, fuck is right, sport. Move or shout, and I'll blow your head off."

Mapathi half-lifted his hands. "My wallet's in my pants' pocket. Take it. Please take it."

The van rolled to a stop beside them. Its door slid open. Hands reached out and pulled Mapathi inside. Beharry rolled him face down, bandaged and cable-tied his wrists, then gagged and hooded him, the van already accelerating away as Joe jumped in.

Tom Mapathi's abduction had taken only twelve seconds.

•••

Joe looked down at Mapathi. "So, Tom. Any idea why you're here?"

The man's eyes flickered around the derelict warehouse, one of many around Washington. It was empty except for the chair he sat on and the thick layer of dust and dirt covering the concrete floor. "No. Why am I here?"

"I thought we should have a chat about the Revival."

Mapathi's body gave the faintest of twitches. "I have no idea what you're talking about."

"Does the name Bruce Kernow mean anything?"

Mapathi stiffened. "No."

"How about Marina Pavel? Cogent? Valle de Banderas? Smallpox? Strain 5524? China? How much more do I have to say?"

"I don't know about what you're talking about."

But Mapathi was having trouble sitting still.

"A lie, but there are better things to talk about than Valle de Banderas, am I right?"

"What the hell are you talking about?"

"How about NBACC's work on the Sin Nombre hantavirus. Or would you prefer to start with Carbonel in Panama?"

Mapathi said nothing.

"Nah, you're right, Tom. That would be waste of time. Tell you what. Instead of the people below you in the food chain, let's talk about the people above."

"I can't."

"You can do anything you want, Tom. We won't tell anyone."

"They're everywhere, you fool. Everywhere."

"Prove it."

"They'll find out if I talk, and then they will kill me."

"What makes you think I won't kill you if you don't?" Joe said.

"Maybe you will, maybe you won't."

"Let's talk about your emails. You talk about the Boss a lot. Who is that? The president? What about the vice president? The National Security Adviser? Come on, who?"

Now Mapathi smiled. "You're a goddammed amateur, aren't you? You're just pulling names out of your ass. Go on, give me some more."

Joe glanced over Mapathi's head to where Adam and Beharry watched from a doorway. "What now?" he mouthed.

"Move on," Beharry mouthed back. "Come back to it later."

Joe turned back to Mapathi. "Tell you what ... Hey, Tom. Tom! Eyes on me... You have to give me something if you want to make it home alive."

"Whatever."

"In a couple of your emails you talked about something called, let me see now ... Yes, you called them 'Slingshots'."

"Yeah. So?"

Joe held out an email. "Here's one. There are more. Tell me; what are these 'Slingshots', Tom?"

Mapathi lifted his head. He stared at Joe. His eyes were narrow with hate. "You don't understand what you're up against, do you? Even if I could tell you everything, the Revival would still crush you."

"You're right, but I still want you to answer my questions. Now, to help you focus, it's time to remind you there are limits to my patience."

Marina Pavel had taught Joe one thing: get brutal fast. He put his pistol to Mapathi's head and ground it into the man's skull. Mapathi moaned. Joe pressed harder. "When I get so pissed with you, I will kill you. The way you're going, it won't be long. So, tell me. Are you ready to die? Because I'm happy to pull the trigger if you are. There are plenty more scumbags like you out there."

Now Mapathi trembled. "Don't kill me."

Joe eased the gun away a fraction and pulled the trigger, the sound of the shot racketing off the walls of the warehouse. Mapathi jerked like a man tasered. "First and last warning, Tom. The next one is in your foot, then your knee and thigh, finishing with a shot to the gut to send you on your way to hell ... and let me tell you, Mister Mapathi, it will be a very long journey, so long you'll be glad when the Devil himself welcomes you in."

"You wouldn't," Mapathi said.

"Yeah, you're right. Too much shooting ... How about I blow your balls off and then put one in your gut? You'd still take a long time to die a very painful death. But you'll have enough time to reflect on the evil you are part of. Now, do we understand each other?"

Mapathi nodded. "Yes."

"For your sake, I hope so. Slingshots. What are they?"

"The reason you're wasting your time." Mapathi snapped with a flash of defiance.

"Tom, Tom, Tom. I did warn you, but I will give you one last chance before I shoot you in the balls. Which foot would you prefer? Right or left? No, perhaps a knee would be better."

Mapathi's defiance vanished. "No, please, no! I'll tell you."

Joe pulled the trigger, but he'd angled the gun so the round skimmed past Mapathi's calf.

"You shot me! You bastard, you shot me."

Joe kicked the chair. "Stop your moaning. I missed because I wanted to. But the next one's for real, so answer my questions."

"I will, I will. Please, put the gun away."

Joe ground the muzzle of his gun into Mapathi's leg, so hard the man squealed. "Why would I? Slingshot. What is it?"

"Military units commanded by officers loyal to the Revival."

Joe's heart skipped. "You mean not loyal to the commander-in-chief?"

"No. To the Revival."

"Just army?"

"Mostly. Some Navy and marines."

"You're full of crap. We are talking about the US military here. Best in the world, so everyone says."

Mapathi lifted his head to look at Joe. "What's the point of having the best if the politicians don't have the guts to use them? For years, the Chinese have pissed all over us, and what do we do? Nothing. But the Revival can, and it will."

"Yeah, yeah. You're bullshitting me."

"I am not."

"Then don't waste my time, Tom. You're not high enough up in the Revival to identify the Slingshot units. You're just making shit up to seem important."

Mapathi was angry now. "I'm not, you asshole."

Joe grabbed Mapathi's head and pulled their faces together. "You're just Bruce Kernow's flunky. All you did was take messages while people like Kernow, Pavel and the rest of the Revival did the real work."

"You're wrong," Mapathi shouted, spittle white on his lips. "Wrong, wrong, wrong."

Joe glanced over to Beharry and Adam. "This is pointless," he called out. "Come on! Let me waste the little toe rag ... I can? Great." He turned back to Mapathi. "There you go, Tom. This is it. Nobody will miss you. There are plenty more lackeys where you came from. Anything to say before I start shooting?"

"The 824th Mobile Regiment. Enough for you?"

"No, it's not. Where are they based?"

"Andrews."

Joe glanced at Beharry.

Beharry nodded.

Joe turned back to Mapathi. "I need names. Which of the 824th's officers are part of the Revival?"

Mapathi shook his head. "I can't give you any names. The 824th only got mentioned the once. I'm not supposed to know stuff like that."

"What other units are involved?"

"No idea."

"More lies. Who's the Boss, Tom?"

"No."

Joe jammed the gun into Mapathi's groin, eased it clear a few inches and pulled the trigger, sending the round through the chair to ricochet off the floor and into a wall.

The man screamed. "Please, no," he whimpered. "Stop, please ... I'd tell you if I knew, but I don't. My emails go to a dropbox. I don't know who has access to it."

"I think you do. And now it's time to say goodbye to your balls, my man."

"I don't know! I don't know!"

Again, Joe pushed the gun back into Mapathi's groin. Hard. The man squealed. "Jeez, you lie a lot. Who's the Boss?"

Mapathi's head slumped. "I'm not saying any more. You're going to kill me no matter what."

"What now?" Joe mouthed to Beharry and Adam.

Beharry crossed his arms across his chest.

Joe put the gun away and went over to where Beharry and Adam sat. "All yours."

Beharry stood. "I'll fetch the Jack Daniels and the little blue pills."

"You sure they'll work?"

"Oh, they'll work. Mapathi is going to wake up on the sidewalk with the worst hangover of his life, with his wallet, watch, and cell gone, and no memory of what happened here."

●●●

"He reacted when you mentioned the president," Beharry said when the video stopped. "What do you think, Joe?"

"Not sure. Because Vandergraaf is the Boss? Or because she isn't?"

"I can't tell … Shit! I thought you had enough to bluff him."

Joe sighed. "I did too, and then I went and screwed it up."

Beharry patted Joe on the shoulder. "Interrogation isn't just asking questions. But you did persuade Mapathi to tell us what Slingshots are, though it came as a shock to hear the 824th is part of the Revival."

"You believed him?"

"I did," Beharry replied. "And when he said there were more units."

"NAVSPECWARCOM for starters."

"What Mapathi's talking about is much more worrying. If he's telling the truth, the Revival has infiltrated right down to the unit level. The risks are huge."

"They are … I don't understand this," Joe went on. "You only need the US military for a conventional attack on China. Even the Revival can't pull that off."

"We're missing something here," Beharry said, "something really important."

"Like what?"

"No idea."

Joe turned to Adam. "You're quiet. Are we missing something?"

"I think we are. I just don't know what it is yet."

Silence, minutes long.

A silence broken by Adam. "The Revival's plan to destroy China has always bothered me, and not just because of the millions who would die. China is the world's largest economy. Destroying it would trigger the worst financial crisis since the Black Death, costing the Gang of 5 hundreds of billions of dollars."

"I've always assumed all they cared about was getting richer," Joe said.

"No, it's not. For all their wealth, the Gang of 5 can only buy influence. They cannot buy absolute power. And absolute power is what they want, what they crave, the only thing in the world money can never buy. Power is what the Revival is all about."

"But what does suborning the US military have to do with anything?"

"They need the US military so they can take over the United States," Adam said. "Once they have, they can destroy China, and the rest of the world falls into line. The Gang of 5 will have power on a scale humanity has never seen. As for the money they've lost, they'll make it up soon enough."

Joe shook his head. "Oh, come on! The US first, China second, and then world domination? Of course it's about making..." His voice trailed off. "Oh, shit! ... All I've thought about is people wandering around China with aerosols full of virus. I never stopped to think what the Gang of 5 really wanted. You're right, Adam."

"I agree," Beharry said. "You don't need the US military to eliminate China; a few busloads of tourists with spray cans full of 5524 can do the job. The Revival needs the US military. It cannot take over the US without it."

Joe felt his chest tighten, the way it did when he was about to push deep into a dangerous wreck, only much, much worse.

"I think it's time we talked with Murata."

—46—

Joe's opened his eyes. He wondered where he was. Then he remembered: the Radiant Sunset Motel, the latest dump in a long line of dumps. And he still had five long hours before the meeting with Murata.

He would never get back to sleep.

He did not try. Instead, he did what he always did: rake through the ashes of the past, trying to see what he had achieved. If he was honest, it was a lot, but still not enough.

The loss of Cogent's Valle de Banderas laboratory was only a temporary setback for the Revival. Marina Pavel had struck Joe as a competent manager; all the work done by her virologists would have been backed-up off-site. The Revival could have a new laboratory to mass-produce a virus to use against China operational in a matter of months.

But instinct told him he was missing something important. The last time he had felt this way was when he'd missed the link between Unit 731 and the *Maroku Maru*.

He forced himself out of bed to make a cup of coffee. Mug in hand, he went to the window and threw back the drapes. The view did nothing to lift his spirits: warehouses and a strip mall, the ground slick with rain and streaked with orange from the streetlights, the road beyond already busy.

Something Beharry said after the attack on Valle de Banderas came back to him, one of those throwaway remarks people toss into a conversation: 'You are the luckiest sonofabitch I have ever met, Joe Lessart'.

Beharry was right. When Joe needed it most, luck had come his way. For starters, why had the Revival found it so hard to track him down? And, even when Revival came close, like when they had shot up the FBI safe house, they had let him slip away. A pickup and two vans full of men with assault rifles, for chrissakes! How could they be so incompetent?

It all felt wrong.

But he was an amateur, as Kemani had pointed out. How would he know what was possible and what was not? Homeland Security had missed the attack on Philadelphia, an attack carried out by islamo-fascist terrorists making mistakes so egregious they would have been funny were it not for the tens of thousands of Americans they had killed that awful Independence Day.

Maybe—like the Philadelphia bombers—Homeland Security's analysts and computers had missed him, the data which might have led the Revival to him a speck amidst the torrent of raw data it had to deal with.

Maybe Beharry had made the difference.

Maybe it was pure blind luck.

Maybe, maybe, maybe …

It did not matter. For whatever reason, the Revival had not tracked him down. There was nothing more to it, he reassured himself. He had to stop being paranoid.

It still jarred though, a finger of doubt toying with his mind.

•••

General Murata's face crinkled in disgust as she walked into the abandoned factory. Lit by a gray, almost ethereal, light filtered through grimy windows, it was crowded with long-abandoned machinery thick with dust and filth, the air rank with the stink of stale urine and feces. Once full of vitality and vigor, it was now a crumbling necropolis, its graffiti-splashed walls another tombstone over the grave of a long-gone America.

She found a box, flicked it clear of dust, and sat down. "I think I'm going to have to burn my clothes when I get home,"

Joe laughed. "Sorry, general. The conference room at the Grand Hyatt was booked."

"Don't apologize. I'm just getting old and grumpy. And I do like your operational security, even if Max Beharry and his friends are army. My faith in our security agencies and the rule of law is not what it used to be. Where's Adam?"

"With Max and the rest of the team. They will cover our egress if anyone comes calling. And we're listening to the local cell traffic."

"Impressive. Now, what have you got for me, Joe?"

"Last time we spoke, we hoped to break into the laptop we recovered from Cogent's laboratory in Mexico. Well, we have. It belonged to the lab's head of security, Bruce Kernow. His contact inside the Revival was a man called Tom Mapathi, and they emailed each other, a lot."

"I've met Tom Mapathi," Murata said. "He worked on Ramirez's campaign and then for Vandergraaf's. Are you saying he's part of the Revival?"

"He was the cutout between Cogent's operation in Mexico and the people who run the Revival."

"Damn," Murata muttered, "those bastards are everywhere. Right, Joe, from the top."

"Yes, general. We had Mapathi's emails analyzed, and they showed…"

•••

Murata sat back. "Impressive work. Your analyst should be working for the CIA. I wish the president wasn't so close to the top of your list."

"Me too," Joe said, "But check the confidence level for her ranking. See how low it is? No, the one who sticks out is Vice President Ramirez. But our analyst is still refining the data from the diaries; she says the more senior the person, the less their diary reflects what they actually did."

"Why am I not surprised? Washington breeds dishonesty. Sorry, go on."

"We've been promised an updated version for tomorrow. I'm hoping we can confirm who the Boss is."

"I hope so too. Let's move on."

"Tom Mapathi and I had a chat, though I had to jam a gun into his groin to make him talk."

Murata sat back. Her eyes widened in surprise. "Are you crazy?"

"Crazy? No. Desperate? Yes. But I figured the risk was worth it. I hoped he'd tell us who the Boss was by making him think we knew more than we did."

"Did he?"

Joe shook his head. "No, but he did say something which made us sit up ... and I hope you're ready for this, general. Mapathi said the Revival has suborned senior officers right across the US military. The units they control are called Slingshots, and one of them is the 824th Mobile Regiment."

Murata's hand flicked Joe's words away. "Not possible. This is the United States of America, not Venezuela."

"Mapathi said it was possible, and we all believed him."

Murata sat in silence for a while, then said, "If the Revival can turn the 824th, where does all this stop?"

"I'll come to that. But it means the Revival is a lot bigger than we thought."

"It has to be if it's penetrated the 824th. But I don't understand why. The Revival doesn't need the military to attack China; their bioweapons will do the job just fine ... Sorry, I don't buy it."

"I didn't want to buy it either, general. But Adam picked it: The Revival's first target isn't China. It's the United States; without the military, it cannot take over the American government."

"What? Like a coup?"

"The critical point I missed, but I am sure of it now."

"Jesus ... I think Adam's right. It's the only thing which makes sense. But I assume the Revival is still interested in the smallpox virus from the canisters?"

"Oh, yes," Joe replied. "Attacking China remains a critical part of the Revival's strategy, but the US comes first. To use a military analogy, they have to secure their base of operations before they take the offensive."

Murata stayed silent for a few minutes, then said, grim-faced, "I hate to say this, but I think you might be right ... This just gets worse."

"It does."

"And it's no secret this country is vulnerable to violent change. Vandergraaf and her people are struggling; there are plenty of people inside Homeland Security and Defense who do not like what she is trying to achieve, and millions of Americans hate the way Washington does business. They have since long before Trump ... drain the swamp, remember that? .... and they are right to. Hell, I don't like the way things are here; this town's not a swamp, it's a cesspool."

"I can't argue with you there, general. The problem we have is time. Adam and I both think the Revival has to make its move soon."

"Why?"

"China is close to taking control of southeast Asia. Only Vietnam is holding out, but not for much longer, not completely cut off from the rest of the world. Once Vietnam is under control, China can consolidate its position before pushing west. The Revival can't let that happen; waiting just makes China stronger."

"It sounds like you're talking months," Murata asked.

"As far as the US is concerned, we think so. Once the Revival is in control, everything it wants to do next—to China, to the rest of the world—becomes much easier ... and much, much faster."

"Then we'll just have to stop them. Anything else?"

Joe slid a pen drive across the table "The video of my chat with Mapathi is on there. Have a look; we might have missed something."

"I will. Mapathi... You didn't... you know."

"Kill the sonofabitch? No, we did not, general. Max filled him with bourbon and pills and then dumped him. He promised me Mapathi would wake up with an epic hangover and no memory of what happened."

"Good. And it's no secret he's a borderline alcoholic; getting shit-faced is what he does best ... Give me three days to think things through before we meet again; we can decide what we do next then. And I'll find out what I can about the 824th without alarming the chickens."

"Do it, general. We'll let you know you where and when."

Murata shook her head as she stood. "Three days to work out how to save the world."

As she left, Joe saw she moved much like Beharry, with the indefinable authority of someone with faith in her ability to get the job, any job, done. He wondered if Murata realized the Revival might be one obstacle she could never overcome.

Joe's mind filled with images what would happen if the Revival prevailed, its global empire built on the bones of millions of innocent people.

It was tempting to paint the conspirators as a bunch of crazies for thinking they could take over the entire planet.

Except, he couldn't. Crazy or not, they might.

Beharry returned. "Let's go, Joe. The general's away, and we should be too."

—47—

"Come on, general!" Joe snapped. "The Revival knows about me. I'm the enemy! The moment you tell Ramirez I'll be in the meeting, I'm dead."

"We're both dead if we can't pull this off. Just your being there should convince Ramirez what we tell him is not only what we believe, it's what we can prove. Think about it, Joe; if you had any doubts, would you go anywhere near him? No, you would not. Which is why this cannot work without you."

"I still don't like it," Joe said.

"Listen up." Murata's voice was soft. "Yes, it's all a huge bluff, but we have to risk it. If we pull it off, we win, and the Revival is over. But, yes, you are right; if Ramirez calls us out, you're dead and so am I."

"What if he doesn't make his move? What if he just sits there and says thanks guys, we'll take it from here? Neither of us will last the week."

"Joe! Stop! I spent months with Ramirez; I know the man. Inside him is a greedy little kid who wants something so badly he'll snatch it from your hand the second he sees it."

Joe turned to Adam and Beharry. "This is crazy. Come on, guys! Help me here."

"Exposing Joe is a bad idea, general," Adam said.

Beharry just shook his head.

Murata shrugged. "Perhaps, but it's the only way we can win. We are too weak to defend. We have to launch a pre-emptive attack, which means risking everything, even our lives. Besides, there is nothing more to discuss. I've already arranged a meeting with Ramirez, 18:00, Thursday, Number One Observatory Circle. And I have told him Doctor Lessart will be there."

A storm of protest broke over Murata's head. Stony-faced, she folded her arms, sat back, and waited for the uproar to die away.

When silence returned, she said, "I do not care whether you agree, Joe; it's done. And I won't apologize for not talking to you. We'd still be arguing a month from now. Ramirez is our number one suspect; forcing him into the open is the best thing we can do."

Joe wasn't sure whether he should be angry or relieved; the latter, if he was honest. He was tired, right down into his bones. This whole business had gone on too long.

He looked at Adam and Beharry. They shrugged. He turned back to Murata. "I know a done deal when I see one, general. I hope it works. What did you say to Ramirez, general?"

"I told him a conspiracy called the Revival threatened the survival of the United States. I knew who was behind it. I had the evidence to prove it. And, since I had evidence which proved he was not implicated, I felt it was my duty as an American citizen to enlist his support to take urgent action to stop the conspiracy."

"That must have shaken him up," Joe said.

Murata laughed. "What? This is Ramirez we're talking about. No, he sounded pleased."

"Why?"

"Because we're offering Ramirez what he wanted: the presidency he thought was his by right until Vandergraaf took the nomination from him. He will grab it, and not just because he want to be president. He hates Vandergraaf, not that hates comes close to describing how he feels about her. And we are going to tell him he can be president and destroy Vandergraaf. It doesn't get any better for him. And, by the time the slimy bastard realizes we've fed him a shit sandwich, it will be too late. We'll have him by the balls."

Joe threw up his hands in defeat. "I guess we're doing this then … Right, Adam and I need to brief Raffa. She has a lot of work to do if we're to get the fake report for Ramirez ahead of the meeting. You should go, general."

"Happy to." Murata kicked a piece of concrete across the floor of the latest abandoned building Max had found. "This place smells even worse than the last one … Max, I want the doctor outside the Glover Park Hotel on Wisconsin, Thursday, 17:40. And don't be late."

Beharry smiled. "I don't how the marines do things, general, but a soldier is never late.

—48—

"Mister Vice President. It's very good to see you again."

Morgan Ramirez patted Murata on the shoulder. "You too, Miyuki. It's been too long."

"You're a busy man, sir."

"I am, I am. Will you be at the party conference next month? Might be interesting."

Murata smiled. "I suspect we'll have more important things to do."

Ramirez laughed, then turned to Joe and extended a hand. The man's face was open and friendly, with lively brown eyes and a brilliant smile which flashed teeth white against tanned skin. It was the face of a man Joe's instincts urged him to trust.

"This is my chief of staff, Carlton Chang," he said.

As they shook hands, Chang eyed Joe like a snake sizing up its next meal. He was a man Joe would never trust.

Ramirez tapped the inch-thick report Murata had delivered to Chang that morning. "This is a remarkable piece of work. Yours, I believe, Doctor Lessart?"

"I'm proud to say it is, Mister Vice President. And even more proud to see it in the hands of a true American patriot. To be honest, sir, it is an absolute honor and privilege to be here today."

Ramirez's shoulders had gone back, his eyes lifted skywards, as Joe's honey-drenched words washed over him. "No, no, Doctor Lessart, you honor me." He bobbed his head at Murata. "The general and I have had our differences, but she is a woman whose judgment I trust. If she tells me I should believe what is in here, then I do. And we have heard rumors of a conspiracy ... What was it called again?"

"The Revival, Mister Vice President." It was a struggle for Joe not to laugh at Ramirez's labored claim to ignorance.

"Yes, the Revival. Your report is the first hard evidence which tells us what the conspiracy's mission is, what its plans are, and who is behind it. America owes you an enormous debt of gratitude. You have done outstanding work, doctor, outstanding."

"You have, doctor," Chang said. He leaned forward. "Your report has confirmed what we've long suspected. But you have to be certain the people you have named are in fact the conspirators."

"I am certain. Everything I gave you is supported by rigorous analysis and verified data, as I am sure you have confirmed for yourself."

"Oh, we have. Your methodology is sound, Doctor Lessart. And we've cross-checked your spreadsheet against our own records, records to which people like you would not have had access."

Despite the crushing pressure he was under, Joe enjoyed seeing Chang's self-confident pomposity. Obviously, the man had never met Raffa.

Chang turned to Ramirez. "We cannot sit on this, sir."

"I agree, Carlton. Just as we suspected, Vandergraaf is the power behind the Revival. I must act; it is my constitutional duty to do so. This is a serious threat... What am I saying? Serious does not begin to describe the danger this conspiracy poses to America, not least because of the people behind it. I cannot recall any time in our history when we faced such a crisis. And to think the president herself is involved. It's incredible."

Joe watched Ramirez. He had swallowed Murata's shit sandwich. And tasted none of it.

"Which is why I have arranged a meeting with the president," Ramirez went on; his eyes glistened. "Tonight, the four of us will cut the head off this conspiracy."

You are right there, sport, thought Joe.

•••

Joe and Murata settled into a Secret Service SUV for the short ride to the White House.

The general's cellphone buzzed. She showed the screen to Joe. "The bastards are moving," she whispered.

"About time," Joe whispered back as he read the text from Beharry. "I was afraid Ramirez would stuff things up."

"Not as afraid as I was," Murata replied. "I'm way too young to die."

•••

As if to take any sting from her remarks, Celia Vandergraaf smiled. Her eyes did not. "I don't enjoy much me-time these days, Morgan. This had better be damn important."

She extended her hand to Murata. "Good evening, general. I'd ask what brings you to my door, but I'm sure someone is about to tell me."

"They will, Madam President. May I introduce Doctor Lessart?"

Vandergraaf's eyes bored into Joe's. Ramirez had made him feel like an old friend, Vandergraaf like a corpse on an autopsy table. "Ah, yes, Doctor Joe Lessart. You were one of the founders of Hydra Research. You sold your company to the French. I can't say I approved."

Joe refused to allow Vandergraaf to intimidate him. He let the silence drift for a moment before he responded. "If America did not live so far beyond its means, we would have found a local buyer, Madam President. But it does, and we couldn't."

Vandergraaf's mouth tightened. Then she smiled and put out her hand. Her handshake was firm. "It pains me to say this, Doctor Lessart, but you are so right. Do you know my chief of staff?"

"Only by reputation. Good evening, Mister Stetterman."

Stetterman was a chunky African American with a reputation as a ruthless political operator. "Good evening, doctor."

"Seats, everyone," Vandergraaf said. "Morgan, the floor is yours and make this quick. My family's waiting."

"Thank you, Madam President. Earlier, my chief of staff received a message from General Murata asking for a meeting on an urgent matter of national security. The general ..."

Joe studied Vandergraaf as Ramirez spoke; he could imagine the mental cogs grinding away as she tried to work out why General Murata had contacted Ramirez instead of her.

"... is a woman of unimpeachable integrity, so I agreed. She provided me with a detailed report, a copy of which I have here. Before I pass it over—"

"Morgan!" Vandergraaf snapped. "Get to the point."

Ramirez dropped the document; it hit the table with a thump. "This document is proof of a conspiracy. It calls itself the Revival. It is a conspiracy at the heart of this administration, a conspiracy to destroy America's democratic institutions by suspending the Constitution and the United States Congress ... and appointing you, Madam President, president-for-life."

In an instant, Vandergraaf and Stetterman were on their feet, shouting, an explosion of such fury it took Murata's stentorian bellowing to restore order.

Vandergraaf waved away the posse of anxious Secret Service agents who burst in. "You have one minute, General Murata, to explain what this is all about, one minute before I have all you arrested."

"The vice president is half-right, Madam President. Yes, there is a conspiracy; the Revival, it's called. It is financed by five of America's wealthiest families. They want to restore America to its position as the world's most powerful nation. To do that, the Revival is developing bioweapons, smallpox most likely. They plan to use those weapons to destroy the greatest threat to their plans: China ... but not until it has taken over the United States government."

"You have to be kidding," Stetterman growled.

"No, I'm not. But the vice president is wrong when he names you, Madam President, as the leader of the Revival. You are not. Doctor Lessart has conclusive evidence the conspiracy is led by the vice president."

"I will make you will pay for those lies," Ramirez shouted, "by god, I will—"

"Sit down!" Vandergraaf's voice slashed through Ramirez's outrage. "General, please go on."

"Thank you, Madam President. As I said, Vice President Ramirez heads the conspiracy. We also have evidence your National Security Adviser, the Director of National Intelligence, the Secretary of Defense, and the Secretary of Homeland Security form the conspiracy's senior management group, along with Mister Chang of course. And it is no coincidence those men and woman are the founding members of New America, the political party the Revival established and funded to make Mister Ramirez the president. We were lucky New America's members had the sense to pick you as their presidential candidate instead."

Vandergraaf's face betrayed the shock of events. "These are extraordinary claims, general. I trust you have extraordinary evidence to support them."

Murata turned to Joe. "Doctor Lessart?"

"Do you recall a man by the name of Tom Mapathi, Madam President?" Joe asked.

"Let's see ... Yes, I remember him. He was one of my campaign team. He drank too much."

"Mapathi was the cut-out between the vice president and a bioweapons laboratory in Mexico. I recovered a laptop computer from the laboratory's chief of security, Bruce Kernow. He had exchanged thousands of emails with Mister Mapathi. From those emails, we were able to determine—"

Ramirez cut in, his voice a half-shout, eyes blazing, tanned cheeks blotched red with rage. "Enough! This is not what you told me earlier."

"You are quite correct, sir. It is not."

"Then what the hell are you talking about?"

"We concocted our report to show two things. First, the president led the Revival conspiracy. And second, you had no role in the conspiracy."

Ramirez rolled his eyes. "Oh, for f... No! I don't. What you said was correct. We checked."

"Not well enough. The real report does not implicate the president. It implicates you."

"Wrong, Lessart, wrong," Ramirez spit. He tapped the report, "This is irrefutable proof the president is the leader of the Revival."

"No, Mister Vice President. It is a fabrication, fraud. All your life you have wanted the presidency. Losing the nomination to Celia Vandergraaf was almost more than you could bear. You felt humiliated, betrayed. And when we offered you the presidency, you could not resist the temptation to take it any more than you could resist the temptation to punish the woman who had so humiliated you. We set a trap for you, Mister Ramirez ... a trap you fell right into."

"Lies, all lies!" Ramirez shouted.

"It's not, and you know it." Murata's voice was thick with contempt.

"You are—"

"Shut it, Morgan!" Vandergraaf said. "Continue, Doctor Lessart."

"Yes, ma'am ... You had to remove the president, Mister Ramirez. She—not China—was the biggest obstacle the Revival faced. But, more than anything you have ever wanted, you wanted her job. When our report offered you the chance to take it, you could not say no. You were so seduced by the idea you decided to use it to confront the president, arrest her, and in the chaos execute the first successful coup in American history."

"Lies, lies lies!" Ramirez shouted.

An aide burst in. "Excuse me, Madam President. I have Anna Jason for you."

Vandergraaf beckoned her over. After a whispered exchange, she waved the woman away.

"My apologies, everybody. Well, Mister Ramirez. I have just been informed the 824th Mobile Regiment's 1st Battalion has surrounded the White House and is not allowing anyone in or out. Is there anything you'd like to tell me about that?"

"How can I?" Ramirez shouted. "You're the leader of the conspiracy, not me."

"Just after the 824th Mobile Regiment left Andrews, the DC police asked for its authority to move. Its commander said she was following orders from the National Military Council—whatever that is—and the cops should move aside or she'd flatten them. Now why would she say such things?"

"What? The Council's orders were very clear; under no circumstances was Colonel Armitage to … I, uh… No, no, that wasn't what I meant to say."

"It's interesting you named the 1st Battalion's commander," Vandergraaf said. "I never mentioned her, though she could be a friend of yours, I guess … No, I think fellow-conspirator seems more likely. What do you think, Doctor Lessart?"

"Fellow-conspirator, Madam President."

"General Murata. Did you hear everything Mister Ramirez said?"

"I did, ma'am. And I am happy to appear as a witness for the prosecution when the treacherous sonofabitch … Uh, my apologies, Madam President."

"`For what? He is treacherous sonofabitch," Vandergraaf turned back to Ramirez. "Your own words condemn you, Mister Ramirez. It's over, so do yourself a fav—"

Ramirez grabbed a stone candle holder from the coffee table and launched himself at Celia Vandergraaf.

Without a moment's thought, Joe burst out of his chair to intercept Ramirez. The weight of his body bludgeoned the man aside, driving him to the floor in a welter of arms and legs. As Joe struggled to contain Ramirez rage, the man's arm swung down and smashed the candle holder into his head.

The blackness claimed Joe.

—49—

Mesmerized, Joe stared at the drama playing out on his television screen.

Thousands of police had flooded the streets as word of the Revival's attempted coup spread. One had just crossed three hundred feet of open ground, alone, her pistol holstered. Now she confronted soldiers from the 824th Mobile Regiment, their armored vehicles and combat robots arrayed behind them, their drones orbiting overhead.

The police officer spoke. The soldiers listened, sometimes nodding. The exchange continued for five minutes or so, then stopped.

The police officer waited.

No one moved.

Until the soldiers laid their weapons on the ground and sat down, joined soon after by the crews of the armored vehicles.

"Give the cop a medal," Joe called out, "one the size of a plate."

He flicked the television off, exhilarated by what he had seen: A lone police officer had persuaded her fellow Americans—decent people following the orders of treasonous superior officers—to accept the rule of law.

Not that things had gone as well elsewhere.

Ramirez had ordered more than the Revival's Slingshot units onto the streets. Within an hour, the paramilitaries had joined the coup; the National Militia Alliance, they called themselves. Heavily armed and driven by Revivalist ideology, they had fought hard. Even now, many refused to surrender, leaving the air over too many American cities hung thick with smoke, their streets littered with the dead and wounded of both sides.

But the Revival had mobilized more armed units than anyone expected. So many, the experts—of which there were hundreds across every media channel, all pontificating on matters beyond their experience or understanding—predicted the Revival would prevail.

But, in the end, few of the Slingshot units fired a shot. Their men and women, confused and angry, had refused to fight when they realized their commanders had lied to them, fatally weakening the coup. But it was the overwhelming show of passive opposition which threw balance in the Republic's favor; millions of ordinary Americans had faced down any Slingshot unit which had hesitated, forcing their surrender.

For a country awash with guns, a remarkable achievement. But it had been close.

A nurse came in, flustered.

"Hey, Jonah!" Joe said, "When will the doctor let me out?"

"Uh, later ... Someone's here to see you, Doctor Lessart."

"Who is ... Oh, whatever." Joe added when he realized he was talking to himself.

Two men appeared. They flashed ID cards. "We're with the Secret Service, Doctor Lessart," one said. "If you're up for a visit from the president, we need to give this place the all-clear."

"Is my hair okay?"

The agent laughed. "It's fine. Ugly bandage though."

The agents declared the room safe and Celia Vandergraaf entered, her face lined and gray. "I wish I felt as well as you look."

"It was only a bump on the head. Madam President."

"I'm pleased to hear it. I can't stay long, but I wanted to thank you myself. General Murata has told me what you've been through. For a turncoat who sold out to the Frogs, you've done well."

Joe laughed. "I try."

"Those Revival bastards almost beat us. Without you, they might have."

"General Murata deserves the credit. She designed the bluff, she tossed the bait at Ramirez, and she understood him well enough to know he could not resist."

"And thank god he didn't. But you still risked your life. Now, before I go, a couple of things. The State Department is trying to find André Tanadi and your crew, while the FBI searches for Skylar Rafiki, Cal Grujic, and Klara Thyaka. My staff will get in touch as soon as they have any news."

"Thank you, Madam President," Joe said, but Vandergraaf had gone.

General Murata appeared. "How was the president?"

"Struggling, I think."

"I cannot understand why anyone would want the job … You okay, Joe?"

"I am; Ramirez didn't hit me very hard … Any news I haven't heard a hundred times already?"

Murata nodded. "Some. Remember when we were talking about Ramirez? We couldn't understand why the Revival had cut him so much slack."

"Yes, I do. It was very odd."

"Well, it turns out we got luckier than we deserved. Director Agnelli told me launching Slingshot was intended to be a collective decision, one made by the entire Revival leadership; none of them ever imagined one of their number would go rogue."

"It's like they had one nuclear missile launch key, not two or three. They were mad."

"Not mad. Too trusting. Most of the Revival's leadership were out of Washington. Only Ramirez and Wilson, the National Security Advisor, were in town. The thought of becoming president so consumed Ramirez he could not ignore the opportunity we handed him. His entire focus became making the coup happen."

"Didn't he and Wilson talk?" Joe asked.

"Ramirez called Wilson in to go over the report with him. Wilson said it was a trap. So Chang takes him into Ramirez's study and beats him to death. The FBI found his body the next day."

Joe shook his head. "Jesus. Imagine those bastards running America."

"I'd rather not. Anyway, it's over, thank god."

"I'm not sure it is, general."

"What? Come on, Joe! The coup's failed and the FBI is busy arresting the Revival's senior people. That sounds like over to me."

"Except it's not. Everyone assumes Ramirez, Wilson, and the rest of them ran the conspiracy. But they didn't; they were just ciphers. The Gang of 5 are the ones with the power. They are the Revival, general. Until the FBI arrests them, the threat's as real as it ever was."

"Hmm … You might have a point," Murata conceded.

"Might have a point? Ramirez and his Washington cronies could not finance the Revival. We're talking hundreds of millions of dollars, money they do not have. The Gang of 5 pays for the Revival, and, in my experience, the people who pay the bills are always the ones who make the decisions. So, please tell me the FBI has arrested them."

Murata shifted in her seat. "Ah, well, uh … No, they haven't, and they probably won't. What you gave to the FBI was circumstantial; it wasn't enough to prove those families were the Revival's founders. They are powerful people, and they are clever, especially when it comes to moving cash around."

"We're not talking pennies here, general. Setting up the Valle de Banderas and Carbonel facilities would have cost the Revival a fortune. Surely you can't move so much money around without being noticed?"

"Director Agnelli told me the Gang of 5 channeled their funding through shell companies in Panama, the Caymans, Turkey, Britain, and from there on through blind trust to godknows where. The Treasury's Office of Terrorism and Financial Intelligence has set up a task force to find out, but it will take years to unscramble that omelet."

"Which means what? The Gang of 5 gives us the finger and carry on as normal?"

"I'm afraid so. Without hard evidence, the FBI can't kick their doors down and drag them off to be questioned."

"Something America will live to regret. Until the FBI arrests the Gang of 5, we've only hurt the Revival. We have not killed it. It will be back, I promise you."

"I don't think so. But it's the FBI's problem now, one I'm sure they can manage. And, to be fair, they do have thousands of cases to process."

"Really? So, we let the Revival regroup while the FBI processes the paperwork?"

"Joe! Enough, okay? You have done your bit. Let the professionals take it from here. Now, the medics tell me they plan to discharge you today. Where can I find you?"

"Adam's got me a suite at the Grand Hyatt."

"I'll be in touch."

—50—

"This is Karl Stetterman, the president's chief of staff."

"Hi Karl," Joe replied. "What can I do for you?"

"We have found André Tanadi and your crew; they're all safe and well in a camp on Mindanao. The Filipinos will have all the paperwork done in the next few days; the president thought you might like to be there when they are released."

Joe's spirits soared. "More than you can imagine, Karl. Tell me where to be, and I'll start organizing my flights."

"No need. The president has arranged for the air force to fly you there."

"Wow! What can I say, Karl?"

"Nothing. We owe you. Captain Morrie Steyn, the Naval Attaché from the embassy, will meet you in Manila. He is a good guy. He'll make whatever arrangements you need to reclaim your ship and move your guys out of their camp."

"Thanks, Karl."

"No problems. One of my staff is on her way to take you to Andrews. Call me when you're back."

"I will, Karl, and please give my thanks to the president."

•••

As the Philippine Air Force helicopter banked into a sharp turn, the loadmaster tapped Joe on the arm and pointed down at the makeshift sheds scattered across a treeless, dusty compound surrounded by razor-wire fences.

The helicopter flared hard and touched down in a blizzard of red dust. Engines ran down and the blades stopped.

An army officer in fatigues stepped forward and saluted. "Welcome, Doctor Lessart. I am Major Jurado, the camp commandant. This way, please."

They headed for a long, low building outside the compound. A tall, thin man stood outside.

Joe broke into a run. "André? Is that you?"

"Am I glad to see you," said his old friend.

Joe took André in his arms and squeezed him hard. The man was all bones. "Tell me you're okay?"

"I am now. Things have ..." André stopped, all choked up. "It was difficult," he went on, "but we stuck together, which made things easier. And Jurado treated us well, because we weren't Abu Sayyaf, I think. I don't how we'd have gone without him. But I knew, we all knew, you would never give up on us."

Joe's eyes filled. "And I never did."

"Come on. The crew are waiting for you."

They broke the embrace and went inside where a tidal wave of Indonesians engulfed Joe, crying, laughing, talking. It took a while to settle things down.

Joe pointed to the helicopter. "There's our ride out of here. The *Sophie Scholl* is waiting for us. We'll spend the night onboard, and then tomorrow I've organized flights for you back home to your families."

This time there was no crying, just whooping and cheering.

•••

Joe came down from the bridge. "I just had a chat with Matti Seppä. Remember him?"

"The Finnish guy? Didn't he run a tech dive shop in Puerto Galera?"

"Still does. Without his help, I'd never have found the *Sophie Scholl*. He was looking for you when the Revival warned him off. I made him bail out to Finland until things calmed down. I owe him."

"What else have I missed?"

"A lot, but I'll tell you everything as soon as Steyn's finished the paperwork and is on his way back to Manila."

"You'd better," said André as Steyn walked into the saloon.

"So, captain," Joe said. "Is the embassy happy?"

Steyn shook his head. "No, it's embarrassed. The illegal abduction of an American citizen by US Navy SEALs is bad enough, but the hijacking of an Indonesian-registered ship in Indonesian waters along with its Indonesian crew and the detention of an Indonesian ferry carrying hundreds of Indonesian civilians?"

Joe had to laugh. "I know it's a wild guess, captain, but it sounds to me like the Indonesians are a bit upset."

"You have no idea. The State Department has its work cut out sorting out what's turning into a massive shit storm."

"I'm not sure we can do anything to help, Morrie."

"Probably not, but if there is, State will contact you. And I'm sorry the US Navy took orders from the wrong people, André."

André grinned. "It could have been worse, Morrie. I put two SEALs in hospital, the CSS was the neatest bit of gear I have ever seen, and being onboard a nuclear sub was a thrill … Well, it was until the crew locked me up in a cupboard. And I didn't much go for the whole hood and orange overalls thing. Or the cable-ties. Or the months behind razor wire. Or sharing my day with Abu Sayyaf assholes, eating shit food, wondering what was going on in the real world."

Steyn's face had flushed red. "What can I say?"

"Nothing would be best," Joe said.

"Yeah ... You sure you don't need anything more from me?"

"We're fine. André and I have a lot to catch up on, and the crew seem determined to ignore my orders to leave the *Sophie Scholl* alone, so we are being well cared for. We'll call if we need you."

"Right, I'm off. Thanks for the beer, guys. And I love your dive boat, by the way. She's a beauty."

"You go first," said André when Steyn had gone. "I want to hear everything. And, when you have told me your story, I'll bore the shit out of you with mine."

•••

André and Joe were still talking when Omar knocked on the saloon door. "Sorry to interrupt, but I need to speak with both of you."

"Sure," Joe said. "Come in. Some tea?"

"No, thank you. I do not say much."

Joe shot André an anxious glance. "What do you want to talk about, captain?" he asked.

"We do not want flights tomorrow. The crew has talked about this."

"I don't understand. Don't you want go home?"

"The *Sophie Scholl* is our ship, Joe. You say take to Semarang. So we do."

"Is this what everyone wants?" Joe asked.

"I tell everyone they go home if they want with no shame," Omar replied, "but they say no. I tried to change their minds, but they still say no."

"What about you?" Joe asked.

"I stay."

"You have spoken with your families?"

Omar nodded. "They understand."

"The monsoon cuts up rough this time of year."

"We are sailors, Joe. And the *Sophie Scholl* is very fine ship."

"If that is what you all want. When will we be ready for sea?"

"Benny says two days to check everything, then we go to San Jose for fuel and supplies; it is arranged. Then we go to Semarang."

"You sure?"

"Sure. Thank you, Joe. Thank you, André."

"Incredible," André said after Omar had left. "I'm not sure we deserve it."

"I'm sure we don't. I still feel guilty about what happened."

"Don't. You came back for us. Now, before I have to listen to yet more of your tales of derring-do…"

"Smartass," Joe muttered.

"…let me ask you this. Are you thinking what I'm thinking?"

"We should make the trip back to Semarang? Too right."

"I'll tell Omar. Now, where was I?"

•••

Joe had not tried to sleep. Why would he? He knew his mind would never allow it.

There was still no word of Rafiki, Klara, and Grujic. No matter what Joe told himself, nothing could relieve the awful certainty they were no longer alive.

He went to the *Sophie Scholl*'s stern and looked to seaward across Camp Sierra's wharf. Had he swum in, recovered the datastores and gotten out as the grenades tumbled down?

He must have been insane.

—51—

Joe wiped the grease off his hands with a wad of cotton waste. "I never want to see that pump again, Benny."

The *Sophie Scholl*'s chief engineer laughed. "For sure. It is an evil pump."

"When we are back to Semarang, tell Rikki you want it replaced. It's a piece of crap. Do you need a hand with anything else?"

"No. Arif will help with the filters this afternoon."

"Right then, I need to clean up. Catch you later."

Back in the saloon, Joe found André sprawled face down on a bench. "Doing it tough, are we?"

André rolled over. "After months locked in a Filipino prison camp with fuck all to do, I have earned the right to lie around doing fuck all."

Joe laughed. It was wonderful to have his best friend back. "Beer?"

"Nah, too early."

"Well I need one," Joe pulled a beer out of the fridge. "Bloody pump. I'm sick of it. I've told Benny to swap it out."

"Good move. Nothing worse than standing in the shower all soaped up when the fresh water goes off."

The phone rang.

"Yeah?" Joe said. "Oh, hi Budi … Ah, okay. I'll come up."

"What is it?" André asked.

"Satphone call. Back in a minute."

"I'll take it in the control room, Budi," Joe said when he got to the bridge.

He picked up. "Joe Lessart."

"Doctor Lessart, this is Karl Stetterman."

"What can I do for you, Karl?"

"I'm sorry, Doctor, but I have news, and it's not good. The FBI has found Klara Thyaka."

A strange, icy calm settled over Joe; he felt remote, detached. "They're sure?"

"One of the people the FBI arrested told them where to find the grave. Dental records and DNA have confirmed her identity. There can be no doubt."

"What about Cal Grujic?"

"I'm sorry to say the FBI has found him too. They were together."

Joe felt hollowed out. "Klara's family? Have they been told?"

"Yes. The funeral is next week. Friday, I believe."

"I'll call her mother."

"Please. Don't hesitate to contact my office if there's anything we can do to help."

"Thank you, Karl."

Joe knew what he had to do. He picked up his cell and punched in the numbers.

"Yes?" the familiar voice of Freddie Kemani answered.

"It's me. We need to talk."

"Of course, doctor. Business or pleasure?"

"Business. I need to find out who killed a friend of mine."

"Name?"

"Klara Thyaka. I'll send you everything I've got."

"No need," Kemani said. "I have seen the news. The FBI found her close to a Revival safe house in the Alleghenies. When can we meet?"

"After Klara's funeral. I'll call you."

"I'll find out what I can by then."

"I'll pay a million for the names of the people who killed her."

"Oh, no. A million is not enough for what you want. I'll need two."

"You are a goddammed bloodsucker."

"No, I'm a businessman, Doctor Lessart. I have outgoings. Two million."

"A third up-front. The rest on delivery."

"I can trust you, so yes."

Joe sighed; the sooner he waved goodbye to Freddie Kemani, the better; the man was costing him a fortune. "Just get me the names."

"Oh, I will. Goodbye."

Paralyzed by guilt, Joe sat in silence until André stuck his head around the door. "What's up?"

"They found Klara. The funeral's next week."

André slid into the seat beside Joe. "I'm so sorry."

Joe had his head in his hands. "Jesus, I'm a sad sonofabitch. I don't think she ever loved me, and now look at the state I'm in."

"Doesn't matter. You loved her."

"I did. Which is why I have talked with Freddie Kemani."

"Your Mister Fixit? Why would you... Oh, shit, you're not going—"

"After the scum who killed her? I am."

"Come on, Joe. You have done your bit. Let the FBI deal with this."

"I can't. She got tangled up in this whole business because of me, and now she's dead."

"Stop this, for chrissakes! Klara's death is the Revival's responsibility, not yours."

"No, André. It is. She'd still be alive if I hadn't got Cal Grujic involved ... No, hear me out. I have to bring the people who killed her to account, and I will. And don't tell me it's survivor's guilt ..."

"Which it is."

"... or I need professional help ..."

"Which you do."

"... or I should leave it to the FBI ..."

"Which you should."

"... because I am not going to do any of those things."

André threw his hands up. "Oh, for chrissakes! You'll need help. What can I do?"

Joe shook his head. "Not now. Klara's funeral is Friday. Then we'll talk."

—52—

Joe handed the photo back to Kemani. "This Charlie Peretz. Are you sure he's the one?"

Kemani tapped the folder on the desk. "I am. Everything is in there."

Joe frowned. "Call me cynical, but how come you could find Peretz when the FBI couldn't?"

"Money jogs people's memories. And, when money didn't work, my guys could be very persuasive. And they could move much faster than the FBI; all you wanted was a name. We didn't have to build a case a prosecutor would accept and a jury believe."

"You're right there, Freddie. The only court Peretz will ever see is mine. So where is he now?"

"Argentina. A place called Estancia Rosita. north of Mendoza, right up against the Andes. Very pretty, I'm told."

"What's he doing there?"

"Staying out of the FBI's hands. Our source says there are another three or four Revival foot-soldiers with him, probably doing the same."

Joe picked up the file. "Let me go through this. I'll be in touch."

●●●

André closed the folder. "Peretz is your man, no doubt about it. Are you still going to—"

"Make him pay for what he did? Yes, I am."

André sighed. "I won't waste my time arguing with you. What's the plan?"

"I'll talk with Freddie about logistics and so on. The hard part is doing the job. I've never killed a professional killer."

"Just the thought of it scares the crap out of me."

"Me too. Come on, it's time you met Max."

●●●

"This will not be easy, guys," Beharry said.

"For chrissakes, Max!" Joe said. "I can't see why. We can be in and out in a couple of days."

"Joe's right," André added. "Peretz is just one man."

Max Beharry leaned across the table. "You two are amateurs. And let me tell you something about amateurs: They don't know shit. You don't know shit, Joe."

"Maybe I don't, but this is what I want to do."

"You're not thinking straight. Listen, both of you. These things always sound easy. Like you say, how hard can it be? Fly into Mendoza, find the target, blow him away, and then exfiltrate the hell out. Any problems, throw money at them, and they'll go away."

"That's how I see it."

"Except nothing in the killing business is ever easy. Things can go to crap in seconds. When they do—and they will—people die."

"Which is why I need you."

"No kidding," Beharry said, "but I have another problem. This whole business is a terrible idea. Even if Peretz killed my own mother, I would not go anywhere near the man, and especially not if he was holed up in goddammed Argentina."

"Come on, Max. Please! I need your help. This is what you do."

Beharry shrugged. "Helping you with the Revival was one thing. Stopping it was worth the risks involved. But killing Peretz is all about revenge, and revenge is not the way to deal with Klara's death."

"Please, Max."

"There's a saying about taking revenge: Dig two graves ... You need to be smart about this, not emotional. Take the file to the FBI. Because it's you, they will take it seriously."

"They haven't so far. Besides, Peretz is holed up in Argentina. Freddie says it will take years to extradite him to the States. Come on. Are you going to help me or not?"

Beharry threw his hands up. "I shouldn't, but I will. On one condition. I run the operation. If I think things are getting too risky, we get the hell out, no arguments. I will not allow you to kill yourself. Agreed?"

"Agreed... and thanks."

"Don't thank me. If it was anyone else, Joe, I'd have walked away. Right, I'll talk with Freddie. We'll need a heap of gear; the sooner he can organize things, the better. While he is doing that, I'll find somewhere we can train in peace. But I have a question for André: Are you planning to go along as well?"

"Of course," André replied.

"To do what exactly?"

"Um, not sure ... Wave a gun around? Act all menacing? I am pretty big."

Beharry gave André a thin smile. "Big men make big targets. But at least you're not trying to bullshit me."

"Let me be honest. While Joe was taking on the Revival, I was sitting on my ass in some godforsaken Filipino prison camp while Abu Sayyaf assholes crapped on about jihad and told me how fucked-up America is.

Now I want to do my bit, perhaps not the best motive in the world, but Joe is my friend. I can't let him do this on his own."

Beharry sighed in defeat. "Fine." He took a card from his wallet and handed it to Joe. "Call this woman. You can trust her. We saw combat in Afghanistan."

Joe scanned the card and frowned. "Angela Liebmann, personal trainer? What's this about?"

"None of you are fit enough, André especially. And you will need basic combat skills to do this mission. Tell Angie you will want her for four weeks, full time. If she says she is too busy, throw money at her until she's not. When she says yes, I'll brief her on what's needed. Right, I'll see you both later."

"Uh-oh," André said when Beharry had gone. "Four weeks with Liebmann sounds unpleasant, Joe."

"It does. Come on, André. Liebmann's world of pain can wait. It's time for lunch with Adam at Addison's, and he's paying."

"You're kidding! Adam never, ever pays for lunch."

"He will. If he refuses, I won't give him the check for the money I owe. And I've spoken to the sommelier; I have arranged for two bottles of burgundy so ridiculously expensive Adam's credit card is going to explode."

●●●

Adam took Joe aside before they sat down. "I wanted to say how sorry I was to hear about Klara."

"Thanks. She had moved on, but I never could."

"She was a fine woman ... Listen, this whole Revival business. For the first time in ages, what I was doing was not about money. I cannot remember the last time I did; when I was a grunt probably. But it has changed me for the better, I think. If you ever need my help, for anything at all, just ask."

"Thanks, Adam, I will. We made a great team."

"Hey!" André called out. "The beer's getting warm."

Joe sat down, happy to let Addison's comforting, understated opulence take his mind off Klara. He reached into his jacket pocket, pulled out an envelope, and handed it to Adam. "Before we get started, this is for you."

Adam tore open the envelope. He whistled. "You don't often see checks these days, and this one's a monster. Thank you, Joe."

"Tell me if my math is off."

"Your math is fine." Adam waved one of the staff over. "Matches and an ashtray, please."

"Yes, sir."

"He'll bring them," Adam said with a chuckle, "but let's see how he tells me I can't smoke in here."

The man returned. "Matches and ashtray, sir. May I show you to the smoking area?"

The three men exchanged grins.

Adam struck a match. "You can relax. I'm only going to set fire to this."

When the envelope was well alight, Adam dropped the flaming mass into the ashtray, and returned it to the waiter.

"You didn't have to do that," Joe said, "but thank you. I think lunch should be on me."

"An offer I will accept. Now, why are you two hopping up and down like someone's jammed pineapples up your asses?"

"Lunch first, I think."

●●●

Adam shook his head. "I know what an ops plan should look like, Joe. Yours is crap."

"Give us a break," Joe said. "We haven't had time to work things through. We're meeting with Max Beharry tomorrow. We'll have a better idea what we're up against then."

"Where and when?"

"Why do you ask?"

André slapped the table. "I do not believe it! You want in, don't you, Adam?"

"Yes, I want in. I may be ten years older than you, but I'm not dead yet."

"Ten years?" Joe snorted. "As if, grandpa."

"At least I was a marine," Adam shot back.

"Years ago. This is not a game. I'm going to Argentina to blow a man's brains out."

André put a hand on Joe's arm. "Whoa, my man. Not so loud."

"Sorry," Joe said. "Listen, Adam. I'm talking cold-blooded murder. Are you sure you want a slice of that?"

Adam gave an emphatic nod. "Yup."

"Sounds to me like you're having one hell of a mid-life crisis. Why can't you buy a Porsche like every other rich asshole?"

"Don't be a smartass. Come on; it's simple: Three people to get this done might be enough, but four is better, so I'm in."

Joe knew better than to argue. "Welcome aboard, Adam."

"I knew you'd see things my way ... Besides, I already have two Porsches. One more would just be crass."

—53—

"Contact left, two hundred," screamed Angie Liebmann, a woman with a full-on 'don't-fuck-with-me' attitude.

Joe, André, and Adam hurled themselves into the dirt, fumbled with their guns, and sprayed rounds at a pop-up target.

"Too slow. Break contact. On me. Move, move, move!"

The trio struggled to their feet and shambled off.

Max Beharry and Freddie Kemani stood on a bluff overlooking the dry creek down which Liebmann hounded her sorry charges.

Kemani shook his head. "What a rabble. They don't fill me with much confidence."

"Adam and Joe are as rusty as all hell, but they'll pick it up."

"The marines were a long time ago, Max. And Joe never was one; he never made it past OCS. What about André?"

Beharry sighed. "I worry about him. He has no military experience, and he was months in a Filipino camp. Angie says he's recovering well physically, but she's not sure about the rest of him."

"He's angry."

"He sure is, and it bothers me. Angry men are unreliable under pressure. I'll talk with Joe so he knows what to expect."

The three men scrambled up a steep slope. Joe stumbled, then slid into Adam and André, the three of them tumbling back to where they had started.

Beharry spit on the ground. "Fuck me! What a bunch of clowns."

Kemani laughed. "I hope Angie doesn't break one."

"I hope she does. It might make the dumb bastards think again."

•••

A sweat-stained wreck, Joe sat across the table from Beharry. He was exhausted. Liebman had put them through yet another brutal day.

"So, Max. What did you want to talk about?"

"You're smart. All the blundering around, all the mistakes, all the 'oh, fuck' moments must have told you combat operations are and always will be a complete mystery to you. Isn't it time you rethought this?"

Joe shook his head. "It's too late."

"It's never too late, so listen to me. Peretz is an experienced, ruthless criminal. He is still alive because he understands the business he's in. His buddies do too; they're all professionals. Peretz is holed up in an estancia built like a damn fort. The terrain's not on our side. And, to make things worse, we will have no real-time tactical intelligence, no drone surveillance, no backup, no casevac support, and you are a bunch of bungling amateurs. All of which makes Peretz a hard target, one even experienced professionals would find a challenge."

"I still think we can do it, especially now Angie's agreed to be part of the team."

Beharry snorted his derision. "You don't have the experience to know what to think."

"But you do, which is why you're coming along. So, give me a straight answer to a straight question. What are our chances?"

"Of killing Peretz? Good. Of Angie and I surviving? Good; we've done this sort of thing most of our adult lives. But your chances of making it out alive? Bad ... very bad."

"We're grown-ups. We can manage."

"Not in the assassination business, you can't. André and Adam are only coming along because they don't want to let you down, André most of all. He feels guilty because you have carried the fight on your own up to now. And the way he was treated by the Revival has left him angry. He wants to pay them back by helping you kill Peretz. As for Adam, he thinks he has to prove himself."

"Which is a problem how?" Joe asked. "We need committed people."

"Not if the commitment is emotional. Which it is, for all three of you... Remember the Afghani girl with blue eyes?"

"I'll never forget her, Max."

"Emotional people always make poor decisions under pressure. As I did, and decent people died. You're heading the same way."

"You're overstating the problem."

"Let me sum up what motivates you guys. You: guilt. André: guilt and anger. Adam: making his life mean something more than money. So don't tell me I'm overstating the problem; I'm not. I'm talking to you because nobody can stop this madness except you."

Joe's face had hardened into a mulish scowl. "I'm not going to, Max."

"Your call," Max said. "Angie and I will be coming home. You three? Sorry, but the chances are you'll end up face down in a patch of Argentinian dirt. Dead."

Joe put his hands up. "Fine, I'll put it to Adam and André. If they agree with you, I don't want you or Angie to come along either. I'll do this on my own."

"You are kidding!" Max said. "If the boys say no, forget Peretz and move on."

"I'm sorry, I won't. Now, let me talk to them."

"I'll be with Angie."

Joe forced himself to his feet and limped over to where André and Adam lay stretched out on the ground, eyes closed, exhausted. He could see Beharry's point.

Neither of them inspired much confidence. But he knew they would not pull out, not now.

—54—

As the latest drone wandered past overhead, Beharry's voice muttered in Joe's earpiece. "Victor-One and Victor-Two outbound with four hostiles. Negative Tango-One, I say again negative Tango-One."

"Goddammit," André whispered.

Joe shared the sentiment. Beharry had been right. Even with five people, killing Peretz was never going to be an easy, in-and-out operation.

Their seventh day on task was almost over. They'd been demanding days: the move from their layup point to the ambush site before dawn, the hours spent waiting for Peretz—Tango-One—to turn up, and then the pull back to the layup point for another cold night without a fire or hot food before starting all over the next day.

What made it worse was a growing certainty all the team's efforts were going to be for nothing. They had seen plenty of Peretz as he moved around the estancia; the red cap he always wore was hard to miss. But there he had stayed. Well out of range. Untouchable.

Victor-One—a battered green dual-cab—rolled past on its way to the highway, Victor-Two close behind. Joe had One's driver in his sights for thirty seconds.

A simple shot.

Joe was an amateur, but even he would not have missed.

He could taste failure, bitter. Another day squandered. Three more, Beharry had said, and they would have to pull out. Joe had started to argue, but the man's face made it obvious there was no point.

"Let's hope he turns up tomorrow," André said. "Water?"

"Please."

André slid back. Joe stared down the empty road. His mind wandered again as the minutes wormed past.

A soft thud.

As Joe turned, a cold, hard shape stabbed into his neck.

A whispered voice. "You move, asshole, and I'll pull the trigger."

Joe froze.

A blow to the side of his head smashed him off his rifle. Red mist clouded his eyes.

"Picking the best ambush site on this road wasn't smart, boys. Our drones had no problem spotting you."

The best ambush site? Joe could not believe Beharry would have made such a simple mistake.

His arms were dragged back, and wrists cable-tied. Hands tore off his radio and headset and jammed a black hood over his head.

A kick in the ribs. Liquid fire. Joe screamed.

"For fuck's sake, stop wasting time," a second voice said.

"Just showing them who's in charge."

"Like they don't already know, ya fucking moron."

Hands hauled Joe down to the road and heaved him into a vehicle. Another body was thrown in beside him.

"André! You okay?" Joe whispered.

"The bastards hit me hard, but I think so."

"Any sign of the others?"

"No. They must have missed them."

Joe swallowed hard. Forget no soldier gets left behind, Beharry had said. If the operation was compromised, those who could were to get out fast. There would be no heroic attempts at rescue; trying would just get everyone killed.

He and André were on their own now.

"I'm sorry I got you into this mess,."

"Don't be. We're partners."

The vehicle jerked into motion. It gathered speed. Cornering hard, Joe and André were tossed around in back until, without warning, the driver slammed on the brakes, driving the pair head-first into the cab.

The tailgate went down with a bang. Hands hauled Joe out and hustled him up steps into what had to be the estancia. It was cold inside; he shivered, but not from the cold.

His luck had just run out, and he knew it.

They stopped. A door banged open. Hands pushed him onto a chair, cut his wrists free, retied them to the chair, and ripped the hood off.

There was a crash as the door slammed shut. The men had gone.

The light was intense. Joe's eyes watered. They were in a small room with whitewashed walls and shuttered windows. Apart from André, also bound to a heavy wooden chair, the room was empty.

"What happens now?" André asked.

Joe knew the answer, but he kept it to himself. "No idea."

•••

When the door reopened, the last daylight leaking past the shutters had long since faded to black.

A man entered. He was tall and overweight, a fleshy face framed by silver-gray hair cut long enough to graze his shoulders. His face was puffy, with full lips below a generous nose. He wore a well-cut jacket over open-necked blue shirt, designer jeans, and hand-tooled boots. Shirt and jeans were doing a poor job of holding back a massive belly.

But it was man's the eyes which snagged Joe's attention; pebbles of gray-blue, piercing under heavy lids.

Angry eyes.

The man strode over, his hand-tooled boots smacking the floor. Without warning, his fist whipped around into Joe's mouth. The blow knocked Joe over, chair and all. His head hit the floor with a sickening thud.

Joe moaned in pain.

The man grabbed the chair. With a grunt, he dragged Joe back upright. He stepped back, face red with the effort.

Joe spit blood from wrecked lips. "You should be more careful, you fat fuck. You're one inch from a fatal heart attack."

The man's fist drove into Joe's stomach and doubled him over, leaving him gasping for breath. "Be polite, Doctor Lessart."

Joe fought to lift his head. "Who the hell are you?"

"Oh, dear. I have forgotten my manners. I'm Mark Dassler ... the Mark Dassler."

"Never heard of you, sorry,."

But he had. He was one of Skylar Rafiki's Gang of 5.

Dassler frowned. "You must have. I'd be number one on the Forbes Rich List if it wasn't for everything the Chinese stole from me."

"Mark Dassler? Let me see ... Uh, no, I don't think so ... Oh, wait ... Yes, I have heard of you. Your brother died. The police said it was no accident, not that they ever laid any charges. You know what, Mister Dassler? You seem like a bit of a psycho; maybe you—"

Another fist. "Shut your damn mouth."

Joe's chest heaved as he fought for air. "Sorry," he wheezed. "Point withdrawn."

"Smart man... You have caused me a great deal of trouble, doctor. And I know why you're here."

"No, you don't. How the hell could you?"

Dassler dissolved in laughter, head back, hands slapping thighs. "Because a mutual friend of ours told me," he said once he had recovered.

"Go ahead; waste your time. I never believe what fat people say to me. It's a character def—"

For a man carrying so much weight, Dassler moved fast. He spun around and drove a booted foot into Joe's bruised body.

The impact catapulted Joe and the chair backwards. Again, his head smacked into the floor. Again, he fought for air, half-blinded by pain. Again, Dassler lifted him back, breathing hard.

"Where were we? Oh, yes. Our mutual friend, Freddie Kemani."

"You're lying." But Joe knew Dassler wasn't.

The man beamed at Joe. "I do like Freddie. He will do anything if the price is right. He knew Charlie Peretz was one of my people; he thought I should know you and your friend were coming after him."

"Fuck off," Joe muttered. But why was Dassler only talking about him and André? How come Kemani hadn't told him about the rest of the team?

"Your problem, doctor, is you still believe in the old-fashioned virtues, things like honesty and trust. Well, Freddie doesn't give a rat's ass for any of those things. Money is all he cares about; how could I say no when he gave me a call and said he could deliver you to my doorstep for such a reasonable fee?"

"He wouldn't do that."

"You're the one sat there, trussed up like a hog."

"Better hog than psychopath," Joe spit.

Dassler kicked André's chair. "Tell me, Doctor Tanadi. How's trusting your life to this idiot working out for you?"

"He's a better man than you'll ever be," André said.

"I don't doubt it. I am evil, through and through; I have never pretended otherwise. Now, I have a question. What were the two of you thinking? That you could just go in with no backup and kill one of my best men? Freddie said you were a pair of clowns. How right he was."

Joe sat there, awash with a sullen despair. His pain-wrecked body made it hard to think. He wasn't surprised Kemani had sold them out; the man's middle name was venal. But why hadn't Kemani told Dassler about Beharry and Liebmann? And where was Adam?

It made no sense.

But then it did.

Sick certainty flooded Joe. Beharry and Liebmann were part of the betrayal. If the Revival had suborned Kemani, they would have suborned them too, though some small shred of decency must have made Beharry try so hard to persuade him to give up on Peretz.

As for Adam, he must be dead. Beharry and Liebmann would have killed him, probably so he did not complicate their escape.

None it mattered now. Nobody could help him and André.

Joe tried to keep his voice steady. "Fine, Mister Dassler, you win."

A manic smile spread across Dassler's face as he bobbed up and down on his toes. "Yes, yes. You lose, Doctor Lessart, and my Revival wins."

"Your Revival? What are you talking about?"

Dassler laughed. "You poor, deluded fool. Mark Dassler is the Revival."

"Then what a clusterfuck you are. Tell me, how did Ramirez work out for you? Oh, yes, not well at all. And then he trashed your coup by going it alone. As for you running the Revival, you don't. Ramirez told the FBI a council did."

Dassler gave a magisterial sniff of disdain. "The council was nothing but a bunch of pompous Washington assholes. They thought they ran things because that is what I wanted them to think."

"I don't believe you. And what about your psycho billionaire friends? They're paying for the Revival too, so you only get one vote out of five, which makes you a lying prick."

That earned Joe a savage kick in the ribs.

"I did warn you," Dassler said once Joe had recovered. "And, for the record, yes, you are right. My friends are funding the Revival, but they defer to me on the major decisions, though it did take some, uh … persuasion."

"I apologize," Joe said when the pain had subsided. "I was wrong. You do make the decisions. You are responsible for the deaths of Klara Thyaka, Skylar Rafiki, and Cal Grujic. You and nobody else. Just you."

A dismissive wave of the hand. "I didn't kill them, though I did give the orders, sure."

"But why?" Joe asked.

"Grujic and Rafiki knew too much. As for Klara, she was collateral damage. Betraying you was the hardest thing she ever did. But I gave her a choice. Either she gave you up, or we would break every bone in her mother's body, one bone at a time. She was smart; she chose to give you up. Of course, I didn't tell her she'd die either way."

From somewhere deep and desperate Joe summoned up an explosive heave that threw him and his chair towards his tormentor.

Who laughed as he stepped back to let Joe crash at his feet.

Dassler ran the toe of his boot through Joe's sweat-matted hair. "You're a dead man, doctor," he said as he heaved Joe upright, "but the Revival will go on. And it will succeed, because the United States and China are too corrupt to stop me."

"I don 't think so. Everything you touch, you screw up, you useless ass—."

Dassler's fist exploded into Joe's face. Not once, but repeatedly. Joe tried to dodge the blows, but he had nowhere to hide. Cuts opened across both eyes, lips split, blood flowed.

By the time his rage was spent, Dassler's chest heaved, his face an unhealthy scarlet. "Guess what, doctor?" he wheezed, fighting for breath.

His face a bloody, frothing wreck, Joe said, "You're having the heart attack I told you to watch out for. You really should see someone about—"

Another fist. More pain. More blood.

Joe spit on the floor. "Hit me all you like, Dassler," he mumbled. "It makes no difference. Thanks to me, you and the Revival are still finished."

"Wrong! Yes, you did hurt the Revival. But you did not destroy it; you never could. Twelve months from now, I will have my bioweapons. As soon as I threaten to use them, the American government will come crashing down."

"Americans aren't stupid; they'll see you're bluffing."

Dassler laughed. "Not when the streets of Hawai'i are thick with dead bodies. Within a month, I will be president for life... And, twelve months later," he went on, "the world will be mine."

Joe could not help himself. "You are insane. Why would anyone let you to do that? Come on, Mister Dassler! Prove to me how smart you are. Or is this just more of your deranged nonsense?"

"America is first. China next; a bioweapon attack the like of which the world has never seen will annihilate it. Then it's the turn of Western Europe, Russia, India, Brazil, South Africa, and Indonesia. They will get one month to accept my terms. What I've done to China will make sure they do, and then the world will have one government, a strong government led by America."

Joe shook his head and said. "You are mad."

"And you're boring. I have done enough talking; now it's your turn. Where are the canisters of hemorrhagic smallpox the Japanese Army put aboard the *Maroku Maru*?"

Joe stared, his mouth sagging open. "All this is about the canisters?"

"You hadn't guessed? Come on, doctor. Tell me what I want to hear. I don't want my people wasting time weaponizing another virus, not when the fine people of Unit 731 have already done all the hard work for me."

Joe allowed himself to enjoy a moment of triumph. He smiled, pulped lips opening to expose bloody teeth. "At last, the truth. Sounds to me like you're screwed. I am not going to help you, Mister I'm-going-to-rule-the-world Dassler. Those canisters are long gone from the *Maroku Maru*. You'll never find them now."

Dassler's face split into the broadest of broad grins. "Thank you, doctor. You've answered my question."

"I don't think so."

"Think again. My good friend Admiral Galadanski ... You know, it's a shame she's been arrested by the FBI; she was doing a superb job running NAVSPECWARCOM for the Revival ... Where was I? Oh, yes. Galadanski. She told me one of your chase boats was missing from the *Sophie Scholl;* the crew said you had taken it and disappeared."

Dassler's face darkened.

"Letting you escape was the SEALs' first mistake," he continued. "Not asking your crew if they'd seen the canisters was their second. Stupid bastards. I shouldn't be surprised, though; marines aren't exactly the smartest people around..."

Joe bit back his response. He'd been kicked enough.

"... Anyway, my people thought you wanted to get somewhere safe. I didn't; that made no sense. You did not know SEALs were going to hijack your ship. You didn't need to run, but you did. Why? Because you were afraid the CIA would be waiting for you when your boat got to Semarang. And they were the last people you wanted asking about the canisters. Not that it matters, not now I know you took the canisters from the *Maroku Maru* and dumped them. I already have a dive ship on its way to Manokwari."

"You'll never find them. The Gulf of Lendari covers a lot of water."

"Give me the raw data from the Indonesian satellites covering the Gulf of Lendari and enough supercomputing power, I can track your chase boat, no matter how bad the weather. And I will."

"Yeah, right. It's hundreds of miles from the wreck of the *Maroku Maru* to where I left my boat. You'll have a shitload of deep water to search."

"No, I won't," Dassler said. "You have a nice video system on your ship, one with lots of high-def cameras. They gave me beautiful, crisp images of you coming alongside. And guess what? No canisters. You didn't have the time to go hundreds of miles, did you, doctor?"

Joe's head slumped. He could not speak.

"You get it now," Dassler went on. "I won't have to search the Gulf of Lendari. The satellite data will tell me where you stopped, probably thirty or so miles to south of where you met up with the *Sophie Scholl*. There's a lot of rock down that way; it's where I'd have picked, and I think you did too."

"So why haven't you got started?" Joe asked. "Why wait?"

"Indonesia is a very complicated place. I know the people who can give me its raw satellite data, no questions asked. What I cannot do is stop them talking about it; Indonesians do like to gossip. My ship has to be long gone from the Gulf of Lendari before the CIA and NSA pick up on it, which is why I had to confirm you had dumped the canisters."

"You're still wasting your time."

"With the resources I can mobilize, I don't think so. Right, you've given me all I need, so we're done. I will see you later, doctor."

"We need water. Please."

"You won't need any, not where you're going."

The door slammed behind Dassler.

And Joe was left to eat ashes.

•••

The door banged, jolting Joe awake. Body and soul, he was a mess: no food, no water, no rest, just despair, pain, and his filth for company. In front of him stood Dassler, flanked by two men.

One was Peretz, red cap and all.

Dassler screwed up his face in disgust. "Jesus! They smell like pigs. I don't want my Range Rover messed up. Take them outside, get those clothes off, hose them down, and find them something to wear. I want them outside and ready to go in fifteen minutes."

"Yes, boss."

•••

Dassler inspected the two battered figures dripping water on the front steps of Estancia Rosita. "Feeling better, are we?"

Joe said nothing, his mouth clamped shut to keep his teeth from chattering.

"I'll tell you this, doctor. It's a pleasure to be able to breathe around you without wanting to throw up. I can be quite sensitive, you know."

Dassler put a hand on the shoulder of the man beside him. "Say hello to the man who killed your Klara ... Come on, doctor! Say hello to Charlie Peretz."

Joe turned his head away.

"No? She put up quite a fight, didn't she, Charlie?"

"She did boss," Peretz said. "Didn't do her no good; she ended up dead like the boyfriend."

Down went Joe's head. Tears of loss and guilt flooded his cheeks.

Dassler chuckled. "Oh, Charlie. You've upset the doctor ... Enough of this. Right! Get them loaded. It's time we went for a drive."

"Wait! None of this is André's fault. Let him go, and I'll tell you where the smallpox canisters are."

"Ah, finally. An offer. You took your time."

Joe's heart lifted. "You'll do it?"

"What?" Dassler said. "No! Why do you think I haven't asked you to tell me? I have what I want."

"I'll give you the exact position. You can put your divers down right on top of the canisters. As soon as you have recovered them, you can let André go."

Dassler shook his head. "We both know you will never tell me where they are."

"Why would I risk André's life by lying to you? He's a brother to me."

"I believe the brother bit, but not the rest. Yes, you could tell me the truth, but you won't. If you did, you would be signing death warrants for hundreds of millions of people. A man like you would never trade one life, even one as precious as André's, for millions. Am I right?"

The man was right. It was over.

Dassler turned to a second man. "Bring the Rover around, Rajiv."

Joe closed his eyes. He could not face André.

•••

Joe lay crammed into the trunk of the Range Rover beside André. Doors slammed, and they drove off.

"Where to, boss?" Rajiv asked.

"The gully past Cathedral Rock," Dassler said. "No point going any further. No one will find ever them out there. God, I love this place. As long as I keep paying the right people, nobody gives a shit what I do."

Joe lifted his head. The morning air was clear and still, the Andes a jagged line of snow-capped peaks cut from a sky of fathomless blue.

It was too beautiful a day to die.

Twenty or so minutes later, Dassler called out, "Far enough. Get them out, Charlie."

Joe took another peek. The vehicle had stopped at the foot of a monolith the size of a six-story office block and flanked by scree slopes.

Peretz lifted the tailgate and leaned in.

Joe took the opportunity, smashing his forehead into the face of Klara's killer.

Bone crunched bone.

Peretz fell back, howling, one hand clutching a shattered nose, the other dragging Joe with him, the pair collapsing to the ground in a heaving tangle of bodies.

But, with Joe's wrists tied, it did not take Peretz long to kick and punch and claw his way free.

Peretz scrambled his feet, chest heaving, blood pouring from his ruined nose. He drew back a boot.

"Stop!" Dassler shouted. "Careless, Charlie, careless."

Peretz wiped his face and spit gobs of blood on the dirt. "Shorry, bosh," he mumbled. "It won't happen again."

"It better not."

Dassler turned away. "Rajiv!" he snapped. "Shovels! Charlie! Get them over to that patch of dirt."

This time Peretz took no chances. Arms at full stretch, he dragged an uncooperative André from the Range Rover. Taking handfuls of hair, he hauled Joe and André across the ground, their feet scrabbling at the dirt to ease the agony. He stopped and cut their wrists free. He pulled out his gun and stepped back.

Dassler took the shovels from Rajiv and threw them at Joe and André. "Dig. Something grave-sized should do it."

Peretz cackled, spitting more blood.

"No," said Joe. "If you want to kill us, just do it."

"I am tempted, doctor, but I love watching a man dig his own grave, a man so close to death he can almost taste it. It adds a certain frisson to an otherwise tragic moment."

"You are one fucked-up piece of shit," André rasped. "You need therapy."

"Didn't I tell you to stay quiet, Doctor Tanadi? Yes, I believe I did."

"And you can go fuck yourself as well."

Dassler pulled out a pistol and shot André in the foot. The gunshot reverberated through the still of morning, a morning now ripped apart by screams of pain. "Oh, dear. Looks like you will have to do all the digging, Doctor Lessart. So best you start, unless you want me to shoot Doctor Tanadi again."

Joe picked up the shovel and started to dig.

•••

Rajiv peered into the pit. "I think we're done, boss. I'll bring the backhoe up later, put plenty of dirt on top."

"Sure." Dassler gave a theatrical yawn. "Right, I'm bored. Out you get, doctor."

Joe pitched the shovel on the mound of dirt beside the hole and scrambled out.

He glanced at his friend.

André's face was gray. "I guess this is it, my friend."

"I'm sorry about the deal I offered Dassler."

"One life in exchange for millions of lives?" André said with a crooked smile. "Never thought I'd be worth so much. Help me up. No way I'm going to let the fat psycho shoot me lying down."

Joe pulled André up into an embrace.

"Come on, lover boys," Dassler said. "I have better things to do than watch two faggots get all mushy. Hey! Turn and face the hole."

Joe put one arm around André's waist and the other on his shoulder. He helped him turn away from Dassler. They stared into their grave.

It was shallow.

Stony.

Cold.

A dreadful place to die.

"We had fun, didn't we, André?"

"Can't complain. At least we—"

Slap ...Crack! Slap ...Crack! Slap ...Crack!

A scream from Dassler.

Joe's heart leapt. A large-caliber sniper rifle. He recognized the sound from the attack on Cogent's laboratory.

He spun around.

Rajiv lay face down, arms outstretched like a priest abasing himself before an altar, blood pooling around his head.

Peretz was on his back. His mouth hung slack, a neat hole between wide-open eyes. He had lost control of his bladder in death, faded jeans darkening around his crotch.

Dassler too was on his face. The man's shoulder was a bloody mess. The shot must have taken him high in the chest between armpit and neck.

But, even now, one arm scrabbled through the dirt, feeling for his gun.

Joe did not hesitate. He brought his foot down hard, snapping Dassler's wrist with a crack. The man screamed.

Joe scooped up the gun and put it to Dassler's head. He lowered the weapon. "I won't let you die on me. I want you in court. Then the world can see you for what you are."

Dassler half-turned his head to look at Joe. His eyes flickered as he tried to speak, but no words came.

Joe rolled Dassler onto his back, ripped off his shirt, wadded it up, and stuffed it into the terrible wound in the man's shoulder. He leaned on it to staunch the bleeding. "André! How're you doing?"

"A lot better now the cavalry's arrived." André said as armed figures flooded the area.

"I thought this sort of thing only happened in the movies."

"Seems not."

A woman dropped to one knee beside Dassler and unslung a backpack. "I take over, sir," she said.

"I want this one kept alive. You hear me? Alive!"

Joe stood and stepped away. Shock was taking hold; staying upright was becoming a challenge. One of the new arrivals came over: a woman in camouflage fatigues and tactical vest, black cap, gun in a thigh holster.

"Who are you?" Joe asked.

"Special Agent Marta Zhou, Doctor Lessart; FBI liaison officer with the PFA, the Policía Federal Argentina. Everyone else is from an Argentinean special-forces unit."

"And I'm very glad to ... Wait a second! You just called me Doctor Lessart. Who told you my..."

Joe's voice faded as all the pieces crashed together. For a moment, he refused to believe what his brain was telling him. But he had to. "You scumbags! You used us to flush Dassler out."

The blind fury in Joe's voice forced Zhou back. "I'm sorry?" she said.

"You used us to flush Dassler out. We almost died."

Joe's rage blew away what little composure he had left. He hurled himself at Zhou, driving her to the ground before hands pulled him away. He cursed, cried, then sobbed, his mental and physical collapse complete.

•••

Joe had to shout to make himself heard over the engines of the Fuerza Aérea Argentina helicopter. "I'm so sorry, Agent Zhou. I shouldn't have done that."

"I'll live. And please call me Marta."

"Nice to meet you, Marta. What happens now?"

"We're heading back to Mendoza. The Argentinean authorities say you can return to the United States once they have statements from you and Doctor Tanadi. We'll have a doctor to check you both out first, though."

"The police won't be happy when they find out what we came to do. How can they just let us go?"

"They've been fully briefed. They see no reason to stop you leaving."

Again, anger welled up. "Because this whole business was a goddammed set-up."

Zhou shrugged "I can't comment. Above my pay grade, I'm afraid."

"Yeah, right," Joe grunted. "Tell me something, Marta. Why did you guys wait so long? Do you have any idea what André and I went through back there?"

"We didn't plan it that way. We lost our satellite datalink with the you-avs."

"You-avs?"

"U-A-Vs," Zhou said. "Unmanned aerial vehicles, drones to you and me. The CIA had two overhead the whole operation."

Joe wanted to tear the woman's head off. "We were an operation?"

"Everything's an operation these days, doctor. This one was Lightning Fish."

"Some operation... You could see what happened. Why did you let them take us?"

"The Argentinians would not move unless your lives were in imminent danger. Dassler's security was tight; we could not risk being spotted."

"How did you know where he was taking us?" Joe asked.

"The CIA had trackers on all the vehicles, bugs inside as well."

"It's no secret Dassler is a psycho. You must have known he was going to kill us. Why didn't somebody bust the door down?"

"Estancia Rosita is like a fortress: thick walls, solid roof, small windows," Zhou said. "The CIA wasn't able to put surveillance inside; we weren't sure where you were being held. You'd be dead if we'd tried to shoot our way in."

Joe took his time. His body ached, his head was a mess of matted blood, and contusions had closed his eyes down to slits. He wanted to find somewhere quiet, cool, and dark to sleep. "Why do I sense you haven't told me everything?"

"Ah … I'm not sure I can."

"You're kidding! Tell me. I think I'm owed that much."

"Yes, you are," Zhou said. "Dassler is an extreme example of someone with narcissistic personality disorder or NPD. You and I would call it megalomania. He feels compelled to tell his victims how smart he is. All he needed was the right audience somewhere he felt safe and in control, somewhere he could let himself talk."

"And you wanted me to be the audience while he performed?"

"I'm sorry if this upsets you, but yes. And not any audience. You had humiliated him, so he wanted humiliate you by showing you how brilliant he was, how nothing you'd done would stop him, how the Revival would take over the world."

"How he was still the winner, even after everything?"

"Exactly," Zhou said. "Dassler has to win and keep on winning. It's a critical part of his world, a world which is more fantasy than reality."

"But why risk our lives? If all he needs is a stage, why not just arrest the sonofabitch and make him talk?"

"Because he wouldn't," Zhou said. "People as high on the psychopathy scale as Dassler never do. The humiliation of being arrested is too much; it's like their brains have imploded."

"You'd have ended up with nothing if Dassler had killed us both."

"We are not amateurs, Doctor Lessart. The CIA had sewed digital voice-activated recorders into your clothing and shoes. They recorded every word the man said. Our people found all your stuff out back of the estancia, and you still have your shoes."

"I hope you sent a HAZMAT team to handle our clothing."

Zhou smiled. "No kidding."

"Did you cook up this Operation Lightning Fish with Kemani and Beharry?" Joe asked.

Zhou pointed a finger skywards "Upstairs did all that. But they were critical to the mission's success. Mister Kuprovic too."

Joe took a deep breath to calm himself down. "Was letting us dig our own graves before Dassler shot us like dogs part of the operation?"

Splashes of red appeared high on Zhou's cheeks. "No, of course not. We're not animals, doctor."

"But you did!"

"Like I said, we had problems with the UAVs. I must admit, I was worried."

"Bully for you. I was shitting myself."

"I'm sorry."

Joe glanced at André; he was asleep. His best friend, a friend he had offered to sacrifice. Guilt robbed Joe of what little remained of his restraint.

"You, the FBI, the CIA," he shouted. "You're all scumbags."

"Calm down, doctor. We had a job to do. We did it."

The anger vanished as fast as it had come. "You're still scumbags," he mumbled.

Zhou said nothing.

Joe closed his eyes and let his head fall back. A minute later, he too was asleep.

•••

A skeletal hand reached up from the pit. It took Joe by the throat and pulled him down, down into the horrors, down to...

"Doctor Lessart," a voice said. "Wake up. We've arrived."

Joe tried to open his eyes. He couldn't.

Blackness. Panic. Terror.

"I can't see!" he shouted. "Help me!"

André's voice was in his ear. "Hold on, Joe. It's just dried blood."

A splash of water. Joe felt his friend's fingers tease open his eyes.

The pit vanished, replaced by André's face, tight with concern. "Better?"

"Yeah, thanks. Sorry. You?"

"The medic says my foot will need minor surgery. The rest of me is fine. You're the one I'm concerned about. Dassler gave you one hell of a belting."

Joe could not fathom why André sounded so relaxed. He had almost gotten the man killed; why wasn't he beating up on him? "I'll be fine."

As the engines spooled down, the door slid open. A head appeared. "You may now disembark."

Joe unbuckled his seatbelt and climbed out. Everything hurt. All he wanted was sleep, somewhere quiet, cool, safe. The sun was bright outside. He blinked in the glare.

Three familiar shapes came towards him.

"Joe, you sonofabitch," Beharry called out. "You had us worried."

Exhaustion had Joe swaying. Beharry took his arm.

Joe shook him off. "Fuck off."

"Ah, okay … I'm guessing Agent Zhou has filled you in."

"I can't believe you set us up. We almost died out there."

"You knew the threat the Revival posed. Don't tell me you'd have done any different if it was me and Angie."

A long pause.

"No, I guess not," Joe admitted at last. "And you were right about one thing: This is no business for amateurs."

Beharry chuckled. "It sure isn't, Joe."

"It worked out in the end," Adam said. "Come, we need someone to check you out."

Joe was too tired to argue. He waited until the medics had loaded André before hands helped him into the ambulance.

•••

Twelve hours later, Adam's plane climbed out of Mendoza en-route for San Diego. Joe glanced over at André, now deep in conversation with Adam, Beharry, and Liebmann, his bandaged foot up on a seat.

Excitement animated the man's eyes. He was treating the whole business as some sort of crazy adventure.

Joe marveled at his resilience. He wondered if André had ever grasped the true evil of the Revival.

Even now, with Dassler arrested, he wondered if the evil lived on.

— 55 —

"Good morning, Doctor Lessart," said Karl Stetterman. "Take a seat, please."

"No, thanks. This won't take long."

President Vandergraaf's chief of staff pulled back his hand, unshaken, and resumed his seat. "Sure."

"I'll give you one chance to tell me what you've been up to. And I want the truth; if I think you are lying to me, I am going to climb across your desk and rip you a new one."

"Calm down. "The President has told me to tell you everything."

"My promise still stands, you asshole."

Stetterman's voice sharpened. "Doctor Lessart! Sit, for chrissakes."

Joe made himself calm down. Anger made poor decisions, Beharry had said, and he was right. He found a chair and sat down. "Talk! And leave nothing out."

"The first we knew of your dealings with the Revival was when General Murata persuaded you to go to the FBI. Director Agnelli was so concerned he briefed the president the next day."

"What? Agnelli promised me he'd keep it tight!"

"I know, but he lied."

"Does anybody in this goddammed town ever tell the truth?" But Joe already knew the answer. This was Washington.

"Agnelli had a job to do," Stetterman said, "and telling you what he knew was not part of it. He had no problem briefing Vandergraaf; she had already told Agnelli of her concerns, concerns which I shared by the way. There was something bad inside New America, but nothing we could pin down. Before you even turned up, Agnelli was so concerned he had formed a task force to investigate. Remember the man who got you away from the Revival safe house before the state police arrived?"

"He said his name was Brad."

"Not his real name, but yes. The FBI planned to turn him; they wanted him to be their man on the inside. Dassler's people killed him the moment he left hospital."

"The poor bastard. No, scratch that. I'm not sorry for him, not at all."

"You shouldn't be; he made his own decisions. Which brings me to your first visit to Mexico. You were lucky to make it out after the kidnapping stunt you pulled in Puerto Vallarta."

"Bullshit! I knew what I was doing."

Stetterman rolled his eyes. "Actually, no, you didn't. You missed a camera upstream of the River Café. It saw you hustling Doctor Pavel away."

"Shit... I was sure we'd spotted them all."

"You didn't," Stetterman said, "but you were lucky on three counts. First, the Revival's security chief, Kernow, waited too long to bring in the Venganza. Second, he thought he was looking for a local. Third, he believed Pavel's story, which is why she is now in Panama, though not for much longer. State told the government hosting a facility dedicated to mass murder on a global scale might not be in their best long-term interests. They've assured us extraditing all the staff will be a formality."

"Marina Pavel?"

"She was arrested two days ago trying to cross into Colombia."

"I'm glad to hear it. She's a bad one."

"For which the FBI intends to make her pay."

"So, there was me doing my knight-on-a-white-charger thing," Joe said, feeling like a fool, "thinking it was me alone against the Revival, and the FBI knew about the conspiracy all along?"

"Not quite," Stetterman said. "Agnelli knew something was up, but not the details. Nor was he aware of the canisters. Their existence was classified Top Secret and access was limited: Only three senior Pentagon civilian staffers and SecDef could access what were called the Case Jade files."

"And SecDef worked for the Revival, which explains how the Revival found out we'd been on the *Maroku Maru*."

"Correct. And, to make matters even more difficult, the Revival's security was good. Agnelli said working out what was going on was like trying to grab smoke. And then you rock up and start to fill the gaps."

"Hang on!" Joe said. "You just made me out to be a bungling incompetent."

"Most of the time you were, but not always. When you found the canisters and took them off the *Maroku Maru*? Outstanding. The attack swim into Camp Sierra? Talk about extraordinary; even the SEALs were impressed, and they don't impress easily. And the Pavel video? Brilliant. It was the first time Agnelli understood what he was up against. The worst day of his life, he said."

"What about the people who attacked the safe house? Were they FBI agents?"

Stetterman nodded. "Of course."

"But why?"

"To make you run. You had a gift for making life difficult for the Revival. We hoped you'd shake something useful loose, and you did."

"You could have just asked."

"We thought about it," Stetterman said, "but there are limits to the, uh … to the activities we can be associated with."

"Like hiring the Escorpiónes to take out Cogent's facility at Valle de Banderas?"

"The United States has worked with some unsavory people over the years ..."

"Now there's an understatement," Joe said.

"... and we will again, but a psychopathic narcotraficante like Hermann Márquez? That was too much."

"The FBI knew about the whole operation?"

"Oh, yes. Agnelli wanted you to kick the Revival in the balls. The intelligence people love when that happens. It shakes people up. They start to worry. They get frightened. They get nervous. They say things to people they should not be talking with. They forget what's secret and what's not. You turned them upside-down; we learned plenty from the fallout. And the you recovered Kernow's laptop; without it, we'd still be fumbling around in the fog."

Joe scowled. "And you just you sat back and let it happen. Incredible."

"Not quite. The President was persuaded to bend the rules and send in the CIA in case you needed rescuing. None of you saw them, and neither did Cogent. Understandable, of course. Kernow's security was slack, and things did get very confused."

Joe stared at Stetterman. "The CIA was there? You're kidding!"

"No, I'm not. And it wasn't the only contribution we made. Did you see the way the lab went up?"

"I only remember a huge explosion. The Venganza had just shot me; things were a bit blurry."

"Ah, yes. Sorry. Well, let's say we helped the laboratory on its way."

"Crap! Even the Venganza would have spotted a demolition team sneaking in."

Stetterman smiled. "But not the A B-2 bomber which dropped a blast bomb on it. The US Air Force argued it was overkill, but we wanted to make sure the facility did not survive... Everything I've just told you is top secret, by the way, the blast bomb especially."

"I bet the locals had something to say," said Joe.

"What could they say?" Stetterman said. "Our sources say they think an illegal drug lab blew up. It wouldn't have been the first time."

"Was General Murata aware of what you guys were up to?"

"You don't think the Ramirez sting was all her own work, did you?"

"I don't believe it. I suppose Kemani and Raffa work for the CIA."

"They probably should, but no, they don't. We were able to convince them cooperation was better than time in the slammer."

Joe shook his head. "I don't need to ask any more questions, do I? We were puppets, with you and the FBI pulling the strings."

Stetterman laughed. "Puppets? No, no. Staying on top of the Revival was like wrestling an ice-crazed anaconda in a swamp. All we could do was keep track of you and take the chances you created. Like I said, you have a gift for creative destruction ... We couldn't have done it without you."

"Thank you... Which brings me to Operation Lightning Fish; what a crap name, by the way."

"You can blame a DoD computer for gems like that."

"I'd have picked Operation Shaft the Amateurs. Or Fuck the Good Guys. But I have worked out André and I were the bait to force Mark Dassler to show himself, so there's not much more to say, I guess."

"No, I don't think there is."

"Apart from us ending up seconds from being shot ... You really are a pack of bastards."

"Yes, we are," Stetterman said. "If it helps, I wish we didn't have to be."

"Yeah, right. Right, I'm done for now. Please thank the president for me. It's always nice when the government's honest and open; it doesn't happen very often."

"No, it doesn't."

—56—

President Vandergraaf took the Presidential Medal of Freedom with its white-bordered ribbon from Karl Stetterman and fastened it around Joe's neck. "The United States of America honors you, Doctor Lessart. I can't think of anyone who has deserved this medal more than you."

"Thank you, Madam President. I wish I could tell people about it."

Vandergraaf laughed. "Perhaps in a decade or two. Karl, a picture?"

Stetterman fumbled in his pocket. "Oh, yes, sorry. Shaking hands, I think."

His cellphone flashed. Two participants, one witness, one photograph, and the ceremony was over.

"Thank you, doctor," Vandergraaf said. "And now, much as I would love to share a beer with you, I have a meeting with the Transportation Secretary."

"It has been an honor, Madam President."

"Goodbye, and once again, thank you. We weren't as up-front with you as I would have liked, but necessity rarely offers us easy choices."

Joe had turned to leave when Stetterman's hand fell on his shoulder. "Come on, Joe, I think I can find us a few beers. But put the medal away first."

•••

Karl Stetterman lifted his glass. "To you, Doctor Joe Lessart: a decent man amongst cheats, liars, and thieves."

"Come on, Karl. Don't be so hard on yourself."

Stetterman laughed. "So, what's next?"

"A meeting tomorrow with the Indonesians and the Center for Disease Control to finalize the plans to destroy the canisters of smallpox."

"You still haven't told anyone where they are?"

"Not yet, but I will when the time is right."

"You still don't trust anyone, do you?"

"Hah!" Joe snorted. "Why would I? One half of the government worked for the Revival, while the other half treated me like a goddammed puppet."

"We've been through this."

Joe put his hands up. "I'm sorry, Karl. You did what you had to do."

"Given the threat the Revival posed, we could not put the welfare of two citizens ahead of the entire United States."

"Don't let the media hear you. They'd crucify you."

"They've already hammered in the nails," Stetterman said. "Everything wrong with this country is the fault of Celia Vandergraaf and her crew of incompetents. If they only knew ... When are you off?"

"We'll join the *Sophie Scholl* in Semarang next week before heading to the Gulf of Lendari to watch the canisters being destroyed. Then we go to Manokwari; liaison officers from the US and Indonesian navies will meet us there along with the relatives of *Orca*'s crew."

"That sub sank a long time ago. There can't be many family members left."

"Fourteen at last count. We will have the captain's son with us, though. The Navy tracked him down in Italy."

"I can believe it," said Stetterman. "It takes war graves seriously."

"As they should. I'm glad we can take Alan Mayer's son to see where his father lies ... Sorry, I have to go. I have to meet with General Murata. Thanks for the beers, and good luck running the country."

"You flatter me."

"I'm damn sure I'm don't, Karl."

— 57—

A sharp, metallic crack punched the *Sophie Scholl*'s hull and the sea over Major Mori's canisters of smallpox virus shivered. An instant later, a roiling fireball from the ring of surface charges engulfed the column of dirty water as it erupted skywards.

The last skeins of spray drifted from the air. Soon only a muddy stain remained to mark the end of the Revival's ambitions.

André put an arm across Joe's shoulders. "Well done, my son. You should be proud of yourself."

"I'm just glad it's over. Let me make sure the Indonesians are happy."

Joe picked up the VHF radio's microphone. "KRI *Banda Aceh*, this is *Sophie Scholl* on 16, over."

"Go channel seven-seven, *Sophie Scholl*."

Joe punched up the new channel. "*Banda Aceh*, *Sophie Scholl* on seven-seven. This is Doctor Lessart requesting Admiral Dasri."

"Roger, standby ... Doctor Lessart, this is Dasri. Go ahead please."

"Salamat siang, admiral. Things seemed to go as planned."

Admiral Dasri's English was precise. "Yes, they did. The drones are sampling the air to confirm the site is sterile, but I have already spoken with the observers from your Center for Disease Control. They are certain none of the smallpox virus has survived."

"I appreciate the confirmation, admiral, thank you. Request permission to proceed?"

"Approved. Dive safely, doctor."

"Terima kasih, admiral."

"Thank you. Dasri out."

Joe put the radio handset back in its cradle. "Manokwari, captain."

He stood at the back of the bridge as the main engines came to full power. Two years had passed since he had unsealed the Imperial Japanese Army's box of horrors.

But there was still one thing left to do.

—58—

Orca emerged from the gloom, its hull a long black shadow against the gray of the seabed.

Joe drifted over the hull of the wrecked submarine. "Surface, this is Joe."

"Go ahead," Budi said.

"We're on the submarine. We'll move to the bridge now, so bring the ROV in."

Joe swam with André to the ball floating above *Orca*'s bridge, tethered to the submarine by a bar-taut wire pendant.

"Divers, Surface. We have you on camera. You can start."

Joe pulled the flag out of a pouch, attached it to clips seized into the pendant, and let it unfurl, the flag waving in the gentle current.

After more than eighty years, the Stars and Stripes flew over the *USS Orca* to honor the last resting place of the men who had fought and died in her.

Emotion overwhelmed Joe. Tears filled his eyes.

•••

The few living relatives of the men lost in *Orca* left alive leaned on the guardrail as their wreaths drifted away on a glassy sea.

Alan Mayer Jr. came over to where Joe and André waited, small, hesitant steps. "Thank you, Joe, thank you, André," he said, shaking each of them by the hand. An old man now, his grip was warm and soft. "I can't tell you how much this means to me. I wish Mom could have seen this. Every day of her life she wondered..."

His voice trailed off. Tears filled eyes faded with age.

Joe's voice was soft. "Your father was a brave man, and so were the men who served with him. I'm glad we found where he rests, and I'm glad we can tell *Orca*'s story."

"So am I," Mayer said. "It deserves to be told."

EPILOG

The old woman in faded blue prison coveralls stepped from the Public Security van. She stopped and lifted her face to the sky. A gray sky from which a thin, icy drizzle drifted. She savored the caress of water on skin.

"Come, mother," the guard whispered. "A few meters more."

"Don't let me fall."

Together, they crossed the yard, its beaten earth long since churned to mud. The Ministry of State Security sent a lot of business Special Purpose Facility 4's way.

They reached a bullet-splintered post in front of a wall of sandbags. The woman stumbled. The escort's hands took her before she could fall.

"Be strong," the man said. "This will soon be over."

The old woman sighed. She was too tired to be afraid. Her life had been full, rich, satisfying. And the Great Navigator had promised her family would be safe.

A promise she knew the Great Navigator would keep.

Hands put the woman's back against the post and secured her wrists and ankles.

A Public Security officer stepped up. He raised a black hood.

"No," the old woman said. "Why would I be frightened? I always did my duty to the people of China."

The officer leaned forward. "We will not forget you, mother. Do not forget us."

The woman smiled. The idea she could help anyone after she was dead was absurd, but this was China; the old superstitions died hard. "I will try, my son. Now, do what you have to do."

Two minutes later, the firing squad had done its work. The woman hung twisted to one side, head down. Blood seeped through the blue coveralls.

The officer returned. He raised his pistol. "Forgive me," he murmured as he fired a single shot into the woman's temple.

•••

A soft tap at the door.

"Come!"

A head appeared. "Excuse me, sir. Minister Ren was executed thirty minutes ago. She went quietly; there were no problems."

"Did she say anything?"

"Nothing, sir."

"The family?"

"State Security have arrested them. They will be executed tomorrow."

The Great Navigator waved the woman away. He stood back from his desk and went to the window. The day was filthy. Wet, gray, miserable, it matched his mood.

He would miss Ren Jieqiong. She had been a loyal, competent, and hard-working servant of the Chinese people. It was her misfortune to be the minister responsible for State Security when it failed to detect the existential threat the Revival conspiracy posed to China and its people.

A failure which allowed China's enemies to take the country to the brink of destruction.

Which was why he had ordered her shot.

And her family. He would not miss them; greedy and corrupt, their exploitation of Ren's authority as a minister had been shameless. They deserved to die.

China would be a better place without them.

He returned to his desk and picked up the phone. "Tell Kuàng I want to see him as soon as I have finished with the Standing Committee. And give him access to the Ren file."

•••

"You have read the Ren file?" the Great Navigator said at last.

"Yes, Comrade Chairman," Michael Kuàng said.

"Minister Ren was extremely popular, especially in the south. You understand her execution may have unfavorable consequences for me?"

"Not if we take steps to ensure those consequences do not occur," Kuàng said.

The Great Navigator nodded. He thought of Kuàng as his weather radar, always scanning the horizon for the next storm. If Ren's death was to create problems, he would know first.

Though he wished the man would drop his first name: Michael, a reminder of the despised English. He hated it.

But Kuàng was as stubborn as he was smart and loyal. 'I do not wish to, Comrade Chairman', he would say when challenged.

"You have some ideas?" the Great Navigator asked.

"Not yet," Kuàng said, "but we must destroy America and its people, as they tried to destroy us. We have no choice."

"But the conspiracy failed."

"Conspiracies only flourish when a country allows them to. Who is to say the Americans will not try again? And when our success shows the even stupidest American the United States is no longer the leader of the world, I think they will."

"You don't think they can be trusted?"

"I don't, Comrade Chairman. You must act to protect China and its people … and yourself."

"Which is why I want you to tell me how we can destroy America. And get me the names of the conspiracy's leaders. You have two months."

"Yes, Comrade Chairman. But I need to see all the information State Security has on this Revival conspiracy. And on China's bioweapons programs as well."

"China does not have any," the Great Navigator said.

Kuàng smiled. "Of course not. But I would still like access."

The Great Navigator returned the smile. "I will speak to Deputy Minister Xuan. Anything else you need?"

"Not now, Comrade Chairman. If there is, I will ask."